Murder
&
Matrimony
in the
Castello

To Kimberly,

Buona lettura!

Tessa

Also by Tessa Floreano

FICTION

Slain Over Spumoni

The Bread Also Rises
(Writers Cooperative of the Pacific Northwest Anthology)

Rockaway Writers Rendezvous
2024 Anthology

Crime & Punishment
(Historical Writers Forum Anthology)

NONFICTION

Italians in the Pacific Northwest

Murder & Matrimony in the Castello

TESSA FLOREANO

BAGATTO
MEDIA

For information and media inquiries, please contact:
Tessa Floreano
tessawriter@tessafloreano.com
www.tessafloreano.com

Cover Designer: Dee Marley
Editors: Michele Chiappetta and Bill Geis

ISBN: 979-8-9913563-8-1 (trade paperback)

Typeset is Bembo and Bodoni (and Blackadder ITC for the notes)

In memory of Livio Lanfrit,
my cousin and fellow book lover,
mi manchi tanto

Acknowledgments

Creating a book is a team effort. I am deeply grateful to my talented editing team at Two Birds Author Services, Michele Chiappetta, Andrea Neil, and Bill Geis, for their invaluable contributions. To Dee Marley at White Rabbit Arts for the gorgeous cover. For their early feedback, I also want to express my eternal gratitude to my LDSN friends and writing partners—Denise, Jayna, Jennifer, Judy, Kathy, Sonja, and Sonya. A big cheer goes out to everyone who cheered *me* on. You know who you are, but special shoutouts must go to *le famiglie* Floreano, Buttazzoni, Bagatto, Lanfrit, Goertz, and Morrison, especially these women—Lucia, Lynette, Antoinette, Ginette, Brandy, AnnaMaria, Margherita, Antonella, Raffaella, Matilde, Virginia, Linda, Casey, Avery, Stephanie, Olivia, Tracy, and Victoria. To my dear friends Anne, Antonella, Audrey, Jan, Jill, Jo, Lisa, Kay, Kelye, Kim, Maureen, Mercedes, Sandra, Sheryl, Suzanne, Valerie, and Wendy, plus all my supporters at the Casa Italiana in Burien, OSDIA Bellevue, and Il Centro in Vancouver, British Columbia—your encouragement has been instrumental in this journey. I am deeply grateful for your support.

I want to give a very special mention to my beloved husband, Jason, for enduring frequent and dramatic displays of creative angst and, a mia madre, Silvia, for her steadfast support. *Ti amo sempre.*

Prologue

Midsummer Eve, 1892
Padua, Italy

"I am ready for the Castle of Love!"

Renata Bombonatti turned away from the massive gilt mirror and beamed at Papà, twirling to show him her outfit. Against Mama's wishes, she was dressed for the city's grandest event of the year. She insisted on wearing a gladiator-styled outfit with a metal breastplate, armored gloves, men's breeches and shirt for modesty, and an open helmet—no dress and floral crown for her.

Though a furrow marked his brow, Papà nodded and pointed at the floor. "Oh, my. You look menacing, Renata. Let's see you walk, but mind the marble, will you."

She paraded up and down the foyer of their sixteenth-century, Palladian-style home, careful not to chip the floor or towering columns with her makeshift sabatons. Shoulders back, arms and weapons by her side, she skirted the protruding Murano glass sconces and half-dozen sgabelli lining the narrow hall. She kept her eye on these protrusions, having bumped into the exuberant back stools on more than one occasion when she used to race out the front door to some adventure or other—something she was still wont to do.

Mama entered the foyer, resplendent in a violet cotton dress with velvet and lace trim. She frowned and set her fancifully plumed hat and frilled parasol on the carved console table. "Husband, do you not think she's too young for this spectacle?"

"Colombina, my dear," said Papà, affixing his straw boater to his head and picking up his lion-topped cane, "it is not every day a city celebrates such an auspicious occasion on our daughter's fourteenth trip around the sun. At this age, she's almost a woman. I should think you, of all people, would be—"

"What are you suggesting? She's barely out of her leading strings, and you are already marrying her off." Mama harrumphed and crossed her arms over her ample chest.

"Please stop. I *am* in the room, you know. Have you forgotten it is my birthday? I want to enjoy myself today with Natalia on the platform." Renata wagged her finger in the air. "That is *all*. No wedding plotting by either of you. I have been looking forward to all the pomp of the Castle of Love because it may never come back in my lifetime, so please, no pressure on me to accept any proposals."

"Pfft," said Mama noncommittally. "So, where are you meeting your friend?"

"She is waiting for me at the Galileo statue in the Prato." Renata waved Papà over. "Please check the straps on my armor. I do not want anything falling off me while I am fighting."

Papà finished adjusting the straps. "I think you are ready for battle, all suited and booted, as the English often say."

"Grazie," she said, blowing him a kiss.

He stood and patted her on her helmet. "You are sure the sword is not too long?"

"Yes, I am sure."

Papà had worked with the stablehand to fashion a small sword from an old gardening spade. He had affixed a sawed-off broom handle and painted the sword gunmetal gray. It was the perfect size and weight to deflect the love bombs the men would throw Renata's way once she was on the castle, and the event began.

"Too heavy?"

"It's fine." She assumed an attack position with her sword, pulling one leg back and stabbing the air between Papà and Mama. "No man will get past me nor claim me for his own. I am Renata Bombonatti, Queen of the Prato, Defender of the Realm, and Empress of All She

Surveys. To the fair citizens of Padua, I intend to carry out my solemn duties to the best of my military abilities. En garde!"

"I see," said Papà, his expression grave.

"Goodness, Sandro, but Renata must have the cold blood of Caesar in her." Mama relaxed her arms and waved one in Papà's direction. "Do you see what your encouragement to read books beyond her maturity breeds?"

"Hmm?" Papà cocked his brow at Mama and said nothing.

"A smart tongue, that's what," continued Mama.

Renata blushed, and Papà bent his head to look her in the eyes. "Renata, are you sure you want to wear this outfit and not a dress with a floral crown on your head like the other maidens? You will stand out, you know."

"No, Papà." She stamped her foot. "A true 'warrior' going into 'battle' must wear the proper attire. You have always taught me this."

"All right, child." Mama rolled her eyes, then finished affixing her hat to her head. "Let's go before you take a fancy to leading a charge across the Rubicon."

Papà smirked and took the weapon from Renata.

"Hey, Papà!"

"I am only carrying it for you until we get there. I have to make sure you do not accidentally poke someone with it. Now, let's march." Papà marched Renata across the foyer and ushered her outside. "We do not want to be late for your grand entrance."

Mama followed them out until the two became three, and their tiny troupe headed for the Castle of Love.

&⌒

Hundreds of Paduans thronged Il Prato—some strolled along the promenade while others lay on blankets and basked in the golden, faint moonlight. The half-square, half-garden piazza was massive, one of the largest piazzas in Europe at almost ninety-thousand square meters. Casa Bombonatti faced it, so the trio did not have far to walk—a good thing, too. Renata's heavy suit and the poorly illuminated park prevented her from sprinting ahead of her parents and meeting up with Natalia before getting a good spot on the platform.

The marble statue of Antenor, the Trojan prince and founder of the city, stood watch over the kilometer-and-a-half elliptical water canal encircling the park's island. The workers erected a wooden castle in front of the twelve-foot-tall stone man. The platform was only six feet off the ground yet ringed in four-foot crenelated wooden walls painted yellowish-gray, mimicking the trachyte stone common to the Euganean Hills. The walls had crenels at the top, like a castle tower through which the girls could fend off their attackers with their makeshift weapons.

A short distance from the empty platform, torches lit up all four sides of the castle. A narrow path led to the stairs the girls had to climb to reach the platform. A gaggle of girls gathered on the east flank while young men clumped together on the western side. At the appointed hour, the mayor would read the event's history before firing a shot in the air, signaling the opponents to take up their positions.

Renata scanned the crowds. Many couples had stopped strolling and found spots on the grass with the most advantageous views. She turned her gaze to the young men already jostling for frontline positions. She recognized a few. Some were her age, while others seemed ready to be real soldiers—restless to test their mettle on a real battlefield rather than a mock one.

"Renata! Ciao, amica mia!" Natalia Ricci called out a greeting and waved as she made her way over.

The two girls were only two years apart, having met one another years before in the park where they now stood. Natalia was dark blonde and green-eyed to Renata's brunette tresses framing amber-hued eyes, and she loved to act like Renata's much older sister,

Papà pulled his pocket watch from his vest and held it near a torch. "I believe the mayor will make his announcement any moment now. You two had best make your way to the stairs. Good luck!" He placed his hand on Renata's shoulder. "We are going to sit over there with Natalia's parents." He gestured to the left side of the Castle of Love, where the Riccis sat. "Go make us proud."

"Yes, do," said her mother, tucking in a stray curl through Renata's helmet, "but be careful. And keep your face covered no matter what."

The gangly mayor with the bulbous nose pushed through the throng until he reached the marble likeness of Antenor. He began by sharing how the Castle of Love came to be in the Middle Ages, his arms talking as much as his mouth.

"My fellow Paduans and visitors, welcome. In the center of this beautiful park, on the once-boggy island of Isola Memmia, your city councilmen have been busy these last few days. They have been directing carpenters to construct a wooden castle, this *Castello d' amore* you see before you. For those new to our fair city, let me share the history of the spectacle you will witness tonight."

He paused until the thunderous applause died down.

"In the late 1200s, Il Prato was the village green, muddy and rutted. A visionary Venetian, Andrea Memmo, transformed the green into the Prato della Valle you are sitting in today. Even then, Il Prato was one of Europe's largest squares and one of its most beautiful. Signor Memmo created a stunning elliptical park dotted with leafy trees and seventy-eight marble statues ringing a vast canal around the green."

The crowd oohed and aahed, craning their necks to observe the towering figures.

"The instant that the painter Canaletto saw this bustling square," the mayor gestured to the ellipse before him, "he wanted to memorialize it. It is unlikely he heard the medieval story of the Castello d'amore. Otherwise, I am sure he would have painted it, too."

Everyone laughed.

"Today our city celebrates its 3075th birthday, and—"

"And your fourteenth," whispered Natalia to Renata.

"That's right." Renata clapped her hands in raucous applause with her fellow Paduans and tried to still her dancing feet while the mayor droned on.

Suddenly, she felt a shift inside her heart and mind. Tonight's Castle of Love was more than a public coming-of-age. Thoughts raced through her head as she tried to pinpoint what had changed.

Looking around, she took in the lively tarantella music, the firelight and starlight, and the aroma of the itinerant baker dousing his focaccia with herbs and olive oil for his customers. The air and temperature had changed from a dense heat to a cool breeze, and she could almost taste magic. Honeyed but sweeter, akin to a promise. A promise of something bigger beyond the Castle of Love and Padua. Trying as hard as she could to grasp what she sensed, she relaxed and turned back into the mayor.

"The city has decided to revive the Castle of Love for this momentous occasion. As part of an Easter pageant over 650 years ago, a similar structure was built on the site of the ancient temple of Concordia, the Roman goddess who personified marital harmony. Every Midsummer Eve, unmarried girls from noble families defended the Castello against budding young men. The enamored men bombarded their love interests with 'ammunition.' These items represented various tokens of their affection. They ceased only when the girls relented, stepped off the castle, and were whisked off the park in festooned carts and carriages to lavish betrothal banquets. The tradition died after the Renaissance, but we are only bringing it back for today."

The young men dressed as medieval courtiers whooped and hollered while the young ladies curtseyed or waved lacy handkerchiefs.

"When I signal, the young men may step up to the Castello, and the 'battle' may commence. The battle will end when the ammunition stores of the men are depleted. Before we begin, a few words of caution for the men."

He silenced the crowd.

"Only the courtiers who have registered their participation with the city council may participate in the battle. When you fire your ammunition, try your best not to hurt anyone. And now for the ladies."

Renata leaned in with Natalia and the other girls to catch the mayor's speech.

"You are not beholden to any man here, even if you accept his tokens. However, it is bad form if you do not at least allow him a few moments of your time after the battle has been waged. Many men have worked hard to assemble an arsenal to rival a lady's dowry, so keep that in mind when making your decision."

A girl, who wore a floral wreath on her head instead of a helmet, turned to Renata. "I am so excited. Do you think the men of our dreams are out there?" She pointed to the men below.

"Perhaps."

After the mayor finished his preamble, he fired the gun above his head to signal the start of the battle.

A mad dash and clash of bodies jostled to their designated spots, and the battle began. Men flung their arsenal at their intendeds—long-stemmed roses, tiny lemons, posies of dried flowers, and scarves rolled into balls. There were wooden hair combs with carved floral patterns, skeins of the finest wool, hand-dyed leather diaries, scented linen handkerchiefs filled with bonbons, and even a sparkly bauble or two. The tokens of affection included verbal projectiles as well.

"See here, signorina," yelled a man as he threw a tiny cake tin at a lady who was quick with her shield. The tin bounced off it, and she set a foot on it to keep it from rolling away.

"Take this, with all my love," crooned another, sending a tiny psalter through the air. He had aimed for a tall girl who lacked decent swordsmanship skills because the bottom of her dress was splattered with orange and red from the jams spilling out of broken cookie bundles.

One man threw caution to the wind and climbed the stairs to the platform. He was so close to Renata that he tried to grab the shirt under her armor. She jerked, and he tried again on a different girl, which was when he lost his balance and tumbled. Oohs and aahs erupted from the crowd, and guards arrived with a hammock to haul him away. Another man, who had been quite persistent in his affection for Renata, stopped to help the injured man. She was moved by his selflessness, instantly understanding that his gallantry might cost him a lady love, but she soon got back to the battle and forgot him.

After almost an hour of the girls ducking and swaying away from all the items thrown at them, the men's arsenals had run dry, and the mayor once more fired his gun, ending the public portion of the evening. The couples started to pair off with their treasures between them and headed to their respective banquets. Natalia stood nearby, flirting coquettishly with a young admirer with dark, ringleted hair.

Renata turned away. The number of people in the castle and its surroundings dwindled until only two remained: she and her suitor. They had locked their eyes once during the battle, and his gaze had been so intense that she had forced herself to break the connection. The young man had repeatedly mouthed, "Amore," but Renata never responded in kind. She could not comprehend the funny way her heart beat inside her chest when she took in the full measure of him staring at her.

She had never seen the man who now held her attention, but in a spark of recognition, she realized he was the same one who had helped the injured man. He had merely removed his Musketeer mustache. The same feeling that came over her earlier when she had perceived a shift in consciousness was with her again.

Contrary to his earlier concerned expression, his current calm demeanor aged him, but not so much that she found his face unhandsome. He neither sported the sparse whiskers of a boy nor the dark shadow of a man needing to shave twice daily to prevent a black beard from forming. Like her amber eyes, his brown eyes reflected golden flecks when he neared a torch, and the light shone on them.

He carried a huge sack full of lovely trinkets that, once his eyes caught hers, he had sent flying in her direction to land at her feet. She blocked each one from hitting her, though seeing his ardor, managed to catch one and smile to show her pleasure. It was a long, leafy branch, and she marveled at the three ripe lemons it held. This token alone told her he came from wealth. Few families in the area had a limonaia that sheltered citrus in a glass enclosure to protect the precious fruit from the bitter cold of La Tramontana winds blowing down through the Euganean Hills every winter.

"May I help you down?" He had broken the spell of her wandering thoughts, and she noticed he held out his hand.

"I-I-I must gather up—"

"Of course. Here is my sack to hold them." He handed her the sack, and she filled it. Tying a knot at the mouth of the full sack, he again held out his hand, and she took it. She slowly descended the short stairs and removed her helmet, setting it on the ground. She gathered and twisted her hair up, using one of the combs he had lobbed at her to secure her affection.

He peered over her shoulder and said, "Are you with … someone?"

"Yes, my parents brought me. They are … over there," she said, pointing to her parents next to Natalia's lying on a blanket under a yew tree.

"Ah, I see them." He retook her hand and squeezed it gently. "I know you must go to them, but before you do, take a turn with me around the park. Your parents can see us from where they are the entire time."

17

"Well, I—"

Renata glanced away only to clap as Natalia and a young man strolled over. The two girls embraced and spoke for a moment. "Let me introduce you to my new acquaintance, Davide Nunzio."

Renata curtseyed, and Davide bowed. "Piacere," they said in unison, greeting one another.

"Davide was my most ardent admirer at the Castle of Love," said Natalia, smiling at the young man. "We are the same age, and though he's invited me to a banquet, we will take time to get to know one another and each other's families first."

"Congratulations!" said Renata and her admirer simultaneously.

"And who is your friend, Renata?" Natalia winked at her friend. "You two are too young for a banquet, surely."

"Oh, um ..." Renata's neck flushed when she realized she had been remiss in introducing herself to her admirer or he to herself, and she had left out Natalia entirely. Where were her manners?

He took the lead and bowed in the direction of the couple. "Placido Pelicani, piacere."

"Natalia Ricci, piacere."

"We were about to walk around the park," said Placido. "Please join us."

"What a splendid idea," said Natalia as she and Davide led the way.

Renata caught her father's eye and waved before falling in step with Placido.

"I hope you do not mind that I introduced myself. I should have done it earlier in our conversation, but we were—"

"So caught up in the moment," Renata said.

"Yes, quite right. And may I know your full name, Renata?"

"Of course," she said, tapping her forehead with the palm of her hand. "I do not know what happened to my manners. I am Renata Bombonatti, the only child of Sandro and Colombina Bombonatti."

He bowed. "Piacere, Signorina Bombonatti. Pleased to meet you."

"I, Natalia, thought I was too young to participate in the Castle of Love."

Placido cleared his throat. "I *am* sixteen. Better too young than too old."

Renata laughed. "Perhaps."

"Forgive me. I should have asked earlier. May I carry the bag with the tokens and your helmet?"

Renata nodded and handed over her things. She could have sworn that she caught a hint of rose on Placido's cheeks as they passed through the lamplight. They talked of everything and nothing as they walked and occasionally joined in conversation with Natalia and Davide. At one point, when the couples were quite a distance from one another, Placido told a joke. Renata laughed until she could not stand upright from the effort and doubled over. When she rose, Placido stood too close. She tried to back away, but he took hold of her hand, brought it to his cheek, and held it there until he released it with a kiss on her palm. Now, it was her turn to blush.

"What is this, Placido?" Each word shook as she spoke. Unsure what had precipitated this sudden turn of events, speaking seemed almost beyond her grasp.

"Our conversation has been so effortless this past hour. Your companionship is so amiable, and your laughter is so very welcome. We have known one another for the briefest of moments—"

She nodded. "'Tis true."

"And yet, I have been at such ease since I first saw you. I do not recall another time such as this with any other girl of my acquaintance. Perhaps the Good Lord has put you in my orbit for a reason."

"Pray tell, what might that be?" She plucked a leaf from an elm tree and ran it down his nose, giggling.

"To be my wife."

Renata stood still, hearing his pronouncement. Wife. The finality of that word reverberated through her bones, and her armor shook a little.

She dared not ask him if he meant it, for she could hear the seriousness of his tone and did not want to insult him. He had acknowledged that they were newly acquainted, that his proposal was sudden and out of the ordinary. However, the conviction of his words enveloped her in a sureness she had only ever felt around her parents.

She giggled and dropped the leaf on the ground. "I am but fourteen."

"I did not mean today," he stuttered, "but I want us to be together one day."

A shudder of relief ran through her body from head to toe. Not today. Thank goodness. She looked at him, her eyes wide, inwardly glad there were no witnesses to this solemn moment. She gulped and willed the fluttering in her belly to cease.

"Renata, from this day onwards"—his voice was strong and sure"—no other woman's name will cross my lips nor fill my heart as yours has." He swung around to face her and eased the helmet and bag to the ground. He took her armored hand and removed the metal glove.

"Oh, Placido." Her warm hand met his, and as she stared at his hand atop hers, she could not tell where her hand started and his ended.

He squeezed her hand. "My devotion has come on so suddenly, it must feel strange. Do you doubt my sincerity?"

"Not in the least." She lowered her head and said, "Though you have surprised me, I surprise myself by agreeing."

Placido placed his hand over his heart and bowed low before Renata. "I am most pleased."

"However, there is a proviso." Renata slipped her hand out of his and waved her index finger at him.

Straightening, he said, "Hmm, I sensed hesitation. Do go on."

She watched as Placido rubbed his chin. "Five years hence, if you still feel the same, you must find me again in this park before midnight on Midsummer Eve, my nineteenth birthday. One day before or after shall render my consent irrevocably changed."

"This, I will do. I give you my word."

"I am not finished. Within six months from that moment, we shall spend the time getting reacquainted. If we are still amenable to one another and my father gives his blessing, we shall wed at Christmas before the century is out, but only after you have completed your military service. I shall not be a war widow."

He cocked a brow. "My goodness, your proviso is, how shall I say, comprehensive."

"I may be young, but my heart is not to be trifled with. Once set, it is thus forever."

He kissed her bare hand. "Our pact is sealed."

Chapter 1

Wednesday morning
December 1, 1897
Padua, Italy

Renata Bombonatti wanted to shout the news from the rooftop but restrained herself lest she need her smelling salts. She stared out across the piazza as the sky became aglow with a tapestry of red and orange hues. She could not believe what she clutched to her bosom—the day had finally arrived when she was invited to the city's most exclusive Christmas literary salon. She would be the happiest of women if she received nothing else for Christmas. And she cared not a whit that it was at the finest palazzi in Padua. She would attend if it were held in a barn because she would follow this intellectual stimulation wherever offered.

She read aloud the invitation:

The Baroness of Calandro cordially invites
you and a guest to attend her Christmas literary salon
on the 3rd Saturday of Advent at 3 PM
Palazzo De Angelis

Renata opened her eyes and ran her finger over the note. The details were embossed in la baronessa's signature navy ink and the gorgeous family crest of four doves sitting in an olive tree. She repeatedly read, "*Il salotto letterario di Natale della Baronessa di Calandro ...*" to ensure her eyes did not deceive her. An afternoon of music, poetry, and polite conversation awaited her and a friend. All she had to do was decide on her dress and which friend would accompany her.

With less than a month until her Christmas Eve wedding, Mama might not let her attend. Mama would claim Renata had better things to do than sit around and discuss books and ideas. Mama liked dancing and balls, where women were seen and not heard. Literary salons bored her. She thought young ladies should not entertain fanciful thoughts and opinions about science, politics, or religion, much less voicing them in intimate settings.

No matter. If Mama forbade her, an appeal to Papà would not be far behind. Until his retirement, Papà had been the Dean of Philosophy at the University of Padua for almost two decades. He was a champion of higher education for women, having come across the work of many learned women in his course of study and teaching. As such, he had seen Renata's schooling as too necessary to end at the country's compulsory age of ten and hired a private tutor to continue her studies. Mama did not support such undue pressure on Renata's mind, but to her dismay, Renata and Papà were united in this effort.

Returning to her task, Renata said, "I must respond immediately to la baronessa."

Renata ran up to her room and pulled out her writing desk. She sat in front of it, a fountain pen and stationery at the ready. In her best penmanship, she replied to la baronessa in the affirmative. She hesitated on a second sheet of her family's stationery, right below the crest of a phoenix engulfed in flames.

Placido or Natalia? Natalia or Placido? I cannot decide who to take, but I must soon.

Her instinct was to invite her fiancé to accompany her. Would la baronessa think it too forward for a woman to ask a man who was not yet her husband? Or should Renata follow propriety and invite her matron of honor instead? Natalia, like Renata, was a baron's daughter, so there would be no messing up the societal mores in that regard.

As for Placido, he was his Uncle Alonzo's heir and would someday inherit the Count of Sica, a most ancient title. A stature far nobler than the Baroness of Calandro and of sufficient peerage that he would be welcomed in any European castle, including the baronessa's own.

Throwing caution to the wind, she invited them both. La baronessa had briefly met all three at the Duchess of Cortina's wedding last year, so it was not as if they were strangers. Renata doubted there would be an issue when all three arrived but crossed her fingers for buona fortuna.

Besides, who among the nobility is not charitable at Christmastime?

Chapter 2

Thursday afternoon
December 16, 1897
Padua, Italy

Renata and Natalia held onto each of Placido's arms as they walked into the Baronessa di Calandro's salon. Lemon-yellow light streaked through the floor-to-ceiling windows, drenching the room in a golden hue. The room was exquisite yet sparingly appointed, with Florentine blue damask on the walls and smoke-gray upholstered settees adjacent to the fireplace. Small round tables with silver-gilt Savonarola chairs arranged around them were dotted throughout. Silver bowls and vases overflowed with evergreens, pinecones, and branches of holly berries.

"Let me help, mi amore." Placido gingerly removed Renata's cloak and handed it to the footman.

"Grazie. You are so thoughtful, Po."

He lightly placed his hand on the small of her back and said, "I always want to be the first man to help you when you need it. You are welcome to disagree, though I hope you allow me this courtesy."

"My Davide is the same way, though he struggles with mild jealousy, of which I shall not discourage him," preened Natalia. "Oh, do say yes, Renata."

"Of course," said Renata, turning to face Po. "My dear, I appreciate your offer to help as long as you realize I am content to try and fix things first myself. Your manners do you justice."

"And your independence does you justice. I may be alone among my peers in this, but I admire it. I give your parents full credit for championing your determination rather than trying to curb it."

Credit was due to her father rather than both parents, but Renata kept that to herself.

Po held out his arms again. "Are you ladies ready to go through?"

"Sì, andiamo," said Renata and Natalia together.

Peeking through the dining room, Renata glimpsed individual floral arrangements of thyme, lily of the valley, red carnations gracing the back of each dining chair, and a table set with fine bone china and crystal. It was all perfectly set for an afternoon of lively yet intimate discussions on whatever topic the hostess cared to introduce.

Renata was glad she had chosen the two-piece cream and navy Paoletti tea gown for the occasion, and Natalia was elegant in her dusty rose walking dress with velveteen trim. They should neither blend into the surroundings nor stand out. Knowing she had been selected because of her upcoming nuptials and relation to the House of Pelicani, Renata wanted to make a good impression on her own merits but adhered to the unwritten rule of la bella figura, a cultural philosophy practiced throughout the peninsula—regardless of rank—and she was ever mindful of its central tenet: outside appearances counted first.

"Hello to the bride and groom."

A slim, blond, mop-haired man and an equally blonde yet very pregnant woman tottered over.

"I wondered if you might be here," said Po, grasping the man's outstretched hand.

Renata leaned in, embracing and kissing the woman. "Lovely to see you, Mariana. This is my friend, Natalia Ricci, I mean Nunzio. We have been friends since our boarding school days." said Renata by way of introduction. "She is my matron of honor and recently married herself."

"And Vito Marzano here," said Po, tapping the man on his chest, "is my oldest and dearest friend … and my best man."

"Congratulations on your growing family," said Natalia to Mariana. "Will you be able to attend the wedding, or is your time drawing near?"

"Yes, I shall be there if someone is patient." Mariana rubbed her belly and laughed.

"Where is la baronessa?" Natalia smoothed her dress and scanned the room. "I am eager to greet her so we can sit down and have our tea."

Placido sniffed the air and licked his lips, pointing to the baked delectables on the tables, groaning with their weight. "She must employ a fantastic baker."

Natalia surveyed the food. "Oh my. She has put out as fine a spread as one might enjoy on Christmas Day. How lucky are we."

Placido continued, "I can smell the sweet, yeasty aroma of the pastries. Right out of the oven, too. It is like inhaling a woolly blanket on a cold winter day."

"There she is ... in the corner ... with Bugatti's aunt." Renata tilted her head to the northeast corner of the room. "Mama met her when she and her artist husband lived in Pusiano, but they live in Switzerland now. She stayed with us while her husband exhibited at the Societé Libre des Beaux-Arts in Brussels earlier this year."

Natalia nodded distractedly. "Ah, right, I remember them."

"You had better stop craning your neck to see who is sitting with whom." Renata tugged at Natalia's sleeve. "La baronessa is headed our way now."

La baronessa walked over to the musicians, whispered something, and they soon struck up Vivaldi's *L'inverno*. Renata thought the opening movement resembled a grieving, struggling person. She did not like what it implied and thought it was a curious choice for la baronessa to request just as she approached them.

"Buon Natale, Signora Calandro," said Renata, Placido, and Natalia in unison, wishing la baronessa a merry Christmas, curtseying and bowing as they did so.

Ever the gentleman, Placido bowed and kissed the signora's hand. "May I say that your ensemble this afternoon is, as the French would say, "Très élégante.""

La baronessa took her hand back. "Oh, with such sweet talk, I should remember to invite you to all my parties."

"He has manners in abundance," said Renata, pleased Po made such a good impression wherever they went.

When the baroness approached, Renata and Natalia both curtseyed again, but Mariana could only drop her head.

La baronessa nodded and addressed the couple. "Buon Natale, Signor and Signora Marzano."

Vito and Mariana returned the greeting.

"Well," said la baronessa, looking at Renata, "it is good that my husband did not argue my desire to enlarge this hall ten years ago. Otherwise, I would have asked your two companions to wait for you in the anteroom."

Renata felt a searing heat color her ears. "My apologies, Signora Calandro. I could not decide who to bring, and so—"

La baronessa leaned in and hissed. "I forgive a slight only once. This time, it works to balance the numbers. Another time, luck may not be on your side."

Renata jerked as if slapped. She willed herself not to react and, instead, threw up a silent prayer to the goddess Fortuna to bring her luck, for she needed a good deal of it.

Placido interjected, putting his arm around Renata's waist. "We came as a show of force to, uh, implore you not to attend our wedding next week. We had not sent an invitation so you would not be obliged to journey to our tiny village of Sica and miss the social season here in the city. Besides, think how forlorn Bishop Callegari will be when he does not see you in your family's pew at the cathedral on Christmas. We dared not incur his wrath by denying him the pleasure of your company for the sake of our little country Christmas wedding. All that said, you would be very welcome at our wedding if you do come."

La baronessa wagged her finger at Placido. "Though the silver tongue has its roots in the Bible, I wager you Pelicanis have possessed one since time began, and each successive generation sharpens their version with the current vernacular."

Placido bowed deeply. "I take your words as a compliment."

"It was not meant as one," said la baronessa, "but you have at least brought your wit, which is always appreciated here." The group laughed, and la baronessa continued, her nose in the air. "Noblemen and women invited to my salon must win my respect as the salon hostess if they wish to advance socially and politically. You will find that education and manners are on full display here. That means everyone must be on their best behavior. Enough of your bowing and scraping. I must get on with my hostess duties."

"Grazie, signora." Renata trailed after a grinning Placido and said, "I echo Placido's invitation. Please come to Sica to see us wed."

The signora swiftly returned and said, "If only you could guarantee that moral elegance abounds, and there will be none of the typical shenanigans the Pelicani boys are known for." With a flourish, she raised her hand and placed the back of it on her forehead. "I can only take so much."

A tight smile froze on Renata's face. She was unsure what the signora meant or whether Placido's behind-her-back whisper of "no promises" was a joke or the truth. Despite the woman's sharp tongue, what Renata knew for sure was that after the minor exchange, they had all had, la baronessa's reputation as THE salonnière of the Veneto was perhaps attributed out of fear rather than earned. Renata just hoped her intended's family wanted a warmer, more welcoming hostess for the salons she would be expected to host.

Their hostess turned, and Renata braced herself for another verbal onslaught. "And as for the bride-to-be, I understand you are an avid reader and are fond of bringing up crime stories at other salons you have attended."

Renata's heart leaped. Perhaps la baronessa had forgiven her infraction. "Why, yes. Is it one of the topics on today's discussion agenda?"

"Absolutely not." La baronessa tapped Renata's wrist with her folded fan. "I only mention it to instruct you to avoid bringing it up. Is that clear?"

Renata nodded and lowered her gaze. "Of course, signora."

A mischievous grin spread across the baroness' face. "However, I have something festive planned to challenge your inquisitive mind."

Renata's head snapped back up. "Oh, I hope it is about Christmas. May I know—"

"Signorina Bombonatti, patience is a virtue with which you seem not very much acquainted. I counsel you to practice, practice, practice." She paused and then winked, taking them all aback. "You will know soon enough. Please sit at the table next to the Vitali sisters, and let's get started."

The quintet moved to the table and sat, exchanging Christmas greetings with the sisters.

After they had settled, Placido held out a plate of biscotti and bomboloni. "It will be all right. Her bark is worse than her bite. How about a pastry, my dear?"

Renata was unsure whether she agreed with Po's assessment of their hostess but could not resist a cookie. "Grazie."

Po was trying to calm her, but her thoughts turned back to the expectations her in-laws had of her. When she moved to Castello Pelicani next week, she would take over as society matron of the county for her husband's widowed uncle. Considering the county had been without a Pelicani hostess for the better part of a decade, Renata hoped they would consider her age and inexperience and grant her some leniency. Po's relatives would be shocked to learn she was not much interested in society functions unless they were of the literary variety.

More than that, she had to ensure that no one caught on to her attempts to mimic Sherlock Holmes to worm her way into helping the local polizia investigate unsolvable cases. The books and magazines she was always reading would help on that score. Starting small and working her way up to the big cases—

Her meanderings were interrupted when la baronessa walked to the front of the room. She stood at a small podium and waited until everyone was quiet. After the introductions, their hostess held up a book.

"I have for each of you the volume known as *The Nobility and Excellence of Women and the Defects and Vices of Men* by the learned authoress, Lucrezia Marinella."

She nodded to her footmen, who distributed copies to the excited attendees in the room.

"If you have not yet read this three-hundred-year-old treatise in which Lucrezia disputes Giuseppe Passi's diatribe about women's alleged defects, fear not, for we have a modern-day learned woman in our midst, a woman of letters."

The buzz in the room grew more frenzied as the guests tried to guess whom la baronessa referred, only to have them all gasp when she pointed at Renata and gestured for her to stand. Renata's heart danced wildly, unsure of what game la baronessa was playing. "Please welcome Renata Bombonatti, daughter of Sandro Bombonatti, the esteemed philosophy professor at our University of Padua. From an incredibly young age, this talented young lady and soon-to-be bride was taught the Roman classics like Aurelius and Tertullian and the words of the great female intellectual Lucrezia Marinella, too. Yes, the very one you hold in your hands."

Renata's stomach began a series of somersaults. Everyone was laughing and staring at her, waiting for her to say something, and then it dawned on her. She looked to their hostess, dreading what was coming next.

"Everyone will read for an hour. At the end of the hour, you will give us your summary of the entire work and your conclusion. Afterwards, the rest of the salon will discuss the summary and whether we agree. I will end that discussion and provide my conclusion. After hearing both, the salon will vote on which conclusion is more aligned with that of the authoress."

The entire room clapped.

"Each table has been assigned a number. I will draw a number after the vote, and if the number matches the majority vote, that table wins. The winning group," she paused, as did the guests, "shall accompany me to Sica next week."

A few tables groaned, and Renata's knees buckled.

"I know, I know." La baronessa pointed to Renata and Placido in turn. "But I have been invited—last minute, mind you—to witness our guest speaker Renata here and her intended," the baroness pointed to Placido, "wed at his family's country pile, Castello Pelicani."

Most guests oohed and aahed, knowing that the Castello Pelicani had not had a public event for many years, but it was not long before everyone who was not so enamored let it be known.

"Those Pelicani are a bunch of rascals!" yelled a white-bearded man with an aristocratic flair.

A broomstick of a woman, tall and bristly, muttered loudly, "And their castle is cursed!"

"Settle down, everyone. This salon has a reputation for polite conversation, and I intend to keep it that way." Unperturbed, la baronessa patted the back of her hair and continued. "We are ready, Signorina Bombonatti." And with that, the lady left the front of the room and sat at her table, leaving the podium devoid of a speaker.

Renata stood frozen on the spot. She glanced at Natalia, whose face had drained of all color. Renata imagined her face looked similar, but she dared not pinch her cheeks to bring a spot of color to them while twenty pairs of eyes were focused on her every move and word.

Yes, she had read the two-hundred-page Marinella treatise, but with only a moment's notice, she was not prepared to give an oral commentary on the work she had read a half-decade ago. Her jaw muscles spasmed. She thought her teeth might start to rattle any minute. Why was this happening?

Then, another realization hit her. In the baroness' eyes, Renata had exercised one slight too many, and a public humiliation would be her retribution. Renata had never met someone who could be so vindicative to someone else, mainly when they had caused no personal harm.

When they met at the Cortina wedding last year, Renata should have paid more attention to the baronessa's behavior. Frantically searching her memory, she recalled that the meeting and conversation had been cordial and witty. It was unconscionable for Renata to be treated in a manner that was not commensurate with the crime.

Anyone in the room could see that la baronessa's purse could stretch to feed another mouth at her salon, so it was not a question of financial harm because Renata had brought an uninvited guest. Unfortunately, la baronessa must have perceived Renata's act as much more than a slight to warrant this embarrassment.

Renata's shoulders sank. Placido had come to her rescue once already. By the looks of his white knuckles on his chair's arms, she did not trust that anything he said or did would not hinder her best efforts. Renata shook her head ever so slightly to warn Po not to create a spectacle in retaliation.

Renata shifted her gaze to Natalia. Her friend's left knee bounced uncontrollably. It was how her body coped under duress. Renata took that and Po's rage as signs that she was alone. She wanted peace with this literary doyenne of society, so Renata had to act fast to ease the woman's ire.

A spark ignited within her as Renata remembered some advice from Seneca, her father's favorite Stoic philosopher. Her father had shared it with her years ago when she had been overwhelmed with life.

"If a man knows not what harbor he seeks, any wind is the right wind."

Renata flipped open the first page of the treatise. She sensed the weight of Seneca's hand on her shoulder and understood it as a sign of perseverance.

Chapter 3

Outside Palazzo De Angelis, Renata, Placido, and Natalia said goodbye to the Marzanos and climbed into Placido's carriage.

Renata looked out the carriage window. Twilight had arrived, draping a velvet blanket over the city.

"How badly she behaved, and for a Christmas salon, too." Renata huffed and arranged her dress under her legs to allow Natalia to sit beside her in the carriage. "The Marinella book had nothing to do with Christmas. Discussing a classic like 'Old Christmas' by Washington Irving or 'To the Tenth Muse' by Matilde Serao would have served as perfectly worthy literary delights for the season."

Natalia took one hand from her muskrat muffler and patted Renata's sable muffler several times. "I heartily agree, my friend."

"Ugh!" Renata peered out the window. "I am done with literary salons run by cunning hostesses with thin skin and even thinner purses."

"My dear," said Placido, settling in across from Renata and Natalia and putting his top hat on his lap, "I believe this is how she tests her guests to see if they can withstand the rigor of her literary salon. Besides, you showed her you were up to the task and brilliantly, too." He tapped the ceiling of the carriage, and the driver set off.

Renata grabbed the lion-headed armrest, then said, "Are you mocking me? Were you aware that this was la baronessa's modus operandi, yet you failed to share that morsel about her character with me? If I had known about her egregious defect, I would not have attended such a farce." From her narrow gaze, Renata shot Placido imaginary daggers.

Placido tilted his head and addressed Renata. "I knew no such thing, amore mia, and heavens no, and I would never mock you or your clever and resourceful mind."

"Of course, he would not, Renata." Natalia sat back against the tufted velvet. "He would never betray you if he had known it was a setup like that. I think your reputation as a sharp mind very much preceded you. I suspect the baroness was not convinced she would proceed with her plan until you challenged her too much, and she swapped out the debater at the last minute. She refused to be bested."

"Hmm. Well, you have convinced me I overreacted, and I apologize for my uncivilized behavior," conceded Renata. "She put me on the spot, and now, all I can think of is taking back the wedding invitation. I do not want her making trouble again, especially at Christmas and on my—*our*—special day. She must be taught a lesson."

Placido sucked in his breath and shook his head.

"There are many rules in the society we travel through," said Natalia, circling the air between them with her forefinger, "but rescinding a wedding invitation is unforgivable."

"Renata," said Placido, lightly rubbing Renata's knee, "I dare say Baronessa Calandro has witnessed how you are more than capable of engaging the high nobility with which she keeps close company. However, she would do well to steer clear of any such mischief in the future. I think it is safe to say she has learned her lesson."

But have I learned mine? Renata asked herself.

Chapter 4

Saturday mid-morning
December 18, 1897
Padua

Renata snapped shut *The Strand* and brought the magazine to her bosom, heaving from the excitement of rereading "A Scandal in Bohemia." Sherlock Holmes was the central figure in Arthur Conan Doyle's short story and equally central to Renata's life. But no one, not even Placido, knew what or how much she read. It was her secret pastime and a subject she had often thought might come up in the many literary events she attended, but it never had.

After what happened at Baronessa Calandro's salon, there was no doubt in her mind another salon invitation was out of the question. If it did happen, she could take satisfaction from outsmarting anyone if the topic of mysteries came up, especially after that woman stood up and said something about Castello Pelicani being cursed. Renata made a mental note to ask Placido about that.

"Are you *still* reading that British magazine?" Mama entered the parlor and startled Renata, who had been reclining on the divan. The petite, prim woman Mama perched on a chair in front of her writing desk and put a hand on her hip, waiting for Renata to reply. "Pfft. Reading about crime at Christmas should be criminal."

"Mama, there is no season for crime or reading about crime, but yes, I am finished." Finished with the magazine maybe, but thoughts of solving a case of her own someday swirled in her head.

Mama waved at Renata. "Go to your room and make sure Alissa packs your trousseau properly."

Renata set her magazine down. "I will have to do it because Alissa is ill and has taken to her bed. I sent a note to the castello that they must provide me with another maid this week until Alissa can join me."

"Oh, bother. I hope the girl recovers soon. Mind that you take everything you need for the wedding and your honeymoon in Sicily."

Wedding. Honeymoon. Placido. It had all happened so fast. Five years had flown by, and the last six months even more. Renata and Placido had exchanged pleasantries and stolen moments in one salon or ball after another until Mama and Papà had decreed that he would do as a husband. And here they were, five years since that fateful day in the Prato.

Renata hugged her magazine and only relaxed when hearing music wafting from the street. She jumped up, but her too-tight corset forced her to slow down. After she had caught her breath, she looked out the Moorish-style window and was thrilled when she caught sight of the zampognari on the edge of the Prato. It was midday, and she shielded her eyes from the bluish-white winter sunlight hitting her eyes. The market and streets were buzzing with Paduans priming themselves for the Christmas festivities. The musicians played "O Come All Ye Faithful" on their bagpipes, and she sang along in Latin.

"*Adeste Fidelis laeti triumphantes,*
Venite, venite in Bethlehem
Natum videte, Regem Angelorum ..."

The pipers, wearing shaggy sheepskin vests, felt hats, and crisscrossed leather leggings, always trek up from the south end of the peninsula to play their bagpipes in the Christmas markets in the north. Playing his piffero, a white-bearded flautista accompanied the piper. Together with troubadours picked up on the journey through the mountains and valleys in the northwest Apennines, musicians of all ages often formed ragtag bands as they traveled throughout central Italy. They arrived late in Padua this year, but Renata cared not a whit. She was thrilled to see them before leaving her hometown for the village of Sica.

Renata let loose on the refrain, her favorite part: "*Venite adoremus, venite* ..."

"You have a lovely voice, dear, but now you must hurry along and—"

Her shoulders sagged. She stopped singing but was too engrossed in the wintry scene below to address her mother's pleas. Renata watched as carriages traversed the snow-covered roads, transporting families and presents from one end of the city to another.

A busker with a mandolin in hand sang from atop vegetable crates on a corner opposite the Prato, hoping to entice passersby to part with a lira or two. Young couples promenaded near the canal and stopped at handicraft stalls on the last market day before Christmas. She loved the sights and sounds of the holiday season and was eager to spend a few days at the castello before the wedding, participating in all the country's seasonal activities.

"When is Natalia arriving at the castello? And the rest of the wedding party? Will Placido's brothers be standing up with him or a friend?"

Mama's questions jarred her back to the present.

"Natalia arrives on the 21st. As for Po's brothers—Giacomo, Fabrizio, and Tommaso—they are not in the wedding party, but his best man, Vito Marzano, as well as his good friends, Ursino Fumagalli and Dario Rinaldo, are already at the castello. Oh, and Vito's pregnant wife, Mariana, will be there, too."

"Hmm, how odd that Placido chooses friends over family to stand up with him at the altar. Though I suppose they are only half-brothers, so—"

"Mama, please. He does not see them as half. Besides, he has his reasons, and ours is not to question why."

"Well, we have got to get an early start in the morning, contessa." Her mother dragged out '-*essa*.' "Castello Pelicani is at least a four-hour carriage ride away, and his lordship expects us for lunch. We cannot be late when your future uncle-in-law is making such an effort for us, for *you*. You will one day be the lady of that manor, and punctuality is of the utmost—"

Renata's thoughts ran wild at the idea that once Placido inherited his uncle's title, she would be known as Signora Pelicani, Contessa di Sica, lady of the manor and the county. She could hardly fathom how thrilling it sounded when she had learned about her future title and role.

Though they had been adolescents, Placido had informally proposed in the Prato at the Castle of Love in midsummer. She thought he had just been caught up in the moment's frenzy, but he insisted he was sincere. Their secret promise to one another had held fast ever since, including throughout his four years of military service. This past summer, Placido reappeared in Padua after many years away.

Unbeknownst to their families, the young couple had met several times in the last few months at various grand palazzi around the Veneto, in the salons of Venice, Vicenza, and fair Verona where the idle aristocracy of fin-de-siècle northern Italy sought out the intelligentsia for philosophical, political, and cultural discourse. It was in those frescoed rooms that Renata and Placido had renewed their acquaintance. Their love had blossomed in reading Dante's poetry, debating Garibaldi's heroism, and viewing exhibitions of Artemisia's art.

While Mama had been busy finalizing a list of suitable prospects for Renata and preparing her for her debutante season, Placido had swooped in and secured Renata's hand. On hearing the news, Mama had been disappointed that Papà had agreed to the arrangement. Mama had lofty aspirations for Renata, her only child. She had set her sights on the great houses of Europe in the hopes that her brunette-tressed, amber-eyed beauty would attract a royal suitor. Even a minor royal would do.

The Pelicani peerage from which Placido hailed was ancient and respectable enough, but when it came to the man Renata would marry, Mama had always wanted more for Renata. More wit. More handsomeness. And definitely more money. If only Renata knew how much more money her mother wanted and needed.

"What are you waiting for, child?"

Renata eased out of her reverie and turned to Mama. "Hmm ..."

Her mother stopped writing yet another of her interminable lists and punched the air with her glass dip pen. "Well?"

"I suppose I wanted a few more moments to myself," said Renata. And many more with My Detective, as she was wont to refer to Sherlock Holmes if she was being entirely truthful. However, she dared not say so aloud lest Mama not only disparage the magazine a second time but once again discourage her from reading so much, especially fiction.

"Get your head out of those silly detective stories and go on upstairs. Honestly, you are a lady. Behave like one." Signora Bombonatti tapped her glass pen in the inkwell. "What *will* your fiancé think of your incessant reading?"

What indeed.

Chapter 5

Sunday morning
December 19, 1897
Sica, a village near Padua, Italy

Renata pulled aside the curtain covering her carriage window and sighed at the sight in the distance. In the shadow of the Euganean Hills, Castello Pelicani rose like a fortress—a presidio over her verdant valley and protector of all her hardworking people. Ca' Peli, as the locals liked to call it, was a play on "capelli," the Italian word for hair. The nickname was an homage to the village children's favorite fable about Rapunzel, a maiden with floor-sweeping flaxen hair.

Against her parents' strong objection that she wed near their home in the historic city of Padua in the chapel of the magnificent university where her father taught the classics, Renata had given in to Placido's urging that they marry at Ca' Peli, his Uncle Alonzo's home and the Pelicani family's country seat.

During their early courtship, when they would meet in the salons of the villas in their hometown, Po would regale Renata with stories of the pony rides and pond swims of his youth here. And as he neared manhood, he embellished the stories featuring exploits of his boar hunts and the bacchanalia that followed. More recently, he began his convincing pleas to marry at the Ca' because the grandeur of the place would so befit the "queen of his eye."

The carriage hit a rut in the road. Ack! Renata bounced off the seat, jarring her back to the present.

She landed in a heap, straightened herself, and peered out the window. Flattening her face against the frosty pane, she pulled back. Ow, ow, ow. She screamed from the pain of ripping her lips off the icy glass, followed by a silent guttural cry. She had just witnessed a man falling to his death. For how could a man who had fallen from a vine-covered turret in a castello be anything other than dead?

A layer of her skin was hanging on the windowpane. She shifted away from the castello and ran her tongue over her torn and bloody lips. Her blood was nothing. Renata imagined the blood gushing out of the dead man's head as he lay on the frigid ground. Her body shook. Her bosom heaved. The questions rushed in.

Who was he? Why had he fallen from the tower? If he had made a noise, had anyone heard him? And more importantly, did anyone care?

"I do, I care," she repeatedly whispered to the empty carriage. She raised her trembling right hand and crossed herself.

The carriage swayed around a bend. Renata grabbed the fraying strap dangling from the ceiling. She willed herself to stay upright and her stomach intact. She licked another drop of blood off her lips. From her purse, she pulled out a handkerchief and dabbed off the blood.

A few minutes later, she twisted her head to see out the other window. It was too fogged up. Drat! She rubbed a corner of her wool cape over the window and jerked. The dead body was gone. One minute, his arms and legs were flailing as he fell. In the next, his body was splayed in an unnatural position. His limbs were all akimbo, then poof! He had vanished.

Nooooooo. She wanted to shout again *I care* but feared the coachman bringing the four harnessed horses to a screeching halt and her head hitting the window. Did she see what she thought she saw? She squeezed her eyes shut and then opened them a few seconds later. She peered out the window again to confirm her suspicions. The ground at the tower's base was bare, but a man was peering over the edge at the top.

Of all the things that could happen before her Christmas Eve wedding, did it have to be a death?

Chapter 6

Renata shivered as the rickety carriage raced over the stone bridge and through the massive wrought iron gates. They passed the vine-draped stone walls and neared the imposing ochre-colored edifice of the castello.

She rubbed her undersides aching from the springs poking her through the thinning cushion. Why had Papà not had the carriage refurbished before her wedding? And why had Mama insisted Renata ride alone while she and Papà took the grander carriage Po's uncle had sent for the ride over?

She did not want to arrive ungrateful but could not help brooding on the accident she had witnessed.

Did Po know about the man who had fallen to his death? Her wondering turned to worry that she had made a mistake coming here, and now her nuptials were cursed before they had begun. With a start, she recalled that the man who had climbed the Castle of Love tower in Padua during the celebrations years earlier had also fallen backward like the accident she had just witnessed. How uncanny.

No, no, no. My worries will only hinder me if I let them.

She shook her head to dispel superstitious thoughts and focused on positive things.

Her heart fluttered thinking of her handsome beau. How gallant he had been at their first meeting. Willing to risk losing a girl to help a fellow combatant. Sigh. She lifted a hand to secure her hat to her fluffy bouffant and smoothed the hobble skirt of her dress lest Po see her as anything less than presentable to his family. Renata was thrilled to have arrived and would soon be in Po's loving arms.

The carriage slowed to a stop, and the driver's boots crunched on the gravel. He opened the carriage door and pulled down the rickety steps. He held out his hand to help her out. "Vieni."

"Please be careful carrying that, Piero." Renata pointed to the wrapped painting on the seat across from her. "That is my wedding gift to my fiancé."

Piero bowed. "Sì, sì."

"Grazie." She took Piero's hand and held her precious nonna's red leather writing box with her other hand.

Once outside, she took three gulps of biting winter air into her lungs before surveying the extensive complex. The castle nestled against a rocky spur on the eastern fringes of the conical, vineyard-covered volcanic hills. She was awed by the beautiful blend of military architecture and a stately home befitting a Renaissance prince.

The grand entrance courtyard was marked by sculptures on high drum pedestals and dominated by the Baroque fountain, which had a strange beast that she vowed to investigate later. She trained her gaze past the exquisite formal gardens to the tower—the scene of the "crime"—and noticed a guard with a rifle on his shoulder circling the tower's roof.

He had not been there a second ago. She would have to find out if a guard was always posted there—perhaps a holdover from when the castello dominated the navigable waterways it was built to control—or a recent addition owing to the unfortunate incident she had witnessed moments ago.

Straining to observe the ground surrounding the tower, a mix of the same frosted grass and hardened gravel that lay near her feet, she could not find a body. Her heart thumped beneath her corset. This was the kind of excitement she felt when she discovered Sir Arthur Conan Doyle's works.

In her before-Placido days, she fancied herself a budding Sherlock Holmes, though better dressed and Italian, not English. Placido would have to take her sleuthing fantasies seriously now that she had been a witness to a potential murder. The question that had loomed since they announced their engagement was this: when would she come clean to Po about her secret pastime?

"Signorina Bombonatti?"

Renata whipped around to face the speaker. A young woman about her age was curtseying. Renata urged her up. "Hello, what is your name?"

"Eletta Bianca."

"All right, Eletta. Piacere. Please show me in and advise the coachmen where they might deposit my bags."

"Si, signora, I mean ..." The woman twisted her apron in knots.

"It's fine. Once I am married, you can call me that. For now, signorina will do."

Renata walked through the arched entrance and beckoned Eletta to follow. It was strange that Eletta was nervous. Thus, Renata sought to put her at ease.

"Come on, take us inside to warm up and then to wherever my beloved waits for me."

Chapter 7

Renata set her writing box on a nearby Empire console table and clapped her hands while admiring the castello's octagon-shaped entrance hall. It was adorned with beribboned pine boughs and holly garlands draped over the second-story railing. Clove-studded oranges sat arranged in silver-flecked bowls on tables. Pinecone sculptures on either side of the staircase resembled those flanking the famous fountain at the Vatican.

She inhaled the oranges' spicy scent and closed her eyes, taking it all in. When she heard a commotion behind her, she opened her eyes to see who it was. Mama and Papà had arrived, and she walked over to them.

"How festive! How fragrant! Do you not think so, Mama?"

"Certo." Mama agreed and crossed the distance between herself and Renata. Renata's trousseau had occupied all the available space outside and inside her carriage. Mama had written to Zio Alonzo to state they would have to rent a second carriage. He had replied immediately and insisted on sending one of his, which Renata suspected was Mama's intention all along.

"Indeed, it is quite grand," said Papà, standing beside Mama.

As Eletta curtseyed to Mama and Papà, a sharply dressed man appeared from an alcove, with his manservant following.

"And we should find ..." The thickly mustachioed man with a shock of white hair and regal bearing paused his speech mid-stride. "Ah, bella Renata. The bride has arrived."

Renata rushed to her fiancé's uncle. She curtseyed before kissing him on both cheeks. "Zio Alonzo, Buon Natale. May I call you uncle like Placido does?"

"Merry Christmas to you, too, my dear. Yes, you may call me uncle. Once you are married, you are welcome to use the title of Contessina, unless I take a new wife to be my Contessa …" everyone laughed, "or Nobildonna, if you prefer."

"Count Sica, Buon Natale," said Mama and Papà in unison, coming up behind Renata, bowing and curtseying.

"Alonzo, please. I only use my title in correspondence or if I need to frighten someone." He winked and waved a hand in dismissal. "Signora and Signor Bombonatti, Buon Natale. It's nice to see you both again."

"Grazie," said the Bombonattis. "Please, we are family. Call us Sandro and Colombina."

"Certo," said Alonzo, nodding. "Welcome to my home." He pointed to the garlands and bowls overflowing with shiny baubles. "We tried to spruce up this old pile for the festivities. We hope you like all the holiday decorations."

"You have a marvelous home." Papà gestured about the entrance hall. Gilded Venetian glass balls hung over the arched exits, and ropes of pearly beads were entwined in the grand stone staircase leading to the upper floors. "Thank you for hosting us for Christmas and holding the wedding festivities here. We appreciate all your staff's effort. Magnifico!"

He bowed. "My pleasure."

"And the groom? Was he not alerted to our arrival?" Mama stretched her neck to look over Alonzo's shoulder.

"Sorry to say, and unbeknownst to me, he left abruptly this morning with his manservant Bepi. His note only said he had to go to Orrico to see about the bedroom suite furniture, which had not yet arrived. Do not fret. He is due back tonight." Alonzo tilted his head at his majordomo. The man stepped forward, bowing his head in one quick gesture.

"Martell, at your service. Welcome to Castello Pelicani, Signor and Signora Bombonatti." Turning, he pointed to three footmen and two maids.

The Bombonattis thanked him and acknowledged the staff. Renata raised her eyebrow. The butler's surname meant "hammer," and she did not doubt that he ruled with one. She wondered if he kept the same watch over the outdoors as he did the indoors, including a dead man who had gone missing.

Renata refocused her thoughts. Soon, she had to speak to Po, then Mama and Papà. Had they seen what she had seen? If not, then what? A flicker of excitement sneaked up the back of her neck. Saliva built up at the corners of her mouth, and she wiped it away lest anyone else noticed. This strange accident could be her moment to shine like Sherlock!

"Lunch is in an hour in the breakfast room." Martell stepped back, snapped his fingers, and said, "Vai." Four male servants wearing aprons appeared and hurried past everyone to help the carriage drivers with the remaining trunks. "We dine at eight o'clock in the dining hall."

Mama nodded. "Very good. Thank you, Martell."

Martell turned to Renata. "Signorina, if you wish to watch or help decorate a tree or two, you can join the staff. After lunch, they will put on the finishing touches in the Blue Room and the ladies' parlor." The butler bowed his head at the Bombonattis, turned to Eletta, and gestured his head upwards.

"This way, signorina." Eletta motioned for the Bombonattis and the servants to follow her up the staircase. The servants were so overloaded with bags that they could easily tip over.

"Oh, before you go," Zio Alonzo held up his hand, and the Bombonattis paused," I always preside at dinner, though I do not eat a midday meal. However, my sons and the groomsmen will be there on my behalf. Also, I have much to attend to regarding the affairs of my estate, so you may not see much of me before the wedding. Please make yourself at home."

The Bombonattis murmured niceties in return.

"And I am busy planning my upcoming trip across America. If Placido has not already mentioned, I will take my three other sons on a reverse Grand Tour of sorts."

"How splendid," said Papà, grinning. "Tours were already out of fashion when my father took me across Europe and the British Isles, but I gained a world of experience, and I regret none of it. Quite the opposite."

Zio Alonzo nodded, then addressed Renata. "When you and Placido return from your honeymoon, Ca' Peli will be all yours for many months. You can settle in at your leisure without the rest of the Pelicanis hovering about. Renata, feel free to begin your salons any time." He winked. "The county matrons are eagerly anticipating their first invitation."

Renata thought back to the mild disaster at the Baronessa di Calandro's salon and did her best not to grimace. "Thank you, Zio Alonzo. I will do my best."

"Yes, she will. She will be the envy of all the salonnières," said Mama, carving a wide arc in the air with her hand, "from here to Milano, Roma, and Venezia."

"Mama!"

"Capital, capital," said Zio Alonzo and left the foyer.

Blood rushed up Renata's face to her scalp and down the back of her neck. In a flash, Renata relived the Baronessa di Calandro's Christmas literary salon and dreaded having to return the courtesy by inviting her to Ca' Peli. The contessa was not the kind of woman who would be bested twice, regardless of who held the salon. If Mama had gotten wind of what had happened at la baronessa's salon, she might not have let on for fear of spoiling the wedding week, and Renata would be ever in God's debt if things stayed that way. She would not relish such a talk with Mama.

Renata walked behind her parents and headed for the stairs when a new voice greeted them.

"Ah, benvenuto. The Bombonattis, I presume?"

Renata looked over her shoulder to see Po's two groomsmen.

"Buongiorno, Dario e Ursino. How good to see you both." She cleared her throat. "Uh, these are my parents, Sandro e Colombina Bombonatti." Her parents climbed down the stairs to stand before the men and shake their hands. "Mama e Papà, this is Dario Rinaldo," Renata said, gesturing to a stocky young man with a shy disposition, then to a much taller man with a thin mustache and a seemingly permanent smirk etched on his face. "And this is Ursino Fumogalli."

"Piacere," said everyone all around.

Dario stepped forward. "Well, we can see that you have just arrived and will want to settle in. Please let us know if we can help. Otherwise, we have, uh …"

"… groomsmen duties to which we must attend. Like Signor Alonzo, we also do not take lunch, so we shall see you again at dinner." Ursino motioned for Dario to follow him. Dario's cheeks reddened, and then he bowed at the Bombonattis and chased after Ursino.

઼ઝ

Renata left Eletta to unpack and trotted off to her parents' rooms. She had to find out if they had seen what she had seen. Walking down the corridor, she could have sworn she had seen the swish of a little girl's white dress, but perhaps it was just a blur conjured by a tired mind.

She knocked at her parents' suite, and her father replied, "Vieni." She entered and locked the door behind her.

Her mother stopped her unpacking and frowned. "Darling, what is it? Why did you lock the door?"

Her father poked his head out from behind the wardrobe door. "Well?"

Renata wrung her hands. "Did you see anything unusual as your carriage approached the castello? Someone with a rifle on the castello's tower, perhaps?"

Mama shook her head. "No. Why?"

"The man rules the county, Renata," said Papà. "It is right that he has a small militia to guard his properties. You best get used to it. This family is rich and will do much to protect their wealth."

"Very wealthy indeed," said Mama, touching the gilded furnishings with one hand and the stunningly carved porcelain figurines with the other.

Her father cleared his throat. "Anything else on your mind, cara?"

Renata nodded. She wanted to discuss the possible death of a man, but after years of Mama's scolding about her unladylike sleuthing, refraining from going into detail about what she had seen would be the wiser move. Though she was days away from being a married woman of twenty, she knew Mama and Papà would not hold back their admonishments regardless of her age and status. And Mama had a superstitious streak that, once aroused, could send the entire household into a tailspin while she ranted about what a particular sign could portend.

Renata clenched her fists at her side. If Mama saw those fists, she would drill Renata for an explanation. Mama could always suss out when her only child was holding back information, so Renata put her hands behind her back, away from prying eyes.

"Oh, uh, ..." Renata gulped. "I thought I saw a cloud of blackbirds near the tower and was curious if you knew what species they were.'

"Ravens. It is always the ravens, never the crows," said her father, snipping his cigar and lighting it.

Ignoring her husband, and without looking up from her suitcase, her mother said, "Renata, cara, is that all?"

"Yes." She rolled her eyes. Papà thought ravens were too clever for their own good, but he did trust the crows. "I am going to go pray for Po's safe return."

"He better be here soon." Mama's shrill voice seemed more pronounced since they had arrived. "He should not have waited so long to see to the furniture. Tsk-tsk."

Placido was not the one making the furniture, but Renata did not mention that fact. Sighing, Renata let her parents be and left.

Chapter 8

Renata stood outside the door and peered down the corridor. She knew the men's wing of the castello was off-limits. She justified being there because, in her self-appointed role as an independent investigator, she had to go where her case led. Picking up her skirts, she padded silently yet purposefully across the promenade that joined the two wings above the empty entrance hall. Though she was glad no one had spotted her stealthy sashay, she looked around and wondered why no servants or footmen were present. Perhaps they were helping guests, preparing lunch, still decorating, or—

"Looking for me?"

At the sound of a male voice, she whipped around.

"Oh, Ursino. I did not see you."

"Well, I am where I am supposed to be in the gentlemen's quarters," he said, stepping closer, his hulk of a chest inches from hers. "Yet you are not in the ladies' quarters where you are supposed to be."

"Ursino, I—" She turned away from his wine-soaked breath.

"Come now." He placed a finger under her chin and turned her face upwards. "You are about to wed my good friend Placido. That means you can call me Fumo now."

His roving eyes unnerved her, and she was glad she still had her scarf on. She had worn it to keep her cleavage covered up and warm during her carriage ride.

Ursino Fumagalli was a rogue. He had earned the nickname "Fumo" because of his habit of roaming around a ballroom and blowing "smoke into a henhouse and stunning the birds." In his case, the birds were ladies he charmed with fancy word spells before selecting a few for his machinations before they realized what he had done. Thus, she wanted to avoid Fumo and knew aggravating the situation would not help.

"I was hoping Placido would greet me when we arrived." Renata took a gander over Fumo's right shoulder into an empty hallway. There was that blur of a little girl again. She shook her head and turned her attention back to Fumo. "Do you know why Po is taking so long to return from Orrico?"

"Hmm…" Fumo said nothing, his eyes fixated on her bosom.

Gritting her teeth, she continued. "When I find Vito, I will demand that he tell me what is going on. You do not want to, and Dario is afraid of his own shadow and yours as well, so—"

Fumo looked up and twirled his mustache, taking a step closer. "What's the hurry? As we said earlier, we groomsmen are awfully busy with our, er, groomsmen duties, but I could escort—"

Her stomach roiling, she cut him off and looked behind her. "Strange that there are so many people missing. Was this the case when you were up on the roof?"

His left eye blinked frantically. "Ca' Pelicani is a massive estate, so if you have not had a tour, I would be happy to—" He offered her his arm.

She ignored his gesture and forged ahead with her questions lest he punted more of them. "Oh, speaking of the roof, were you up there a few hours ago?"

"Yes," he growled. "We were rehearsing a tableau vivant for the wedding night. Why are you so interested in the roof?"

"Just curious." She paused and scratched her head. "Why was it necessary to practice outside in the cold and so high up, on the roof no less?"

The scar above his eyebrow twitched, and his jaw tightened. "Dario, Vito, and I grew up fighting with the Pelicani brothers, and often it was on that roof."

"But Vito is an expectant father. Why would he take such risks, and in the cold, too?"

Fumo's eyes blackened for a split second, and Renata looked away. Then, he puffed out his chest before answering. "The temperature matters little to us warriors when we are in the midst of battle because—" He hesitated, and she watched as his features returned to normal. "Let's go back to why you spend so much time in the men's wing." He took another step closer. "To maintain your reputation, I could forget I saw you if we were to—"

Renata had had enough of this wily creature when he dismissed yet another of her questions. She stepped to Fumo's left, but his arm shot to the wall, blocking her.

"It is time for lunch, and everyone is waiting for me in the breakfast room, so I will just—"

A slow grin spread over his face. "Lunch can wait. It is not too late to change your mind about the wedding. I assure you it is not, especially when there are other ... more enticing options."

Rascal, she wanted to shout but kept quiet. He was still too close. She stepped on his toe and twisted away from him swiftly.

"Ow!" He bent to check his foot.

"Sorry, I have to run," she cried as she flew off.

Moments later, she was back in her room with the door locked. Renata caught her breath and then flopped onto the tall armchair near the fire that Eletta had stoked.

Rats! She hated getting caught and by none other than Fumo, too. Oh, why did Placido keep him as a friend? The man was impossible, and all her friends who had met him at the engagement party agreed with her. Ursino was a different man when Placido was about. Perhaps Po was loathe to let him go because they had known one another since they were in leading strings. Besides Po's kindness and generosity to his friends, it was the only reason that made sense to her.

Retrieving a handkerchief from her purse, Renata spotted an envelope above the mantel addressed to her. Placido! She would recognize his handwriting anywhere. Why had she not noticed it before? Had someone slipped into her room when she was sneaking around the men's wing? She leaped up to grab the note, but the bustle and bulk of her dress prevented her, so she forced herself to rise slowly. When would she learn to be less physically impulsive?

Finally, with the note in hand, she sat at her vanity. Her hand trembled while she slid the letter opener under the sealing wax. It came right off in one piece, and she caressed Placido's crest, the letter *P* riding the back of a pelican. Placido Pelicani. Renata Pelicani.

Po, my love, she thought, *soon I will be your wife and have a stamp like this all my own.*

She placed the wax seal over her breast and held it there a moment.

Remembering the letter, she dropped the wax onto the table and opened the letter. It read:

I am but temporarily from thee.

Where is your (im)payshient existance?

Truly, V° P, are safe and flee, but—

Remember: our love will defy all distance.

She had been sitting for twenty minutes and reading the atrociously-spelled note a dozen times. Renata raged at the ceiling and waved the note at it.

"Po, this is as clear as the mud in the Battaglia Canal. What have you done, and where have you gone?"

Papà was pounding on her locked bedchamber door. Her yell must have alerted him. She ran to open the door to keep him from busting it down. As she reached the door, she spotted another note on the floor.

This one had been pushed under the door, and she hurriedly hid it in her bosom. If it was anything like the first one, she need not involve her father until she had read it first.

Papà pushed past Renata. He surveyed her suite of rooms and returned to where she stood. His arm swept the air, as it was often wont to do when he was agitated. "Why were you shouting? What's happened?" He crossed his arms and waited for her response.

She thrust Placido's note at her father. "This."

Her father scanned it and then slapped it with his hand. "What is the meaning of it? It makes no sense to me."

"Papà, do you not see? It is Placido's handwriting. Zio Alonzo told us Po has gone to Orrico, though there seems to be more to it, and he is trying to let me know with this note."

"I am not interested in your love gibberish. Tell me where he has gone if he is not in Orrico." Her father thrust the letter at her. "He should be here. Why did he not meet your carriage? Hmmpf. I know neither his father nor mother were around to raise him into adulthood, but his uncle has manners enough that he should have taught the boy that at least. And we all acted like it was normal that he was not here to greet us. For shame."

"Papà, I think this note is just a-a-a joke the groomsmen are playing. As for Po, I assure you that he has not gone on a fool's errand." She cast her eyes down and then back up, widening them while she forced her lower lip to tremble. "I overreacted, and I apologize for disturbing you and making you come to my room."

He tapped his foot and pulled at the skin of his Adam's apple, then stopped.

"How far is this town of Orrico anyway? A man of Placido's stature could have sent a servant." Her father's foot had gone from tapping to stamping.

"I do not know, Papà. I have just asked Ursino, and he, uh, he told me not to worry." She placed her hand on Papà's forearm and the other hand behind her back, fingers crossed. "And we should not either. Go finish your cigar before we have to go down for lunch."

"Find his manservant, Renata." Papà punched the air with his index finger. "Get him to bring Placido home. Your mother and I ..." He mopped the sweat from his brow. "We are ... worried for you. That is all."

Renata's shoulders fell. "Yes, Papà."

Papà pulled out his pocket watch to check the time and snapped it shut seconds later. "Dio, we have seven hours to bathe, dress, and be downstairs for dinner. It is all your fault that we got a late start but never mind now. If your groom is not downstairs for dinner, I will demand that Alonzo send out the cavalry to bring him back. The Bombonattis will not be humiliated. I will see you shortly for lunch."

Renata followed her father to the door and locked it after him, shaking her head at his incessant timekeeping. He seemed worried about something beyond the fact that Po was missing. Though she could not put her finger on it, she would ask him about it at lunch. Meanwhile, she returned to her vanity table, fished the new note out of her bosom, and opened it.

When your groom returns, tell him I wish to speak to him privately.

F

It was signed simply with the initial *F* and one too many flourishes on either side. Fumo! Ugh. Two notes in the space of a half hour? Who knew young men were so prolific with their letter-writing?

Renata placed the notes side-by-side. She read and reread them. Finally, she came to two conclusions. First, the handwriting was not identical. Second, she did not believe the *V* and *P* in the first note—

Vito and Po, respectively, were in trouble, though she did think Fumo knew much more than he had let on. The trip to Orrico just before she and her family were due to arrive was suspicious, but was it enough to warrant more sleuthing and keeping her guard up?

Chapter 9

"Are you a new lady's maid?" Renata tried not to show her frustration with how Eletta had styled her hair. Renata had wanted it to look a certain way for her first night here and Po to realize what he had missed all day, so she fussed with it.

"Yes, I am. If you are not so pleased with me and think me not suited for this work, I will let you know that I was recommended by one of the groomsmen."

"Ah." He must have been bedding her and got her the job. Renata scolded herself for jumping to conclusions, though Vito had a pregnant wife, and Dario was interested in paramours of his own kind so that only left Fumo.

From the mirror, Renata watched as Eletta lowered her head. Renata paused and pulled out her face powder. She dabbed the puff gently all over her face and décolletage. "Is there other work to which you are better suited?"

"I am a trained seamstress, signorina." Eletta straightened her shoulders and stood a little taller. "I am a fifth-generation seamstress. My great-great-grandmother Lucia was taught at the court of the Duke of Ferrara. She left his employment when she had saved enough soldi to open a little shop, Moda Bianca, in our village of Sica."

Renata furrowed her brows. "If you have a shop, how do you handle your duties here?"

"I am here but recently. We will have to close our shop due to, er ..."

"Due to?" Renata encouraged Eletta. She had been fidgeting with a hair comb, and Renata took it so the maid would stop and focus.

"The Marzanos! It's their fault," she burst out. Embarrassed, she ran to bring Renata her satin shoes, but Renata waved her away when Eletta knelt to buckle them on.

Renata gulped. She took the shoes Eletta handed her and put them on the floor. "Do you mean the noble Marzano family of Padua?"

"Yes, the very same. They are connected to the Pelicani family. A century ago, the current conte's great-grandfather was trying to build up our village of Sica with shops. He hoped his actions would attract many craftsmen—a blacksmith, a tailor, several woodworkers, leather toolers, and so on. Hearing of her husband's plans, the then-marchesa demanded a shop for the ladies."

Pointing to her head, Renata said, "A smart thinker, that woman."

"Well, when word got out, it reached Ferrara. My great-great-grandmother applied and was accepted as a shop tenant."

"Rare for a woman of that time, but I tip my hat to her."

"Yes, she was ahead of her time. Everyone said so, signorina, though I doubt the current Signor Marzano thinks so."

"Why is that?"

"He claims his relative likely never intended to extend the lease to four generations of Bianca women. He said as much to Signor Alonzo when I tried to bring the matter to the conte's attention. The worst part is that your future uncle-in-law believed him!"

Renata jerked. "No. I cannot believe Vito would be so cruel or that Zio Alonzo would agree. Could there be any other reason Vito is behaving this way?"

"No, just plain cruel. Signor Marzano served us an eviction notice for the end of the month after your wedding. He does not believe in the Christmas spirit. Ack!" Eletta pulled at her hair. "Neither Babbo Natale nor Gesù Bambino would condone such an uncharitable action, would they?"

Father Christmas and the Baby Jesus? Goodness, but this girl was over the top. "Mmmm," said Renata.

"No, they would not," hissed Eletta. Her shoulders sagged. "Oh, what am I to do, signorina?"

Renata set the hair comb on the dressing table.

"Well …" She did not want to get into a philosophical or religious discussion with Eletta. The maid had brought up the white-bearded man in the red suit and the Baby Jesus in the same sentence, but Renata did not want to take the conversation further with a woman who was so distressed about her dire circumstances. She changed tactics. "Is there someone taking over the lease? Unfair, I grant you, but might that explain his hurry?"

"He intends to allow Signor Salucci, the bookseller next door, to expand into our space because he will pay double what we pay." A fat tear rolled down Eletta's face and plopped onto Renata's hand. Renata wiped it off before handing Eletta a handkerchief to clean her face. "The ladies of Sica will have nowhere to shop for dresses, and we will lose our one-hundred-year-old business. I cannot afford to move my business to another town. Even Arquà is too far."

"That's quite a sorry tale." Renata thought a moment. "I wonder if—"

"And we still have the leasehold papers!" Eletta planted a hand on each hip and pouted until her other eye released a tear. "If only a magistrate would hear our case, but the Marzanos and Pelicanis are too powerful. A ruling against them would be a stain on their name. They must be held to the original arrangement. Can you do something?"

"You know that Vito Marzano is my fiancé's best man," Renata began.

"Forget that greedy Marzano. Ask your husband or his uncle. I tried with Tomm—"

"You spoke to Placido's brother, Tommaso?"

"Briefly, but he could not offer advice on how I might proceed. Maybe you could try Signora Marzano?"

Renata bit the inside of her mouth. She was losing her patience with this desperate, demanding girl. "I am not yet married to have enough sway with my in-laws, much less my husband's best man's wife."

"Fine, but they will get their due." Eletta went to the wardrobe to put away Renata's day dress.

Renata was stunned. Her family's servants were not this bold about their private matters, nor were they so disrespectful in the way they spoke to their employer. Being in a forgiving mood, Renata could see the young woman was distraught and sought something to say to soothe her. "All right, I will try, but you must find Vito so I may speak with him."

Eletta whipped around and put her hands together in a prayer position. "I will be forever in your debt."

&

Fifteen minutes had passed since she sent Eletta to find Vito. Renata only realized now that the maid never promised to look for him. Renata knew staring at the clock on the mantle would not bring her answers about Vito's whereabouts. She resigned herself to going downstairs before her mother sent up a servant. Unlocking her door, a shiver ran up Renata's spine, and a strange thought settled at the base of her neck.

What if Vito and Po were unsafe and "free" meant something else? Perhaps the man she saw fall from the tower was the missing Vito, and Po had had to "flee" to be free? And what had Eletta said to Po's half-brother Tommaso? Renata reminded herself to find all three half-brothers and find out what they knew about Po and the Marzano-Bianca leasehold dispute.

&

Renata sat at her vanity table, holding a warm lavender-filled compress on her forehead. Dinner with her parents and Zio Alonzo had been a barrage of inquiries—all directed at her and none at Dario, Fumo, or her fiancé's brothers. The young men had all sat at the table eating, drinking, and laughing, not appearing as perplexed as everyone else about the whereabouts of her fiancé and his best man. She wanted to wring all their necks.

From how Po had described his circle of friends, they had been thick as thieves for a thousand years. They knew everything about one another. Fumo and Dario's many furtive glances between them, when they did not think she was looking, gave them away. How odd. Something was amiss, and they were keeping it from her. Were Zio Alonzo and the brothers involved in this trickery, too?

The groomsmen and Po's brothers had excused themselves before dessert, claiming they would continue their search for Vito. Two of the most important men of the week were missing. However, it was strange that no one had yet to mention the fatal fall she had witnessed. She did not want to alarm her parents or Zio Alonzo about the accident, though she was sure someone in the wedding party or the house must know about it. Zio Alonzo assured her he would send someone to look for Placido in the morning if he did not return tonight.

She silently vowed to continue her investigation in the morning, and if nothing turned up by noon, Renata would take everything to Zio Alonzo.

Chapter 10

A knock at the door and Eletta entered with a breakfast tray.

"Buongiorno. Here you are, signorina."

Renata put down her compress. "Any news? He has been gone for two days."

"No. I have asked everyone downstairs. Signor Placido's valet and Signor Marzano's valet are missing, although everyone suspects Signor Placido took his valet with him to Orrico. A stable boy has formed a search party among the field hands. I have asked him to report to you with anything they find."

"Thank you."

"And Signor Marzano? Anything?"

Eletta shook her head. She poured a cup of coffee, added some cream, and then passed it to Renata.

"Thank you, Eletta. Please return in an hour to dress me."

"Sì, signorina."

"Wait." The maid had turned to leave but came back when Renata called her. "What did you mean yesterday when you said, 'They will get their due?' And that you had spoken about the leasehold dispute with Tommaso?"

Eletta jumped, her hands shaking and her eyes blinking rapidly. "Um, did I say that? Ha ha. If I did speak to Tommaso, it was probably because I was upset, and the sentiment arose from that moment. Think nothing of it, signorina." This time, she turned on her heel in lightning fashion and slammed the door on her way out. From the force of the slam, three candles blew out, engulfing the room in semi-darkness.

"Oh!" A shiver ran up her spine, and her headache worsened immediately.

Though she had had a fitful sleep, she was determined to decipher Po's note correctly in the hopes it would provide her with a clue or two to solve the case of the missing men. It was the least she could do.

Though Renata had long wanted to work a criminal case, she wished the opportunity had not presented itself during Christmas week or involved anyone in the wedding party. Perhaps it was her imagination, or too early to say, but no one else seemed as concerned or dedicated to solving the mystery as she was. Half-worried and half-excited, her pulse quickened. There was nothing else to do but roll up her sleeves and get down to the business at hand: her first case!

She lifted the lid on her traveling desk and retrieved her stationery, a glass stylus, and her favorite bronze-colored ink. "Right, I will take it line by line."

Her head throbbed again.

See, I am but temporarily from thee

Yes, okay, he has not abandoned me at the altar. He knows my impatient streak, all right, she thought. It had taken him long enough to finally propose properly, the informal Castle of Love proposal notwithstanding.

Where is your (im)payshient existance?

Hmm, is he trying to tell me to be patient regarding his absence? Well, he better return soon. And I will have to get on him about his spelling—again, it's so atrocious. What did he learn at that military academy in Modena, anyway?

Truly, V°P, all safe and flee.

Renata tapped her stylus on her blotter and ruminated.

"Flee" must have been a mistake. He had meant to say that he and Vito were both "free."

Renata paused. She was on line three, and only some words were being used straightforwardly. Perhaps "flee" did mean "flee," and the two men were safe because they had fled. But where? She read on to the fourth and final line to see if "flee" clarified whether it meant "flee" or "free" or both.

Remember: our love will defy all distance.

He mentioned "love," so that was reassuring. But "distance?" What could that signify? She thought for a moment. Maybe his distance from her in Orrico was for a higher purpose and not about checking on the furniture. Was Po trying to protect her? Did Po and Vito flee because they had information that could put them in danger, and was distance the only way to keep them both safe? And her as well?

It was plausible that Po's chivalrous nature had gotten the better of him, but how did Vito fit in? Did one of them see the man fall from the tower? Or worse, who pushed the man over? What did the valets know? And what of Mariana?

Renata's headache was no better, yet she had to get dressed and tour the castello with her mother to see about the wedding preparations. Po's note made her uneasy, but at least he had not left without telling her something. He knew she loved a good puzzle. As for Fumo's note, she had thrown it in the fire. She was not going to let him tell her what to do. She made a mental note to discuss Fumo seriously with Po and the suitability of a continued friendship. If she were to judge Fumo based on his behavior from their talk in the hallway alone, he would not be a "friend."

Renata took Po's note and debated burning it, too. Instead, she did something she had never done but had dreamed about many times. She pulled out the Fabriano diary her maid Alissa had given her as an engagement gift. It must have cost the girl many months' wages. The slim diary was red linen, matching her nonna's red leather writing box. It had a sleeve in the back, and she tucked Po's note in there, then turned to the first page and wrote *My first case.*

She had just converted a diary into a casebook. A bride and sleuth in the same week. What had she just bitten off?

Chapter 11

"Though the current conte uses only a fraction of them, there are, in fact, 190 rooms in the castello." Martell opened the shutters of an enormous leaded glass window. "See here?" He opened the window and pointed down. "This is one of two external staircases built for horses."

Renata and Mama made appropriate sounds of appreciation, Mama more so than Renata. Renata was amazed by all the details Martell knew about such a sizable fortress as Castello Pelicani and could see he was enjoying his role as their tour guide.

Martell continued, "During the late 1500s, when the castello was built, the then-count and other nobles did not have to dismount to reach the first floor. They could bring their horses inside the fortress. The built-in ledges in the wall are still visible. Il signor Sica no longer rides, but when Master Pelicani and his younger brothers were children, they used those dismounts. Still do."

Mama peered at the poem painted on the wall next to the window. "Was the castello always owned by the Pelicani family?"

"You can confirm in the Libro d' Oro in the library, but I believe it will be three hundred years as of tomorrow," nodded Martell.

"Right up to my wedding day," said Renata, pleased. "What timing."

"And this way ... is where your reception will be held," said Martell, opening the broad double doors into the main hall. Once again, Renata thought she saw the flouncy hem of a girl's white dress, but she kept the vision to herself because no one else remarked on it. "The workmen are finishing touch-ups to the laurel wreaths and swords in the ceiling. There were a few cracks, and Il signor Sica wanted you to have all six salons as perfect as can be. For the wedding and Christmas."

Renata looked up as they walked around the room. Forty feet above her head were platforms with men on platforms atop them—caulking, sanding, and dabbing paint here and there to cover up cracks in stunning centuries-old frescoes. The oval in the center depicted an armored man with angels on either side of him, one bestowing a wreath over the knight's head while his foot stepped over a black cloud encircling a naked man's body underneath. A hero was defeating his enemy, and heaven rewarded him for his effort. Ah yes, the family's exploits in full view—to be admired and feared in the same breath.

"This room is exquisite. How lucky that Renata will be able to see it every day. I do not envy Alonzo the cost of the upkeep. How many servants must it take—"

"Mama," said Renata, tugging at Mama's arm. "Our ballroom in Padua may not be this grand, but—"

"It is not, nor will it ever be." Mama dabbed her left eye. "For we cannot now afford such a one if we wanted to."

Renata gave Mama a quizzical look and switched the subject. "Martell, who is the supervisor of this work?" Renata pointed to the Soldier of Fortune fresco cycles emblazoned on all the walls. "I would like to thank him."

"Ah, that would be Brizio." Martell bowed and left them to fetch the man on the other side of the hall. He returned with the foreman in tow and introduced him.

"Signora e Signorina Bombonatti, ecco Brizio."

The man stepped forward and bowed his head quickly. His work shirt and pants were covered in dust and paint. What little hair he had was all flat due to his work cap, which he had removed and now scrunched in his hands.

"Brizio, thank you so much for doing all this work to prepare for my wedding and the following Christmas celebrations. Placido would tell you if he were here, but he's away. So, on behalf of both of us, your men are doing—"

Renata's head snapped back. She was unprepared for the man's pinched expression. His muscles tightened around his lips, and his eyes narrowed when she uttered Placido's name. Renata fumbled for a moment, words failing her. Then, the clouds covered the sun in the sky, and all the natural light streaming into the room vanished. Renata shivered.

In a tone that suggested she was not the least aware of Renata's discomfort, Mama asked, "Have you worked here a long time, Brizio?"

"Sì, Signora Bombonatti," said Brizio between rattling teeth. "My brother Rodrigo and I grew up here with all four Pelicani boys. In those years of our youth, I venture to say the six of us were nearly indistinguishable."

"Ah, wonderful," said Mama, clasping her hands before her. "We are sorry to have kept you from your vital work. Martell, we should press on. Could we meet with the cook now? Or the florists? Or the ..." Her voice petered out as she left the room, Martell following right behind her.

Renata dared not move. Brizio's face had stayed the same. They stood facing one another for a few seconds, but it felt like minutes. The man knew Vito's whereabouts. When she had mentioned Placido's name, Brizio's eyes had shifted rapidly, giving him away, but her eyes remained fixed on his, and from his twitching eyebrow, she could tell her stare had unnerved him.

Abruptly, Brizio turned and jammed his cap on his head. "Troppo lavoro. There's much work to do." His stomp across the terrazzo floor to the scaffold drowned out the other worker's voices. His behavior only confirmed her suspicion.

Renata called after him. "I will catch up with you later, Brizio." She made a mental note to add his name to the suspect list in her casebook.

Chapter 12

Claiming her headache still had not cleared, Renata begged off seeing the cook and the florist, assigning the final approval to her mother.

Letting her mind meander, she wandered up, down, and around various wings of the castello with a fully fueled lantern leading the way. For all anyone knew, Vito was holed up in an unused wing, and Po and Mariana were tending to his wounds.

She also wanted to get to the roof, ascertain what might have happened to the fallen man, and see if a guard was still on patrol. Before getting far, she stumbled into the Blue Room, where maids teetered on ladders decorating the tree. Outside, the melodious tune of a hymn playing on a mandolin wafted up to the room as Renata entered.

"Sorry, Signorina Bombonatti," said the tallest of the three maids. "We usually finish decorating by the Feast Day of the Immaculate Conception, but we are behind schedule with the wedding."

Renata picked up a handful of tinsel and placed a few strands on the lower branches. "Not to worry. I am glad to see so many trees in the castello. Our family decorates only with Papàs' family's ancient Nativity set. The family tradition from my Mama's side is only what can be found in nature this time of year. Things like tree boughs, pinecones, cyclamen, and holly berry, but no full-grown trees like you have here."

The maids smiled, nodded, and continued their work.

"I am curious and wondered if you might help me." The three maids stopped their work and stared at Renata. "On my carriage ride here yesterday, I thought I saw some men on the tower roof. Do you know why they were there?"

"I believe they were rehearsing a tableau vivant, signorina," said the boldest of the three maids.

"Ah." That confirmed what Fumo had told her. She placed a bit more tinsel around the tree. "Do you know who all were up there?"

Again, the bold one spoke. "Signor Placido, his three brothers, the best man, the two groomsmen, and I believe a footman or two to round out the numbers."

"I see." Renata busied herself, looking into the crate stuffed with ornaments lying in thick hay to protect them. "Seems no one has seen Vito Marzano since then. Do you know where he might be? Or his valet? Or his wife Mariana? So many people—"

Just then, a breeze blew in from nowhere and scattered all the tinsel. Everyone gawked at one another, the bare tree, and the mess on the floor. Renata's eye twitched, and her mouth was momentarily devoid of saliva. It was as if the castello heard her questions but did not want anyone to give her the answers. She ran out of the Blue Room without a goodbye or a look behind her.

𝄔

After about an hour of running scared, she had finally shaken off the eerie sensation she experienced in the Blue Room. She wished her superstitious mother had not had such an influence on her around these kinds of things. On the second floor of the castello, Renata found a nook overlooking a courtyard and rested there against the chilly windowpane. She pulled her shawl tighter about her shoulders before sitting in the niche, observing the comings and goings of the castello below.

The kitchen staff were slaughtering chickens in one corner, the gardening crews were tapping branches to unburden the trees of their snow, and Mrs. Trevisan, the housekeeper, was directing the delivery of food and furniture into the house from vendors who had been engaged to provide for the wedding and the Christmas festivities to follow.

Martell had insisted she meet Mrs. Trevisan before Renata left him with her mother. From the few moments she had spent in the housekeeper's company, it was clear to Renata that Mrs. Trevisan knew just as much, if not more, about running the household than Martell did—though she was sure the woman would never admit it aloud. And the woman was thoughtful. While on her rounds, she spotted Renata sitting alone and invited her to the kitchen.

"Signorina Bombonatti, will you have a bowl of soup to warm you? You must be freezing sitting in that nook beside that frosty window. You will catch a chill before your ceremony, which will not serve anyone. Come, let us get you downstairs."

Renata followed the housekeeper down a level to the kitchen. "Now sit there." The woman motioned for Renata to sit at a small table near the hearth, brought a steaming bowl, and set it in front of her. "I hope you do not mind ribollita with a few leaves of cavolo nero thrown in.

"Not at all." The vegetable soup was hearty and thickened with kale and day-old bread.

"Cook is not quite ready with dinner, but we had some soup left over from the staff lunch. Though I am from Rome, and we have our soups, I have grown fond of ribollita since I have been here."

"I have our cook make me this same soup every winter. Thank you, Mrs. Trevisan. It is delicious. My compliments to ...?"

"Signor Succo, but we just call him 'Cook.' " Mrs. Trevisan nodded and went off on her merry way.

While she ate, Renata pulled out her casebook and pencil from the secret pocket in her dress. She always paid her dressmaker an extra fifty centisimi to put them in and not tell her mother, who frowned at such unladylike embellishments in her garments. She would have to ask Eletta if she did the same for her clientele.

Besides Brizio, Renata jotted down everyone she had suspected, all that she had heard and witnessed, and everything that was still outstanding, namely, the location of the groom and best man since she had arrived at Ca' Pelicani less than twenty-four hours ago, plus two valets and one errant wife.

Though Sherlock did not use one, Renata knew her converted diary would serve her well. It was a notebook within a notebook. The handmade papers within were designed with an accordion fold, so at first glance, it resembled a regular ladies' diary. On closer inspection, the papers could be unfolded to reveal her case notes—perfectly hidden away from prying eyes.

"Ah, there you are, signorina," said Eletta, coming up and curtseying. "But why are you eating peasant food? And where is Mrs. Trevisan? She would not be pleased to see this."

Renata closed her casebook and tucked it back into her pocket. So much for a moment's peace. "Do not concern yourself, Eletta. Mrs. Trevisan herself brought me this ribollita. I love this soup. It always fills me up. Our cook makes it for me every winter."

"Hmph." Eletta pursed her lips. "Well, your matron of honor has arrived, and she wishes to speak with you."

"Right, of course." Renata slurped up the last of the soup, then rose. She padded after Eletta, carrying two lanterns to light the way out of the dim rabbit warren on the lower floor.

Chapter 13

"Natalia, cara, come stai?" The two friends kissed one another on both cheeks. "I am so happy to see you."

"And me, you," said Natalia, patting her friend's hand. Natalia's maid took her cape and picked up a suitcase. Eletta led the way upstairs to Natalia's room carrying the other bag.

Renata slipped her arm through Natalia's and followed the maids.

"Davide's mother is sick, so I came alone. If she is better, he will come the day before the wedding," said Natalia.

"Sorry to hear that, but I am thrilled to have you to myself for a few days."

Once they had reached Natalia's rooms, Renata said, "Now that you know where your room is, come and have coffee with me in my suite. Eletta, please bring us a tray with extra biscotti and ensure Natalia's maid has something to eat."

"Yes, signorina." Eletta disappeared down the back stairs.

Closing her bedroom door behind them, Renata led Natalia to the settee. They talked about this and that and got caught up on almost everything since they had last seen one another at the Contessa Calandro's salon.

"Everything seems to be running smoothly, and yet. What have you not told me?" said Natalia, raising eyebrows. "What has happened since you arrived here?"

"My parents act strange and seem overly concerned about money and luxury. My fiancé has gone missing, as has his best man and their manservants. Did I mention Mariana, the best man's wife? Because she is missing, too. Oh, and I saw a man fall off the tower to his death when my carriage was but a short distance from the castello grounds. And no one has said anything about it. I do not know if my exhausted state imagined it or if they were all trying to keep the bride from worrying or, worse, running away from a tragedy. I am already building a list of suspects, but no one stands out." Renata's words tumbled out while her arms flailed around her. "There, that is all of it."

"You cannot be serious. Is there something wicked afoot? You should have told me all this right away instead of letting me partake in idle gossip." Natalia jumped off the settee and paced in front of Renata. "The wedding is in three days! How did it all go so wrong? What does your mother say? Is your father out looking for them? Or Signor Pelicani's men?"

Renata felt a familiar throb on her forehead and rubbed it. "I have not been able to do very much because—"

A knock at the door brought a finger to Renata's lips, and Natalia nodded.

"Entrare," said Renata.

The maids entered with a tray laden with a coffee pot, porcelain cups with the Pelicani crest, two liqueur glasses, a flask, and a copious quantity of pastries and biscotti.

"Here you go, signorina." With trembling hands, Eletta set the tray on a stool adjacent to the settee where Renata was sitting and left. Renata thought it odd that Eletta was nervous again. She seemed nervous a lot. She was new to being a lady's maid, but she had also teetered during her curtsey and could not get out of the room fast enough. Renata vowed to ask her questions about the fate of her family's dress shop and the groomsman she had befriended.

Natalia returned to the settee and poured two cups of steaming coffee with a dribble of milk and two cookies on each plate. "Here, you need to eat a ricciarelli and a cantucci with your coffee unless you want something stronger to accompany them." Natalia grabbed the bronze flask and swung it before Renata's face like a hypnotist swinging a pendulum.

"Si, una goccia." Renata held up her fingers with a small space between her thumb and forefinger to indicate the small quantity of dessert wine she wanted.

Natalia handed Renata a cup and saucer. "Un caffè corretto."

Corrected coffee—with a drop or two of brandy—was always how Papà took his evening coffee. Renata grew up tasting it, though she had never tried it at full strength. If Natalia were willing, then she would, too. It might just give her the courage to face more challenges in the days ahead of her nuptials.

They sipped and chewed in silence, each woman deep in her thoughts. Renata breathed in the solid almond scent of the ricciarelli and the orange-vanilla aroma of the cantucci. The familiar smells calmed her and reminded her of the halcyon days of her youth when she would help her family's cook bake for the festive season. Natalia set down her cup and broke through the quiet between them.

"I can help you, Renata. Tell me everything you know. Hold nothing back. We will figure it out, including your parent's strange behavior."

Reluctantly, Renata pulled out her casebook and showed Natalia everything she had documented. Natalia listened and read each page of notes as Renata explained her evidence and assumptions. She picked up the pencil resting in the crease and handed it to Renata. "I have some suggestions if you are willing to listen. I am no Sherlook, like you."

"Sher-*lock*. Also, two syllables, not three." Renata shook her now headache-free head. "I have told you a hundred times how to pronounce his name."

"Pfft," answered Natalia, shooing away Renata's correction. "Do you want to hear my ideas, or will you play schoolteacher?"

Renata grabbed another cantucci and stuffed the whole thing in her mouth. She hovered the pencil over the casebook, signifying her acquiescence.

"Very well, I shall begin," said Natalia, sitting up. "In addition to your questions, I have four of my own."

Renata cocked an eyebrow and sat forward on the settee. She set down her coffee cup and smoothed the open notebook on her lap.

"Number one: You have yet to examine where the man fell," Natalia began. "Number two: You must question the stable boys and gardeners, for surely they would have seen or heard something. No one falls from that height without screaming or being too severely injured to hobble away without being seen."

Renata fidgeted at the vision Natalia painted and nodded.

Natalia cleared her throat. "Number three: Why was your maid unable to find or question the manservants?"

Renata scribbled a note in her book. "Bepi is Po's manservant, and Eletta claims Vito's manservant—I do not recall his name—is missing, too."

Natalia sipped her coffee. "That is four missing people. Has il Signore said or done anything? Has anyone informed Vito's family? What about his wife?"

Renata gulped. That had occurred to her, but she was too scared to write it down lest someone should find it and accuse her of not doing her duty to inform the family. "I assumed Mariana had accompanied Vito here, but I have not seen her. We must search the women's wing, although perhaps she is arriving separately?"

She would not know about her husband's fate, but Renata did not want to speak those words aloud. Mariana bumped the tally of missing people to four. Four. Realization of the enormity of their situation manifested into boulder-sized angst and dropped into Renata's stomach. Now what?

Natalia continued. She used her fingertips to count her questions and held up four fingers. "Number four: Why have you not shared your suspicions with Signor Pelicani? It is *his* house and *his* nephew. I would want to know if I was him. Besides, guests are arriving at all hours. If they catch any of the staff talking, they will be worried, and your wedding may fall apart before it has had a chance to start."

Natalia slumped. "Even Christmas is looking gloomy."

Renata let out an exasperated breath. "How can you talk of Christmas when death and missing people abound?"

Natalia furrowed her brows. "Well, as much as I want to support you, this is a big mess. Perhaps a bride should not be sleuthing as much as you are."

"I am determined in this effort, with or without you." Renata raised her chin. "Besides, the sooner I figure out what happened, the faster I can return to focusing on the wedding preparations."

Natalia brightened. "All right, if I help, do you promise you will try to enjoy Christmas, too? You may draw too much attention to your investigation if you do not. You will soon be the new Signora Pelicani and the future Contessa di Sica. The eyes and ears of the entire household are on you now and forever, so perhaps some circumspection is in order."

"Very well. I will feel guilty spending time away from solving a potential murder. However, I will only participate in some of the castello's activities because I do not want to draw too much suspicion."

Natalia patted Renata's knee. "I will do my part to distract you. Now, what about Po's half-brothers—Giacomo, Fabrizio, and Tommaso? Where are they in this mess?"

Renata tapped her pen on her notebook. "They live in Padua but come and go from the castello as they please. I have spent little time with them and have not asked them hard questions. I must tiptoe in that arena."

Natalia crossed her arms over her chest. "How privileged they are that you are leaving them alone when they would have witnessed the fall the same as you. They are full of information."

Renata put her pencil in the crease of her casebook and closed it on her lap. "All right, all right. Let us start by examining and answering your questions, which seem to increase by the minute for someone who has been steadfast in her disdain for investigative work. Then, God willing, we will work through my questions if I have the strength. To answer your first and second questions, I have not had time to slip outside to examine the crime scene, nor have I seen much of the castello's interior."

"Fancy words." Natalia poked Renata in the arm. "Are they from those Cher*lock* stories you are always reading?"

"Sher—oh, never mind." Renata stifled a yawn. "I am tired from searching inside the castello. This morning, Martell, the butler, showed Mama and me around, but I did not ask him for a map because I did not want him to get suspicious, but I know I have not seen all 190 rooms."

"Oooh la la," said Natalia. "That is a lot of rooms so that I can commiserate. This castello is bigger than the entire village of Sica."

Renata interrupted. "Question number three has me stumped, too. Eletta is acting strangely—I had not yet written that in my casebook. Number four is ... complicated."

"What is? Are you afraid of Alonzo? The brothers?" Natalia furrowed her brows.

"A little bit." Renata bit her lip. "I am on good terms with the conte, and to some extent, his nephews, and as Po and I plan to live here awhile after our honeymoon, I do not want to stir up trouble in case it is nothing. I should give up the sleuthing and focus on the myriad things I still must do before my wedding day."

"Do nothing?" Natalia's voice rose an octave. "You said yourself a man fell from a tower. That is a death on the lord of the county's doorstep, and he should be informed about it— to say nothing of the polizia—before the staff spread it like wildfire around the castello and county. And if I have not heard you talk about wanting a case of your own for the last year or so, then I should have my hearing checked because this is just like those you read and tell me all about in excruciating detail."

"Ow!" The throbbing in her head had returned. The police? Her Po? Involved in a missing persons or accidental death case, maybe even a murder? She could not and would not believe it. She was a bride and about to be the most senior woman in the castello. Perhaps it was too much.

Natalia forged ahead. "You may not want to be the one telling Signor Pelicani, but the falling man may be related to Vito's disappearance. He has the right to all your information and anything about the suspects. Who better to tell him than you? In your inimitable way, you can present things logically and succinctly without hysterics, which I am sure he will appreciate."

Renata nodded slowly. The questions and potential answers were all competing for her attention, and despite her better judgment, she poured herself some liqueur and took a long swig. She put the glass down and wiped the corners of her mouth.

"But Natalia, give me your honest opinion. Should I continue investigating?" Renata clenched and unclenched her hands. "It is one thing to follow an investigation in a novel or a newspaper, but quite another when it involves one's own family."

Natalia grabbed Renata's hands to stop her agitation. "Po will soon be your family. Do you not owe it to him and Vito to do something before the police show up? And do you not think it is odd that four men are missing and no one seems too concerned? Including Po's brothers, who were on the roof?"

Renata bent at the waist, put her hands on her head, and closed her eyes. She ought to tell Zio Alonzo and let him deal with it. Po's note was short on words, though no great cause for alarm. She had to believe he was in Orrico and was not involved in this chaos, but Vito was another matter.

Her nerves were heightened because of the wedding, nothing more. She was resigned to letting her casebook remain idle until a much later, undefined date. After talking to Zio Alonzo, she said she would embrace her role as a bride and enjoy these final few days as a single lady. She promised herself another Christmas activity or two, too. Satisfied with her decision, she sat up and collected herself.

"There, that's my stalwart friend." Natalia patted Renata on her knee. "Now, what are your questions?"

Renata was about to start when a knock on the door interrupted her. "Come in," she and Natalia both said in unison.

Natalia's maid entered the room and set about gathering up the dishes. Renata looked over the maid's shoulder. "Where is Eletta?"

The maid stopped her work and addressed the women. "I do not know, signorina. She was acting funny when we left here. After she showed me to my quarters, she left hurriedly, and I have not seen her since."

Renata stood and brushed a couple of crumbs from her dress. "Did she say anything before she left?"

"She muttered something like, 'Those damn Marzanos.' I did not know what she meant, nor was it my business, so I—"

"Thank you. That will be all." Natalia stood, too, and dismissed her maid. She reached for Renata's hands. "Look at me. We have but a little time until we must get dressed for dinner. We will split up and try to get some answers. Do you agree?"

Renata waved her index finger. "No. Mama will be none too happy to find me poking about. She is always telling me my sleuthing is unladylike."

"An old refrain from a very traditional woman, much like my mother. Perhaps the two of them should have written *The Rules of Polite Behavior* instead of Giovanni della Casa."

"True," said Renata, and they both burst out laughing.

"Come on. What do you say to a sleuthing partner?" Natalia elbowed Renata in the ribs.

"I could use the help, but only if you follow my lead." Renata walked to the bed. "I am going to lie here because my head is throbbing. You find Mama and tell her. She will run up to check on me, so you should accompany her. Once she sees me sleeping, you convince her to leave me alone and invite her to a game of Scopa while I rest. After you leave, I will find Zio Alonzo and hunt about some more."

Natalia's shoulders slumped. "You get all the fun."

"My dear, we have different ideas about what constitutes fun. Scopa can be a fun game if you play your cards right." Renata winked and squeezed her friend's shoulder. "I know you are unhappy about it, but I promise to make it up to you."

Natalia's eyes widened. "How about I search for Mariana and see if she knows where Vito is?"

"Excellent idea. We shall meet back here in a few hours."

Chapter 14

Renata slipped out of her room and raced down the hallway to the other end of the castello. As far as she could tell, no one saw her step outside through one of the doors she had found on her earlier stroll.

Staying close to the castello's walls, she spotted a forest and headed to it for better cover until she reached the tower. The estate's forest was peppered with oaks, walnuts, common hazels, and paulownias, while the fields had frozen stalks of wheat and corn sticking out of the snow. On the canal side, the farm hosted a multitude of animals. In several fenced-in areas, she counted sheep, hens, ducks, geese, cattle, and donkeys, plus a dozen cages full of rabbits and a massive, covered pen full of pelicans.

She remembered Martell saying that the surrounding land, including the castello totaled thirty hectares. She knew some groundskeepers were provided housing, though she did not see anyone milling about in their enclave. Many outbuildings ringed the castello, including the enormous tobacco-drying barn where previous barons and marchesi grew and later sold Kentucky-style tobacco for the Toscana cigars.

Finally, Renata reached the tower she had spotted from her carriage. Before coming out of the relative safety of the forest, she pulled her cape's hood further down her face. She scanned the surrounding grounds and the tower roof in case a guard was patrolling. Seeing nothing and no one, she left the forest and headed straight to an ancient bay laurel tree. Its branches were hefty and provided some cover. She surveyed the tower's bricks and saw no sign of blood. The torch mount with the rail below it that held the family's standard was bent at an unusual angle, and the standard's colorful cloth was torn.

Renata's heart raced like a mouse caught in a corner by a cat. Did the rail break the man's fall? She rushed to the tower, not caring that her hood fell back as she flew. There were many sets of footprints near the tower. So, someone had seen the fall and sent men to either help an injured man or pick up a dead body, but which was it?

She surveyed the muddied snow under the torch mount. She walked around the nearby fountain. Nothing stood out.

The wind picked up, and she returned to the tree for shelter. Again, she surveyed the ground with less snow because the bigger branches may have taken the brunt of the man's fall. There were boot prints. She noticed they were all one type—one type from one man. The size of the prints looked identical, though one track was smeared as if the man was dragging his foot.

She looked up into the tree. Two burly branches were broken, and several twigs were scattered around beneath. She looked back at the torch mount with the torn standard. The man's clothing must have caught on the mount, and his weight had bent it. Perhaps his clothing had torn, then fallen again, and the bay tree broke his second fall. That meant ... the man might have survived the fall.

She raced back to the forest, covering her head again and holding her hood. After forty feet into the densest part of the woods, she slowed her pace and let the questions pour forth.

Who was the falling man? Where did he go? Who had come looking for him? What did they do when they did not find a body? The person or persons responsible for the dastardly deed were probably connected to the castello. If so, they would be frightened of being found out, even if it were an accident. Why was it all being hushed up?

She repeatedly turned over the questions and possible answers in her head, stopping under a stately walnut to scribble furiously in her casebook. At last, she reached the barns, storehouses, and the orangery where the stablehands and gardeners worked. As inappropriate as it would seem, she had to question them. A man had fallen from the tower. They were outdoorsmen. They would have been bound to hear something, an unavoidable scream. But would these men open up to her? They did not know who she was. Should she tell them the truth or fabricate a plausible story?

She would decide what story to spin when she reached the barn. Encountering no one on the well-worn pathway to the large stone barns, she slipped through a side door. Thank goodness it was open, for she was not sure she would have the strength to unlatch the heavy front barn door, much less open it. From her initial once-over and inexperience with such things, the sturdy iron hardware looked original, as it was built in the late Renaissance.

It was dark inside, with only a few windows at the top of the barn letting light in. It was enough to see the horses and donkeys in their stalls, and she could smell them, too.

Oink!

She jumped. Of course, they had pigs. She placed her hand over her heart to slow the rapid beating and decided to be bold. "Hello?"

Lots of noises, none of them human.

She tried again. "Hello?"

"Planning on a ride, signorina?"

"Oh!" She turned to an adolescent boy coming up behind her.

"A ride, then?" He held up a riding whip.

"Uh, no. No."

He pushed his cap back from his forehead. "Did you bring apples?"

"No." Renata shook her head and walked to him. "I am, uh, Elisa, Signor Pelicani's, uh, cousin. I have also been studying at the Anatomical Theatre in Padua. And I have come looking for a body. And I understand there was one here yesterday."

She took a breath and scolded herself for breathing and talking so unnaturally.

"I believe it was an unfortunate accident. The man had no family, so, uh, the university sent me to find out if we could have the body." She put her hand out to reassure him. "To study, of course. And we shall give him back to the family for a proper burial once we are done."

"I-I-I do not, uh—" The boy grabbed his stomach.

She pressed on. "Perhaps you saw where they put him, hmm?"

Renata looked around. Lifting canvas cloths covering hay bales and old crates, she saw nothing that stood out. Her frustration was heating her face, and she had to turn away so the boy would not get suspicious as one lie followed another. They were flowing faster than a burst dam. She might pull this off if she could keep her confidence level high.

"I never saw a-a man. They came looking for a man, but I never saw him."

"I see." Well, what she could see was that he was frightened, yet his responses confirmed her suspicions. "Is there anyone else I could talk to? Is the stable manager nearby?"

"That would be me. Who is asking?"

Renata squinted and could see a shape coming from the donkey stalls. Had he been there the whole time? She could not see a door frame over there. "I am Elisa Pelicani, Signor Pelicani's cousin. And I have been studying at the Anatomical Theatre—"

"Signor Pelicani has never mentioned you."

She gasped when the man was within a couple of feet of her. "Brizio! Why ... I did not know you manage the barns and a construction crew?" He looked the spitting image of the man she had met near the scaffold hours ago.

"You are thinking of my identical twin brother." He spoke and laughed in the same deliberate, somewhat condescending tone as his brother. "We share a last name. That is true, but I was born two hours *after* my brother. I am Rodrigo."

"Oh, I see." Once again, she did not see, though she had to act fast because this number two man was not buying her story. "Well, like I said, I am studying at the university, and we need bodies for our anatomical studies. We heard there had been an unfortunate accident and that there was the body of a dead man without any family here. Of course, once we are done dissecting, I mean, studying the body for medical purposes, we would offer him a decent burial."

"As I said, I know of no cousin, Sign-o-ri-na Pel-i-ca-ni," he said, drawing out her name, "and I do not believe Il conte Sica would ever support a female member of the family studying at the university."

Renata did not like his derisive laughter or how he spoke to her. She pulled her shoulders back and said, "Does the conte need to tell his workers about his private life? Do you dare question a blood relative of this grand estate that you are so fortunate to be able to work at? Is the word of a female Pelicani not good enough for you? Shall I get my cousin to come speak to you?"

Rodrigo pulled himself up to his full height, three inches shorter than Renata, and scratched his chin. He studied her the same way his brother had. When he spoke, his eyes narrowed to slits.

"There was no man. Your information is ... inaccurate."

"But this boy here ..." She turned to the stable boy. He was gone.

"Which boy? I do not see anyone but us. You city girls may not know your boys from a four-legged beast, but I can assure you, around here, we know the difference." He turned on his heel and disappeared among the donkeys again.

Chapter 15

Shaken by the incident in the barn but not defeated, Renata opened the big creaky door to leave and almost hit Zio Alonzo in the face.

"Oh, pardon me, Zio."

"And where are you off to?" He picked up his fallen cap and dusted it off before replacing it. "Has one of the stable hands been showing you around, or did you wander out alone?"

"Alone. After my carriage ride the other day, I was itching to stretch my legs and take advantage of the good weather."

"Indeed." He looked up, scanning the sky from right to left. "Well, I am glad to find you here, for I have two gifts to give you. Follow me."

"How curious because I have been looking for an opportunity to speak to you alone."

"Here's your first gift." He handed her a polished yet slightly knobby walking stick. "I fashion them out of fruitwood, and everyone in the family has one. I made many as a boy but have mostly given up the craft. Your arrival prompted me to pick up my old woodworking tools again."

"It is a fine stick, thank you." She fingered the pelican insignia he had carved near the handle and smiled. "I shall take it with me on all my country walks."

"See that you do. "There is much uneven ground here, and you must mind the bumps and gaps." He swung his stick in a wide arc over his estate. "In time, I hope you come to love this land as all we Pelicanis do."

"I am sure I will."

They walked past several outbuildings before arriving at a fenced enclosure. "What is this place?"

"The aviary for our pelican pod, but we generally refer to it as the pen."

"Po never mentioned you kept birds." She marveled at the two-story birdhouse with its myriad perches, a bamboo forest, and a long rectangular pool with floating logs and rocks jutting out of the water like shards.

They stood outside the gate while he talked. "Our family has kept pelicans here for over five hundred years. It is usually the job of the second son to act as the bird keeper, which is Tommaso's role. This may be why Placido never mentioned it. He is less invested in the 'feathered' branch of the family, though Tommaso's not much fond of the role either. He would rather rule over a real castle than an aviary."

Renata laughed and decided to use the moment of levity to talk to her uncle-in-law but was thwarted by the mention of his next gift. "Zio Alonzo, I wonder—"

"Let us go deeper into the aviary, and you can pay your respects to the pelican I have chosen for you."

"A bird of my own?"

"Why yes, every family member has one. It would help if you visited it regularly so it gets to know you and, eventually, eats out of your hand. We breed only Dalmatians. Fortunately, this variety of pelicans does not migrate south during the winter. It is mild enough here that they prefer to stay and feed in the inland deltas and estuaries because they tend not to freeze over."

"Ah." Two approached her: one with silvery-grey plumage, whereas the other was a dingy brownish-grey who spread its black-tipped wings in greeting. "Why, hello. I am Renata. I am new but will visit you often over the coming months."

Zio Alonzo continued his schooling. "They are mostly silent except during mating season when you hear all grunts, barks, and hisses. The male pelican is much larger than the female, and I have picked a female for you. She was born about six months ago, soon after you and Placido announced your engagement.

"Where is she?"

"There, the one with the dull yellow bill which turns a deep orange-red when it breeds."

She watched it fly from one rock to another and then to a post with a high perch. She faced Zio Alonzo. "Thank you again for the gift. I shall name her Gisella, which means 'pledge' because I pledge to care for her. It connotes resilience, strength, and bravery. When I was younger, I used to have a parakeet by the same name, and when she died, I was too distraught to raise another."

He nodded. "A fine name."

They watched Gisella fly, splash around, and groom herself. After a while, Renata said, "The cold is seeping into my bones, and I must get back. Will you walk to the castello with me?"

"Certo," he said, holding the gate open for her and closing it when she had passed through.

Their feet crunched virgin snow as they walked. In the distance, the soft, snow-capped peaks of the Euganean Hills blended seamlessly with the white landscape. Reaching the vineyard, Renata was struck by the stark grapevines in neat rows on the central plain, seemingly marching like thin wooden soldiers to vanquish Venice, Padua's rival. Here and there, plumes of smoke from the tenant farmers' houses rose and mingled with the low-lying fog that had yet to lift from its morning visitation.

Pulling her attention away from the beauty of her surroundings, she forged forth with her question. "Zio Alonzo ..."

"Yes, Renata?"

"On Sunday, as my carriage approached the castello, I thought I saw a, um, soldier patrolling on the tower roof. Do you usually have guards on your roof?"

"Yes," he growled, "occasionally we have poachers. Some do not have enough in this harsh climate, so they come after our livestock, poultry, and even a prized pelican or two. I cannot always be lenient and let them get away with it."

"Oh dear, I did not realize you had poachers." That was not the answer she expected nor was it the question she had wanted to ask first. She wondered what his lack of leniency meant but kept that to herself.

He pulled up his drooping coat collar so it better covered his neck. "This winter is particularly cold, and I dare say Europe will break records."

"Hmm …" Further questions raced through her brain, and she carefully selected the best one from the list. "I wonder … could there be another reason a guard was stationed up there?"

He stopped, piercing the snow with his walking stick with more vigor than was necessary. "What are you implying?"

"Only Po, his brothers, his groomsmen, and some staff were up on the roof around that time practicing a tableau vivant for the wedding entertainment. It was not long after that—"

"Ah, there's the butcher." He twirled his stick in the air in the butcher's direction. "I must speak to him about which animals to slaughter for the wedding feast." He patted her hand atop her stick. "Sorry, dear. I will see you inside later."

How's that for honesty?

৪১

Renata entered the kitchen through the courtyard. She scrubbed the muddy snow from her boots on the round bristle brush just inside the door and almost got pushed into a tower of potato sacks when a vendor came in carrying a gigantic saw. She smiled, remembering the old peasant tradition in Veneto of a just-married couple sawing a log together. If the newlyweds could work together and cut through the log, tradition held that the marriage would last because husband and wife had succeeded at overcoming their first obstacle.

Tears threatened, and she wiped them away. She missed Po. It was her second day at the castello without a sign of him. His note had sounded like a lament. It seemed he longed to be with her, but maybe her deciphering skills were not what she thought they were. Her conversation with Zio Alonzo left her angry and unsure of what to do next except move quickly out of the way of the saw coming at her.

Renata pushed herself off the potato sacks and looked around the room for Mrs. Trevisan. A discordance of voices, hissing pans, and boiling pots greeted her. If it were not rude, Renata would have covered her ears. There must have been twenty or thirty people milling about the hall. The modern stoves and ovens were at one end, chopping and other preparatory tables were in the middle, and at the other end, there was an open fire with comfortable chairs around it. Applewood burned in the hearth, filling the room with a fruity aroma.

She spied Mrs. Trevisan in a rocking chair, her hands wrapped around a steaming mug of something hot. She wanted to ask Cook if he might have seen something, but he was not in the room, so she thought she would ask Mrs. Trevisan.

"Mrs. Trevisan," said Renata, walking up to her.

The woman struggled to rise, but Renata insisted she stay where she was. "Please, do not get up on my account. I am looking for Signor Succo."

"He's with the butcher and his lordship, Signorina Bombonatti. Your mother already met with Cook and approved the menu for your wedding in two days. Is there a problem?" She feigned ignorance and sipped from her cup.

"Oh no, no, not with the menu, no. It is just that I, uh ..." Renata looked about the busy room, hoping that Cook would appear and she could speak to him without further explaining to Mrs. Trevisan. "I have a question for him, but it can wait." She smiled through the lie, then tried again. "However, there is a question you might be able to answer."

"Yes, signorina?" Mrs. Trevisan held her cup and saucer aloft.

"I know this is Martell's area, but since you are right here," Renata said, taking off her cape and holding it near the fire, "I thought I would ask you first."

"All right." Mrs. Trevisan rocked in her chair—her response tentative.

"My fiancé has not returned from Orrico. His best man, Vito Marzano, is missing, as is the best man's valet." Renata spread her cape over another rocking chair and faced the housekeeper. "I wondered if you knew anything about their whereabouts. Where they might have gone and such."

The woman took a long sip before answering. "I know you are new here and do not know how a house like this operates. However, I am surprised your mother has not taught you that it is not the responsibility of the housekeeper to monitor the activities of the male members of this castello, whether their rooms are upstairs or downstairs or if they are visiting another town."

From the tone in Mrs. Trevisan's voice and the tightening lines around her mouth, it was obvious Mrs. Trevisan was offended at the line of questioning. The housekeeper's tone was bold, though it was probably a test to see if Renata, as the top female in the house, was made of stern stuff. She knew all the staff had not had a Signora Pelicani to answer to for almost a decade and that it would take some time for Renata to earn their respect and gain allies.

Meanwhile, Renata noted to watch for a pattern in the woman's behavior. This was not the first such servant at Ca' Pelicani who had some gall. She would talk to Po about it later, but for now, she needed answers.

"Mrs. Trevisan, I am ever so sorry. I did not mean to suggest—"

"You did not mean to suggest … yet you are apologizing for it now … so whether you meant it or not … does not negate the question." Like the Roman she was, the woman's accent was full and confident.

Renata closed her eyes and rolled her shoulders. She needed Mrs. Trevisan on her side now that she was marrying into the family. Renata had to own up to her assumptions and deal with the woman's attitude later. She opened her eyes and did her best to put a contrite expression on her face. "You are right, Mrs. Trevisan. I apologized, yet you have not accepted my apology. Very well," Renata pointed to the tray of coffee and biscuits on the side table next to the woman, "I shall leave you to enjoy your break."

Mrs. Trevisan eyed her over the ridge of her steaming mug and said nothing. She was a veritable maid of silence.

Renata tried one more time. "You see, I am desperate for answers, and I … never mind. I will intrude on your time no further. Good day, Mrs. Trevisan." Renata picked up the cape, folded it over her arm, and strode past the housekeeper. Renata was about twenty feet away when the woman called out. Renata whirled around to face her.

"They were up until noon on the tower roof rehearsing a tableau vivant as a surprise for you. That is the last time I heard about any of them. As for the manservant, I think Martell might know where he is. They all report to him, even the visiting ones."

"Thank you, Mrs. Trevisan. You have been a big help to my frayed nerves."

Chapter 16

"Future Signora Pelicaaaani. Oh, future Contessa di Siiiica. Are you awake yet?" Between the rolling of her body on the bed by two pairs of hands and one loud laughing voice, Renata could not help waking up.

"Natalia. Eletta. What are you doing here?" said Renata, bleary-eyed and grumpy.

"Signorina, it is time for you to dress for dinner, but first, we must take your boots off. It looks like you slept with them on." Eletta took a boot hook and began undoing Renata's boots. When she was done, she returned to help Natalia pull Renata upright.

Renata opened one eye and scanned Natalia from head to toe. "My, my, you picked a fine gown."

"Davide picked this out for me when he was in Barcelona. It is a bit somber with the black lace at my breast, but the claret is a fitting color for the season, do you not think so?" Natalia twirled so Renata could see the dress front and back.

"Would the navy velveteen suffice, signorina?" called Eletta from the wardrobe.

Renata rubbed both eyes and yawned. "Sure."

Renata went behind the Oriental screen, and Eletta helped her out of her day dress and undergarments. After a short, warm sponge bath, Renata slipped on fresh undergarments. Over them, she stepped into a gold and floral-embroidered evening dress that showed her neck and bosom to the full advantage.

"So, tell me, Natalia. How was your afternoon with Mama? Did you let her win?"

"Every time. Six games until it was time for siesta. I could have wrung your neck for making me play a useless game, but you were not here. I mean," Natalia glanced at Eletta, "you were sleeping, so you were absolved from our card games."

"Well, I hope at least you cherished your siesta time," said Renata. "In all seriousness, did you get any information out of Mama?"

Natalia shook her head. "Sadly, no, but we can talk about that later. After the game, I finished reading *Il Corsaro Nero*, Salgari's latest swashbuckler. Oh, how I wish I had married a pirate." Natalia flopped on a wing chair near the fire.

"I know you, Natalia." Renata chuckled. "You would be bored after a week of hearing all his tales. You would beg him to sail to the Caribbean for a great adventure. But in a matter of hours, you would ask him to turn the ship around because you would be beset by seasickness."

"Hmmph. Do not spoil my dreams." Natalia picked at an imaginary piece of lint on her dress.

Renata emerged from behind the screen. "That is why most people read novels like Salgari's. To dream, so dream away." She walked over to her vanity, selected an impressive cameo from her jewelry box, and handed it to Eletta. Eletta pinned it to an amber velvet ribbon and tied it around her mistress' neck.

"There, signorina. You are ready." Eletta picked up Renata's laundry and left the room.

Renata checked her hair one final time. She dabbed on some perfume and stood. "Ready?"

"Yes, I am. I was going to ask Eletta if she could inspect me a final time, but she left without being dismissed. I hope you will not forget Alissa and bring her here as your proper lady's maid once she's well again." Natalia gestured with her thumb to the door. "She is much better trained than this one."

"It was such bad luck that Alissa caught a cold before we left for Ca' Pelicani. Eletta is trained as a seamstress, so the role of a lady's maid is not her forte."

Natalia pouted. "I would never have guessed."

"Stop it, Nat. Zio Alonzo assigned Eletta to me, and she is doing her best."

"Oh, Signor Pelicani assigned her, did he?" Natalia strained her face over a mirror and pinched her cheeks to make them bloom pink.

"She is preoccupied with some, uh, family matters." Renata waved her hand dismissively. "I cannot blame the poor girl for not getting everything right. I can certainly sympathize. I know something is bothering Mama and Papà, and I cannot concentrate either."

"So, you do not think Alonzo has her spying on you? Or sabotaging the wedding by loaning you an inexperienced lady's maid?"

"What a thing to say. Of course not." Renata laughed it off, but deep down, she could not shake the feeling that there might be a grain of truth in what Natalia said. The real question was what purpose the spying would serve. Could it have anything to do with what was nagging her about her parent's behavior?

Ω

Mama passed Renata and Natalia on the staircase and pointed to a room ahead. "We are in the small Sala della Francesca tonight."

"Thank you, Signora Bombonatti," said Natalia. Once Signora Bombonatti was safely away, Natalia leaned into Renata behind a potted palm on the second-floor landing. "Do you think the groomsmen will be at the dinner tonight?"

Renata looked over her shoulder to ensure no one was within earshot before she replied. "This was one of the questions I had. Fumo cornered me in the hallway. He relayed nothing about what happened at the tower, but Mrs. Trevisan, some maids, and Fumo said the brothers and groomsmen had been on the roof rehearsing a tableau vivant Po wants to surprise me with."

"A tableau vivant! How fun! The castello could use more revels. It is not just your wedding, but Christmas, too."

Renata glared at her. "Is that all you can think of? Fun?"

"I do apologize." Natalia cleared her throat. "But did the housekeeper say anything about someone falling off the tower?"

Renata shook her head.

"And the other friend?"

"Dario? At dinner last night, neither Dario nor Fumo claimed to know what had happened to Vito. They left early, claiming they would look for him and the manservants. The brothers were off to see what was keeping Po in Orrico. It was all I could do not to go off with them."

Starting down the last flight of stairs, Natalia patted Renata's hand. "Mariana is missing, too. If Vito is the man that fell and survived, then she must be with him, caring for his wounds."

"Ugh. Four people unaccounted for." Renata wrung her hands as she followed her friend. "I cannot believe none of Po's brothers or his groomsmen said anything about a man falling from the tower. If we believe everyone, they were all up on that roof! And Eletta heard nothing from the staff at breakfast, so I doubt whether the men put any effort into their search last night."

"I know you are frustrated, Renata dear. I am, too, but cooler heads must prevail if we are to get to the bottom of a potential murder."

"Ugh, I cannot bear to think that is true." She covered her mouth with her hand.

Natalia eyed the guests on the landing below, who had looked up when they heard Renata moan. To reassure them, Natalia waved and smiled until they all turned back to one another. "A body fell, and it was not found. Somebody is responsible. If the act was intentional, that is murder, is it not?"

Renata bit her lip from shouting again and alarming everyone. While she had guessed the man survived, perhaps fresh snow had already covered the tracks of the other footprints, and her assumption in the barn had been incorrect. Instead, the men to whom the other footprints belonged may have been able to pull a dead man out of the tree and carry him away.

Were these men connected to the incident, or were they innocents who either saw the man fall or happened upon him afterward? Perhaps Vito had injured his head and could not remember who he was. Mrs. Trevisan said that Po's friends were rehearsing a tableau. They may have been dressed in costumes, and therefore, the fallen man was not recognizable as a noble, so the men who found him may have thought him a wanderer, and—

"I can hear your mind spinning fantastical conclusions," whispered Natalia. "Will you share one or two? I am here to help."

"You made a point I had not considered, and I was just thinking it through." Renata saw her mother motioning for her. "We will talk more after dinner."

Though the room was considered the smallest of the dining rooms, the glittering table was set for sixty people. Renata and Natalia, along with other guests, wandered around the room. Renata whispered to Natalia about the stunning frescoes of Bacchus adorning the ceiling and walls of the great room. They oohed and aahed at the finery of dishes and flowers set on the table. Filigreed candelabras with long, green-flecked candles were spaced every three feet.

On either side of them were shallow rectangular dishes with floating camellias. Renata had seen several camellia bushes in the orangery on her tour with Martell and had asked for some for her bouquet. How fortunate that Zio Alonzo had a limonaia and an aranciera to supply him with fresh lemons, oranges, and flowers all year long—a luxury reserved for the very few with similarly vast and successful estates. She made a note to ask Eletta about the odd-looking candles. They had a slight camphor aroma, but Renata thought they smelled divine and would be perfect for the chapel.

Renata swallowed a lump in her throat and said a silent prayer for her beloved's safe return. Martell rang the bell to signal that dinner was ready. As the guests started to move, Zio Alonzo beckoned her and her parents over to him.

"Please wait here a moment until everyone has gone in. It will not take long."

Renata looked at Mama and then Papà, but both looked and acted as clueless as she was about why Zio Alonzo was holding them back.

At last, the room was empty, and Martell closed the doors behind the last guest.

He swigged the last of his aperitivo, cleared his throat, and began. "My dear family, it is with some sadness that I must inform you that Vito Marzano has had an unfortunate accident, and he and his wife have gone missing."

The Bombonattis erupted in a mix of shock and surprise.

"Please, hold your questions until I am done." Everyone quieted, and Renata reached for Mama's hand. "Placido and his friends were rehearsing a tableau vivant on the tower roof. Why they had to go all the way up there, especially with Vito about to become a father, I do not know."

This was precisely what she had asked Fumo. It was odd that Zio Alonzo said Po's friends were rehearsing yet conveniently neglected to mention Po's half-brothers as participants.

I knew I should have questioned Zio Alonzo before now.

"The tableau mimicked a sword fight. Vito got too close to the edge, and we believe he fell over. He seems to have survived, but he has gone missing. Placido would not have authorized such a location for a rehearsal. Still, we imagine he is distraught about his missing and possibly injured friend, so why he chose to go to Orrico with nary a notice is perplexing."

I doubt that, but I will find out when he returns.

"My dear," he turned to Renata, "please do not worry. This is sad news, but Placido will be back, and we will go forth with the wedding. I sent his brothers to find him and accompany him home. He had sent word earlier that snow had collapsed the only bridge leading out of Orrico, so he and his manservant were stuck trying to bring home the furniture. I demanded he leave the furniture and return at once to be with his bride."

And his missing best man.

Mama fanned herself. "Where could Signor Marzano be? How could he have fallen from such a height and then walked away? Is he hiding alone or with his pregnant wife? What about needing medical attention?" Mama could not help but blurt out her concerns.

"Mama, hush with your incessant questions." Renata looked at Mama disapprovingly and encouraged Zio Alonzo to continue with his announcement.

"Let us have our dinner and discuss things in the morning. We should know more then. Signor Marzano is likely resting at one of our tenant's cottages. We will find him. Renata, we can bring a cot into your room if you wish. Your maid can stay with you, so you are not alone."

"Thank you, Zio Alonzo. You are too kind, but I am fine on my own." She did not want to be watched over like a child, although she may have to concede that Natalia was right and that Eletta may very well be his spy. The thought made her angry and resentful that Po was not here to defend and protect her.

Renata blinked back tears. Would Po return and honor their promise to each other at the Castle of Love all those years ago?

᪥

Renata took the empty seat at the dinner table next to Natalia. She was grateful the place card had her calligraphed name on it. When

Natalia gave Renata a quizzical look, Renata whispered, "Later," and allowed the footman to place her napkin on her lap. The footman had poured Prosecco all around the table, then filled Zio Alonzo's glass once seated.

Zio Alonzo looked like he wanted to be anywhere other than hosting a roomful of people. His eyelids were drooping, and his cheeks were colorless. The news must have caught up with him.

She looked over at Fumo and Dario. Their faces had drained of color. They were fidgeting in their chairs and kept their eyes downcast.

The mood in the dining hall had turned from sad to somber, with everyone whispering and wondering what had happened. Renata just wanted to run up to her room, curl into a ball under her bed covers, and stay there awhile. And she would, but not before she figured out three things.

How had Zio Alonzo learned about Vito? Why had it taken him this long to make his announcement? And why had he neglected to mention that his three older sons were also rehearsing on the tower? She had seen Vito fall yesterday before noon. Others would have, too. Why had so many people kept such a big secret? And for so long. What else might Alonzo and others be hiding?

☙

Renata followed Natalia to her room and gave her the news. They agreed to discuss it further in the morning. When Renata returned to her room, there were two more notes. One in the usual manner, with wax and a seal impressed upon it. The other was most unusual, for it was written on her vanity mirror using her cheek cream. The rose-colored rouge spelled out:

Stop snooping around unless you want to end up like Vito.

Renata grabbed the back of her vanity chair to steady herself. Her sleuthing was getting in someone's way, and their response was to threaten her. Her knees wobbled, and she sank into the chair to keep her legs from buckling. That was when she noticed the note in her hand. Thank goodness, it was Po again, and she tore off the wax this time instead of saving it. Another cryptic note. She crumpled it up, hurled it against the wall, and then thought better of it. She retrieved it, smoothed it out, and read:

All is not what it seems.

And what is seen is not all.

Young families must be protected.

But only where the walls are not thin.

It was unsigned. Did Po think this was a game and her heart a game piece? She considered the fire this time but chose to test her tired brain before bed in case the note contained a clue to help her better understand what was happening. She retrieved her casebook and began at the beginning.

The "all" he referred to in the first and second lines must be the incident and the injured Vito. So, the whole thing was a farce, and she had been right. Vito was alive. She clenched her teeth and growled slightly before continuing with her endless questions.

Which young families? Po did not have any children, nor did any of his friends, so who could he mean? Renata scratched her head for a moment. Ah, he must mean Vito and Mariana and their unborn bambino. Was Po trying to tell her that they were all safe? Was Po somehow with Vito and not at Orrico? That could not be right.

Had the Pelicani brothers found them? If so, why had they not all arrived back at the castello already? And if Mariana and a manservant were nowhere to be seen, had someone gotten word to them to meet Po and Vito somewhere other than the castello? Could Natalia be right that someone had tried to murder Vito, and as such, he had been carried away to a safe location?

Renata reread the note. The last line glowed like a bright candle. Perhaps Po was trying to tell her the castello was unsafe for Vito, Mariana, the baby, or himself.

A chill swept over her body as her eyes moved from the note to the mirror, where the menacing note in red was scrawled across it. Who had left *that* for her? And was that person the reason her fiancé was hiding? And away from his soon-to-be wife?

Chapter 17

A sliver of amber peeked through the heavy damask curtains and stirred Renata awake. First, one eye opened, then the other, and she grudgingly pushed back her duvet and padded to the window. Orange flames streaked the clear winter sky, enveloping the grounds in a colorful glow. She gazed at the beautiful scene below, hoping for fresh insight into her worries. Renata had tossed and turned during the night, too many questions swirling in her mind. She must start her day and answer them, much like Sherlock would.

For My Detective would not dally like me, she thought.

She turned to her wardrobe and pulled out a cypress green woolen skirt and matching jacket she was sure Sherlock would approve of. Next, she spotted a lace-collared high-neck shirtwaist—perfect for the outdoors, where she hoped to spend time today. Her head was sure to clear quickly in the chill.

☯

Renata was at the buffet cabinet when Martell entered the breakfast room. He said something to Zio Alonzo and left the room. When Martell returned, he announced, "Ispettore Grasso and Officer Damiani."

All eyes turned to the newcomer. The inspector was stout and turnip-shaped, though he had a look that could take command of any room as soon as he entered it. His assistant bore a nondescript face on a lanky frame, with a demeanor that was ever attentive to his superior's needs.

"Ah, Ispettore Grasso and Officer Damiani. Benvenuto a Ca' Pelicani." Zio Alonzo did not rise from his seat at the head of the table, though he waved the policeman in.

"Signor Pelicani." The inspector addressed Zio Alonzo before greeting everyone else. "Saluti a tutti."

Everyone nodded or mumbled hello in return.

Zio Alonzo cleared his throat and looked around the table. "By now, you have all heard the news that Vito has died. I informed the polizia early this morning, and they sent Ispettore Grasso to investigate. I imagine the inspector would like to speak to some or all of you, so please, I know this is a trying time for everyone, but answer his questions the best you can."

Turning to Grasso, Zio Alonzo said, "For the sake of Placido and Renata's wedding in two days, man, see to it that the matter is settled before the wedding. And Christmas. I will not have either event spoiled. I have said all I want to say. All yours, Ispettore."

"Grazie." The inspector acknowledged the head of the house and then faced those seated at the table. "I am Giorgio Grasso, the most senior policeman in this part of the region. During this investigation, my officer and I have taken rooms at the Pensione Cavallini, so you may contact me there when I am not here." The inspector stood as tall as he could with his hands behind his back and bellowed. "Now, enough chitter chatter. If someone could show us the tower, its roof, the grounds, and so on."

"Sì, sì," said Zio Alonzo, nodding. "Martell, please have one of the footmen accompany the inspector wherever he needs to go."

Renata watched the inspector's face tighten at Il conte Sica's instruction that he should always be accompanied. She surmised he was not much used to being supervised or having his wandering restricted. She smiled for the first time that morning.

Ispettore Grasso put his hand over the grip of his gun in his holster and turned on his heel to follow the footman who had somehow appeared without being summoned. She had never inspected a weapon up close and suddenly wanted to do so. She had to know if it was a

Beretta, a Bodeo, or a Fiocchi. Papà had accumulated quite a collection from his service in Ethiopia, but he had never let her near his guns alone.

However, she could not very well announce her intention in front of everyone. Mama would outright forbid it. If Mama could only know that the mere thought of guns had sent a rush of blood to Renata's neck, she doubted even the most potent smelling salts would stir Mama from the shock of Renata's arousal.

After breakfast, Renata whispered to Natalia. "Distract Mama, will you?" Renata pulled her shirt collar higher on her neck. "I am following a hunch. I shall explain later."

Natalia gripped Renata's arm. "What? Again? No. I thought we were going to the Christmas market in Arquà today. It is my favorite of all of them."

"Yes, later. Please do this for me." Renata released Natalia's grip. "I promise to buy you some piping hot bomboloni with chocolate when we get to the market."

Natalia crossed her arms over her chest. "I will let you bribe me with doughnuts, but this is the last time I shall be so easily swayed."

Renata wasted no time standing and addressing her mother. "Mama, I must ask Cook about the wedding dinner. I shall see you later." Renata waved away Mama's protestations and left the room.

She soon caught up with the policeman and the footman in the foyer. "Ispettore Grasso."

The man was not surprised at her approach and gave her an appraising look as she drew near. "Signorina, scusi, but I do not know who you are."

"Renata Bombonatti," she said matter-of-factly.

"Piacere. You must be the bride." He tilted his head. "Can I help you?"

"Sì, uh ..." She cleared her throat before scanning the octagonal room to ensure no one was eavesdropping. "Signor Pelicani thought you might have questions that, uh, the footman could not answer, so he asked me to help."

"He did, did he?" The irritation in the inspector's voice was unmistakable. "Let's get on with it. I have a busy day ahead of me." His gruff manner did not bother her if she could watch everything he did. It would be worth it if she learned something that might help the investigation. The gruffness only added to her desire to spend time with a man in uniform. It would be a first, though it was yet another desire she had never expressed outside her diary.

The footman led the way up the winding stairs to the tower roof. The higher they climbed, the colder it got. Thankfully, she had thrown on a shawl before coming down to breakfast. She made a triangle using the shawl, crossed the long pieces, and tucked two corners into opposite sides of her skirt's waistband.

She sent another note of thanks to heaven for choosing a shirtwaist and skirt combination instead of a dress for her shopping excursion with Natalia today. Bundled as best as she could be, she walked past the inspector and the footman, who was holding the roof door open for her.

Out on the roof, the mighty morning wind from the conical Euganean Hills dispersed the mist lying low over the Venetian Plain. Within moments, the ochre plains became bright, clear, and still. The view was spectacular, and she let it carry her away until she heard the footman yell, "Signor!"

Renata rushed over. Officer Damiani was inches from the inspector, sweat trickling down the edge of his sideburns as he watched the inspector balance precariously among the stones.

The policeman stood on the crenel between two merlons fronting a parapet. It was where a soldier might have fired arrows if a marauding army attacked the fortress. He looked over the battlement to the ground of the bailey below and wrote something in a little gray notebook. Jumping off, he moved to the next crenel and the next until he had stood in the middle of each one.

Ah, thought Renata, *he is taking measurements and observing what stands out from each angle.*

She scribbled that observation in her casebook.

"Signorina Bombonatti," he shouted, though he need not have done so, for his voice carried over the wind, "do you know where Vito Marzano fell?"

This was where she could either tell the truth or feign ignorance. She decided to test the waters of his congeniality with the former. "Why, the one closest to the laurel tree."

He jerked, then followed her until she found the opening above the tree with the broken branches.

"Voilà!" She waved her arms, much like a magician revealing a trick.

He stepped into the crenel and peered down. Rapid strokes flew across his notebook before he turned the page to accommodate still more words. Finally, he stepped down, looked up at her, and licked his pencil. "And may I ask how you knew the exact crenel?"

"I happened upon the laurel tree below during my walk yesterday, and ..."

Renata drank him in. The aroma of his soap. The wet wool of his policeman's overcoat. Even the hint she had seen of his proud streak and hot temper was attractive, both quite the opposite of Po. She knew she should back away, yet she could not quite bring herself to do it. He, in turn, searched her eyes, face, neck, and heaving bosom. The air was crisp all around except between them, where a rising heat had to stop, though neither moved.

A moment later, the taut wire that had run from one body to the other snapped. They pulled apart as fast as if a lightning strike had hit them. She gulped, then pointed down and away from her, trying to regain her equilibrium. "I noticed thick branches were broken, too big for the snow to have done the job. I saw many footprints nearby, and the story came together naturally."

He sucked in his cheeks. "With whom else have you shared this theory?"

"No one."

He rubbed his chin. She liked it. It showed he was a thinker, and she liked thinking men, hence her penchant for literary salons, though the Baronessa di Calandro's may have soured her on them. Watching him, Renata suspected the inspector did not jump to conclusions either.

"What can you tell me about this Marzano fellow other than he was a good friend to your fiancé?"

"Vito is the youngest son of the previous Conte di Marzano. Though Vito was the prodigal son who had just returned to Sica for the first time since he left five years ago, he had never felt at home here, always 'bigger than his boots,' or so my fiancé said. Vito took no money from his father when he left Sica to apprentice with Zanellato, the famous goldsmith in Vicenza."

"Hmm …" His eyes shifted left to right in rapid succession.

She continued. "Vito was there only five years before opening a bottega specializing in his famous love knot jewelry. It is how he met his now-wife, Mariana. She saw him putting an enormous knot pendant in his shop window when she was passing by and—"

"Sì, sì. I gather his enterprise is a success." The man tapped his notebook with his mechanical pencil. "Do you know who might want to bring him harm? Any rivals, new or old?"

Renata detected an emphasis on "old." The policeman was angling for information, though his patience had a short lifespan. She had noticed it right away after Zio Alonzo had introduced him. At first, it irritated her, but now she realized he was a man who was focused on his work and did not want to waste time. There was a resemblance to Sherlock's mind she could not deny. She could learn from this man, and outside of the grizzly tutors her father had hired years ago, she had not been around many men who were professionals in their field. It was intoxicating.

"Well?"

She cleared her throat and shook her head. "No rivals that I know of."

There *was* Eletta. And Fumo. Though she did not know the dynamics between her husband's childhood friends, throwing Fumo or her maid into a fire without hard evidence was amateurish. Sherlock had taught her that. When the sight of Fumo came up in her mind's eye, she faltered for a moment and almost gave him up, if only to see him squirm under a policeman's barrage of questions. She chuckled to herself, but Grasso caught her.

The inspector held up his field notes. "Something funny you wish to share, Signorina Bombonatti? Worthy of my notebook, yes?"

She blushed. "Oh no, a silly joke popped into my head."

Ispettore Grasso grumbled and flipped a page of his notebook, his pencil ready. "Why was Marzano on the roof? Was he alone? About what time was he here?"

Back to the cold business at hand. She welcomed it. "He and my fiancé's friends were in costume and masks rehearsing a tableau vivant to perform at o-o-our wedding." Her hand flew to her throat. She almost choked on the last word. Days ago, it was an absolute. Today, uncertainty had crept in, but she reminded herself: *C'è ancora domani* There's still tomorrow.

The inspector gave her a sideways glance. "Go on."

She gulped. "I believe they were practicing late morning and into lunchtime."

He held his pencil in the air. "Please list the names, signorina."

"Let's see . . . Vito Marzano, my fiancé's best man, plus Dario Rinaldo and Ursino Fumagalli—all childhood friends. And his three half-brothers—Giacomo, Fabrizio, and Tommaso. Perhaps more, but those are the only ones I know." She looked at the footman, who had not spoken during her banter with the policeman. "Were you here?"

Renata and Ispettore Grasso were both surprised when he spoke. "Yes."

"Well, man, why did you not speak up earlier?" The inspector stomped his foot.

The footman shrugged. "You did not ask."

"Impertinent." The inspector wrote something in his book and,

without looking up, asked, "Who else? Who else was here during the rehearsal?"

"Three other footmen plus one other person I did not recognize. A small but wiry man. Seemed to want to fight, particularly with Signor Marzano."

"Why did you not recognize him?" The words tumbled out of Renata's mouth before she could stop them. The policeman scowled, and his knuckles turned white, holding his pencil.

"We were in costume and wearing masks. The wiry fellow disappeared soon after Signor Marzano fell, so I could not make him out beforehand. I did not remember that part until just now."

"There must be something else you remember. Think harder."

"No, I cannot—"

Crack! The inspector swore. He had just broken the tip of his pencil and smeared his notebook. "I am done here."

Chapter 18

Renata and Officer Damiani walked outside behind Ispettore Grasso and back into the servants' hall, where the inspector questioned maids and other footmen. Despite nervous glances from the staff, she took as many notes as the inspector did. Occasionally, he glanced over, scowled, and said nothing.

Two hours later, after he had exhausted the staff, the inspector flipped shut his notebook. "If you are right, Signorina Bombonatti, that Signor Marzano is alive, then the moment Signor Marzano and Signor Placido, or their manservants return, they must come immediately to the pensione where I am staying. I will interrogate them there."

"Of course, inspector," said Renata, assuring him she would see to it herself.

"Take Officer Damiani with you and bring me Il conte Sica, and Signori Fumagalli and Rinaldo. The footman here will take me to somewhere private to interrogate these men. Perhaps in the library?"

"Certo. We shall meet you there," she said and left with the officer.

"I am told the library is quite renowned in these parts," said Officer Damiani, adjusting his tie as he walked.

"So I am told. I have yet to see it myself."

When they found Zio Alonzo, Fumo, and Dario, Renata and the officer walked behind them, and Zio Alonzo led them all to the library.

Officer Damiani held Renata back just as she was entering the room. "May I warn you about something?"

Renata's pulse pounded, but she nodded.

"Ispettore Grasso has a long fuse. However, once lit, he explodes. His temper takes a while to come off the boil. Also, he is not very forgiving, and his memory is remarkable. Bear all that in mind and watch your step as this investigation proceeds."

She twice tapped her index finger to her nose. "Praemonitus, praemunitus, as my grandfather used to say."

He bowed. "Forewarned is forearmed indeed. I am glad that you took it as such."

Renata was not sure what to expect other than a dark, oak-paneled room much like her family's library, but what lay before her was something else entirely. Gray light filtered through semi-circular rondels and leaded windows, filling the gold-and-cream decorated room with a hazy glow. Each shelf-covered wall ran three-quarters of the way up to a two-story vaulted ceiling.

Lying open on an intricately carved lectern was the golden book of Italian nobility, Libro d' Oro. No doubt it was open to the page detailing the Pelicani family's titles, land grants, and coat of arms, but she did not take the time to confirm it.

She sat in a wing chair while he perched himself on the edge of the desk. It was not long before a knock at the door brought Po's friends and his uncle into the room.

Zio Alonzo sat in the other wing chair facing Renata while Fumo and Dario stood beside Renata.

The policeman flipped open his notebook and pointed his pencil at Dario. "Signor Rinaldo, please give us your recollection of the morning of December 19th."

"We were all on the roof in costume and masks, practicing the fight as part of the tableau we would perform at the wedding. I heard a scream, and Vito fell from the tower in the blink of an eye. We looked down, and he was on the ground, not moving. We were stunned for a few minutes but scrambled down the stairs. He was gone when we got outside next to the shrub where he had fallen. We have not seen him since."

"You looked for him?"

Dario straightened. "Yes, of course."

The policeman did not look up from his notebook. "Where, and for how long?"

Dario looked at Fumo and then back to the inspector. "About an hour and all over the nearby grounds and stables. The pelican aviary, too."

"Everyone who was on the roof formed the search party?"

"Well, uh … not exactly." Dario shuffled his feet.

The inspector squinted at the groomsmen and pursed his lips. "You," he said, pointing to Fumo, "Out with it."

"My friend may be mistaken. He thinks a short man on the roof disappeared after the fighting stopped, but I do not recall such a man rehearsing with us."

Renata sat forward, her eyes shifting back and forth between the two men. Dario had corroborated the footman's version of the incident, but Fumo disagreed.

"Placido was the first down the stairs, and we could not find him either. Maybe he found Vito and hid his body. Maybe he was too distraught to face us. Maybe he caught someone taking the body away, and they chased him. Maybe he left suddenly for Orrico because he felt he was in danger."

"That is many maybes," said Renata, rubbing her temples.

The inspector recrossed his legs and raised an eyebrow at Zio Alonzo. "You knew about the accident before your nephew left for Orrico?"

"No." Zio Alonzo pounded the arm of the chair with his fist.

Dario jumped at Zio Alonzo's voice, and Fumo steadied him.

"He left me a simple note saying he had to go to Orrico. Only recently did I learn from my stable manager Rodrigo that he had found Vito. He advised Vito to rest, and he went off to get supplies to tend to his wounds, but when he returned to where Vito was hiding, he was no longer there. He was afraid to tell me the truth, fearing he would be implicated."

"Of course, he is implicated because he was withholding evidence." Ispettore Grasso took a note and then barked. "And you are only telling me this now?"

"I was hoping we could find Vito without involving la polizia. And we did not want to frighten Renata and her parents."

Renata gave him a weak smile.

"Is that why you brought me in late? Do not answer that. I already know." He scribbled furiously without looking up. "So, where was he?"

Zio Alonzo opened his cigar box, selected a cigarillo, lit it, and, in a shaky voice, said, "In the back of the small tobacco barn. Rodrigo found Vito and hid him as he asked, and then when Vito escaped, Rodrigo came out to help the search party so as not to draw suspicion that he was harboring Vito."

The inspector turned his attention to Fumo and Dario. "Did you two look in the barn?"

They looked at each other. Fumo nodded, and Dario shrugged.

The policeman shook his head and swore. "May I?" He pointed at the cigar box, and the count nodded. The inspector lit his cigarillo with shaky fingers and began anew. "He could have made it to the barn under his own steam, but why did he not stay where he was and wait for help?"

Renata's lip trembled. The groomsmen hung their heads. Zio Alonzo took a deep drag on his cigarillo, shook his head, and pounded his fist again on the armrest.

Ispettore Grasso stubbed out his cigarillo and closed his notebook. "I will stop by the stables and interrogate this Rodrigo fellow on my way out. I shall return tomorrow at which time I expect your four nephews to have returned from Orrico. Have them ready to be interrogated when I arrive. Signor Placido better have answers, or else I will bring in the army to search this house."

Zio Alonzo rang the bell pull, instructed the footman to show the policeman out, and stormed out of the library after they had left.

Leaving Dario and Fumo in the library, she walked between rooms, looking for Martell. Mrs. Trevisan thought he would know what may have happened to the manservants. Neither Renata nor the inspector had asked him, which was one of the big questions yet to be answered in her casebook. She found the man in the breakfast room, supervising the table setting for pranzo, the midday meal.

"Ah, Martell. Just the man I wished to see."

She had entered the long rectangular room and walked half its length to reach the butler. Bent forward, he was busy measuring the space between plates and from the edge of the plates to the edge of the table. He did not acknowledge her, so she waited while he conducted precise measurements. After her run-in with Mrs. Trevisan, she knew she had to bide her time to win over the servants.

She scanned the wall and rather liked the pretty wallpaper in this room. The color palette of light neutrals, earth tones, and the muted green of the acacia sprigs evoked tranquility and classic elegance, transforming the room into a haven of timeless charm.

Straightening from his bent position, Martell set his measuring stick on the table and looked down from his giraffe height. "How may I help you, Signorina Bombonatti?"

"I have a question to ask, but while waiting, I could not help but admire the décor. I would not change much from the few castello rooms I have seen thus far. The previous contessa had an excellent eye and refined taste."

"Indeed. Before her and her …"

"Yes? Her and her …?"

He cleared his throat. "Before her untimely demise from a sailing accident, the late contessa, Signora Paloma Pelicani, had completed a very tasteful update of the decor and furnishings of the main salon rooms and bedroom suites."

"Ah." Just as well because until the Pelicani babies started arriving, and possibly after, Renata hoped she would find many cases to solve as an independent investigator: a missing person's case, a robbery, maybe even a lost heirloom. At any rate, she wanted to keep busy with her own pursuits rather than fill her days with the type of domesticity expected of her. She did not care much about keeping house like she had been taught at boarding school, though she would not share that plan publicly.

"You had a question …?"

"Oh yes. You see, my husband's best man, his wife, and their manservant are missing. Might you know where he has gone? The last time anyone saw him was during the tableau vivant on the roof."

"Only Bepi is under my purview. Marzano's man is no concern of mine." With that, Martell returned to his measuring.

"All right, but—"

Martell stopped and raised himself to his full height once again. "Do not think me rude, signorina, but the master has sent out a search party. In due course, we shall have answers enough to satisfy."

Even you. He never said those words at the end of the sentence, but the implication was clear. His tone was confident. This made her think he might know something about Vito and that it might be good news. She also knew when her probing had reached its limit.

"Thank you, Martell."

He nodded and resumed his work.

જી

Climbing the stairs to her room, Renata's arms and legs felt like they weighed as much as a wheelbarrow full of bricks. Each step was harder than the previous one until, at last, she reached her room, threw her shawl on the floor, and collapsed onto her bed.

Observing everything the inspector did and answering his endless questions had made her—for a brief moment—want to give up her sleuthing. She was no further along now than when she started two days ago. And there was still no Po. Her handsome, adoring Po had tested her patience with his notes and forced her into a guessing game.

She took off her jacket and threw it on the bed. "Aaaaaaaaargh!" she screamed at her ceiling.

Natalia came racing into the room. "What's wrong?"

Renata raised her head an inch off the duvet. "Everything," she said and dropped it down again.

Natalia picked up the shawl and hung it in the wardrobe. She sat on the bed beside Renata and played with her friend's hair. "You have not told me what you discovered in the barn or what progress you made with the handsome policeman."

Renata pushed her friend's hand away. "Oh, you are wicked. I am about to get married. I do not see him that way."

"You are going to marry, not go to your grave," teased Natalia.

They both burst out laughing. Renata felt much lighter.

"Come on, future Signora Pelicani." Natalia pulled Renata to a sitting position. "Let's go to Arquà. When we get back, I have an afternoon surprise for you."

૪૦

When they arrived, the carriage driver had attached a sleigh to the horses and removed the hot pans from under the blankets on the seat.

"Oh my, how wonderful," said Renata, "I have never ridden in a sleigh before. The perfect Christmastime activity if there ever was one."

"Step in, ladies. Let me help you." The rosy-cheeked driver settled them under the warm blankets.

"Yah!" He snapped the reins, and they were off.

The driver carved a path through the castello's snow-laden fields rather than take the snow-and-dirt-packed roads. With the sleigh, the horses flew by the barns and outbuildings of the farm with little effort. As they passed woven grapevine fences and small laurel groves, Renata filled Natalia in on all that had happened.

"So, Vito is *alive?*" said Natalia, sotto voce so the driver could not hear her.

"Yes, we, that is, the inspector and I, believe so. Thanks to God." Renata crossed herself. "Martell did not say so specifically, nor did he show me all his cards. He held back what he knew of the manservants' whereabouts."

Natalia tapped her chin. "Hmm, he must have a good reason to withhold that information."

Renata adjusted the blanket and tucked it tight under her thighs. "It makes no sense when the entire household is under investigation. Unless ..."

"Yes?" Natalia leaned closer to look into Renata's eyes.

"Unless they are in hiding for their protection because Vito's fall was no accident. Perhaps Po is safeguarding Vito and Mariana, and the manservants are with them."

Natalia grabbed one of Renata's hands through her muff and squeezed it. "They do not know if the perpetrator will strike again, and they need to remain hidden."

"And safe," said Renata.

Renata and Natalia both nodded as the realization dawned on them.

"So, you agree?" Natalia searched Renata's face.

Renata bit her lip and murmured in agreement. "But the question remains: where are they?"

She looked over the cloistered town and took it all in—just an hour. That's all she wanted—a few moments to let go of the situation they had found themselves in. It was real and awful and was not going away.

But this one afternoon, she sought a respite for her brain and to enjoy a bit of Christmas, too.

The driver maneuvered them onto a roadway lined with cypress trees that stood like sentinels. Leafy olive groves, bare jujube shrubs, and vineyards, denuded of their fruit, dotted the white countryside. The sleigh swooshed along the untouched snow as they approached the outskirts of Arquà Petrarca, the pearl of the Euganean Hills. The soaring bell tower of the Church of Santa Maria loomed over the hamlet—its noon chimes sonorous among the midday bustle of the town.

Minutes later, the friends dismounted a few feet below Casa del Petrarca, the last abode of the famed Renaissance poet, Petrarca.

"Signorina Bombonatti, the skies have darkened, and the Bora is rising," said the driver, pointing up to the steely clouds above. "I can feel the brutal wind in my hands. You will need to cut short your visit lest a snowstorm catches us unawares and we get stuck here. The sudden ones are quite fierce this time of year."

Natalia harumphed. "But I had planned a surprise after our shopping!"

Renata quieted her friend and reassured her they could come back another time. "Very well, driver, we shall comply. Now let us be."

"Let's hurry to the bombolone vendor and peruse the market," said Natalia. "If we have time, we can visit Petrarca's tomb, his ivy-covered cottage that I love so much, and—"

"All right, Natalia. You are as excited as a child on Christmas morning when they see all the gifts Babbo Natale has left them."

Natalia's face lit up, skipping ahead of her friend, undeterred.

They walked the cobblestone streets and greeted the townspeople. Everyone was in a good mood because it was the season of Christmas. As they passed Petrarca's house, Renata blew a kiss at the Moorish-style windows of the library set into a corner of the scholar's last home and promised to return soon.

The women turned the corner into the square and were instantly assaulted by organ grinders, a horse-drawn omnibus, and all manner of food vendors. Stone masons ate roasted turkey legs next to a merchant tending a fire in a metal drum that held turkeys on a spit. The candymaker dipped small apples on sticks into a kettle of hot sugar syrup that hardened around the fruit when he lifted it. A baker had a giant vat full of hot oil. A crowd of children chattered away next to him while waiting for their precious donuts—a rare yet much anticipated holiday treat in these parts.

A cap was passed to those listening to the canticles that told the Nativity story, thus securing a few coins for the musicians singing and playing. Natalia made a mad dash for the baker's queue and clapped her hands in time with the music. Renata joined her, and when it was their turn, she ordered four donuts, and Natalia beamed with gratitude. They strolled through the stalls, enjoying their sweets. Renata bought Eletta a Christmas present—an embroidered handkerchief of tea-stained linen—to thank her for her help that week. Next, she bought a set of yarrow-dyed linen squares for her maid Alissa, who was back home sick with a cold.

"There's a glover over there, and I must see him about this hole in my left glove. I will not be long." Natalia trotted off, and Renata wandered until she spotted a stall with a row of pendants. Drawn to jewelry from a young age, Renata could not help herself and strolled to a Roma woman's cart to peruse her wares.

"Good day, signorina. Can I interest you in a ring or a pendant?" Renata had barely set foot near the Roma woman, and she was already peddling.

"Good day to you," said Renata, scanning the merchandise. Nothing grabbed Renata's attention after touching and holding several pieces until she spotted a pendant lying on the bench behind the woman. "May I see that pendant?"

"Why, I just finished it. One moment." The woman busied herself polishing the pendant made of gold and silver rings to a bright shine, then moved on to the silver necklace it hung on. Before she handed it to Renata, she paused.

"What is it? Let me see it." Renata reached for it, but the woman pulled it back and dangled it next to her face.

"Traditionally, a man buys this for a woman. In my country of Algeria, a love knot symbolizes a beloved's eternal love and devotion. When a woman wears it, we believe it can bring the couple closer together."

Renata wondered if Vito's love knot jewelry had a similar tale to tell. The necklace would give her something to remind her of Po and hold onto until he returned.

"I will take it," said a gruff voice. Renata whipped around and faced Fumo.

"You!"

He smiled like a tiger, ready to pounce.

"Hello, Renata."

"W-w-where have you been?" She clutched his forearm to steady herself and dropped it like hot coal.

"Just browsing these fine vendors' wares." The timbre of his voice dropped two tones.

"Have you met with the inspector yet? What did you tell him?" Her pitch rose three tones.

"That I was quite far back from the crenelations. That I saw and heard nothing until Vito screamed. And that is the extent of information I provided." Fumo pulled out his cigarette case and lit a cigarette.

She was about to rant and demand why he had not shared this information with her earlier when she saw two drops of blood on the inside of his cigarette case. She felt faint and held onto the corner of the jewelry cart.

Renata opened her purse to grab her smelling salts. Something rough brushed her hand, and she heard a soft clunk. Something had dropped in next to her compact. After sniffing her salts, she reached into her purse to put them back and pulled out the Algerian love knot wrapped in a strange handkerchief a second later.

"Fumo, no!" She turned to see the woman in copious skirts, aprons, shawls, and necklaces counting her money. Horrified, she tried to give it back to the woman.

The woman hissed, "I cannot return it and sell it to someone else. Bad luck."

"It is a love token, but between friends, not lovers," Fumo said, almost too softly for Renata to hear. "I know if Placido were here, he would have bought it for you, so think of it, of me, as—"

What *would* Placido think of such an extravagant gift? It was the tradition in these parts for the best man to buy a ring for the bride to wear on her right hand, but Fumo was not Vito, and tears threatened to spill down her face at the thought. Fumo was watching her intently. She could read neither his eyes nor his face. As she tried to understand what had happened, another thought occurred.

"I will accept this gift, Fumo." He beamed at her change of heart. "On one condition."

He took a step toward her. "Oh? Pray tell."

She willed her body to stop shaking and her voice to ring clear. "You must come with me to the tomb. There is something I wish to ask you there."

"Very well, I shall see you there in a half hour."

Renata watched his retreating backside until it was lost in the crush of peddlers and peasants. Once he was gone, she remembered she had to find Natalia and realized she was still holding the pendant. She was about to open her purse to drop it back in when a red splotch on the corner of Fumo's handkerchief poked out of the top.

Pulling it out, she gasped. Several very dark and substantial red spots were just below the first one. Her hand trembled as she brought the reddened rag to her nose. She almost gagged. There was no mistaking the iron scent of blood, but whose was it?

Chapter 19

The entire town of Arquà Petrarca was built from stones—houses, walls, fountains, churches, and steep, cobbled streets. Past the column of the Venetian lion on via Valleselle stood the house that the poet, Francesco Petrarca, and his daughter's family inhabited from 1370 to 1374. This time, Renata did not blow a kiss to her favorite room.

Instead, she kept a brisk pace until she reached La Chiesa di Santa Maria Assunta. Petrarca's tomb, a carved coffer of Verona red marble, had been placed in the center of the churchyard six years after his death. Many literary-minded Europeans made a pilgrimage here, but that was not why Renata had insisted Fumo meet her here.

Tradition held that one could settle a dispute when an untruth lay at the center of it. The two parties would agree to visit Petrarca's tomb to resolve the conflict. Once there, the accuser of the lie insisted the accused hold up their right hand in the direction of the poet's head and swear they were telling the truth. This was Renata's intention, too. If Fumo were lying, a righteous God would strike his hand down as proof of his lie.

The churchyard was empty except for the enormous tomb. Fumo stood before it. Renata stopped in front of the copper head at the top center of the tomb.

Fumo patted the marble. "An interesting place to ask a question. This is where people come to confess—"

"Yes, precisely that." She squared her shoulders and said, "Raise your right hand."

A sly smile spread across Fumo's mouth. "Renata dearest, there is no disagreement between us, so I see no need—"

"I am not your dearest, now raise your right hand, Fumo." She ground out her request through a clenched jaw. Sighing, he did as he was told. "Now, do you swear that you did not kill—"

"Renataaaaaaaa! There you are." Natalia came running over with their carriage driver in tow. "The driver is insisting we return to—oh, forgive me. I do not think we have met." She held out her hand. "I am Natalia Nunzio."

"Molto piacere." Fumo kissed Natalia's gloved hand but did not let it go.

"Signorina Bombonatti, we must go." The driver was wringing his cap in his hands. "You got out of my sight, and I was worried. If I do not return with both you and Signora Nunzio, your parents will kill me."

Kill. It was such a strong word. "I will join you shortly," said Renata, waving dismissively at the driver. "I just have this one thing I must do with Signor Fumagalli, and we must do it privately."

"Signorina Bombonatti! I cannot allow such a thing. You are betrothed to—" The driver stomped over to her. "We must leave now."

"Not yet. Oh, very well." Renata turned to Natalia and saw her friend's cheeks were flushed red. "Natalia?" Natalia ignored her and kept her focus on Fumo.

Renata shook her finger at Fumo and said, "And I am not done with you," but he did not acknowledge her. She sat in the sleigh, fuming. After a minute, Renata twisted herself in the sleigh to look back at her friend. Fumo was still caressing Natalia's hand, no doubt spewing sweet nothings.

"Natalia, andiamo! Subito!"

"Coming, coming." Renata watched as Natalia pulled her hand from Fumo's. She sashayed backward until she reached the sleigh, waved at Fumo, and then mounted the sleigh.

ဆ

Renata was still fuming on the sleigh ride home and spoke not a word to Natalia no matter how much she cajoled. The snow was coming down hard and fast, befitting Renat's mood.

The driver was lamenting the fact that they had stayed too long and that he had warned of a potential snowstorm. He was ranting through the scarf wrapped around his mouth that the storm had become a blizzard, his visibility was next to zero, and he was having trouble steering the horses. As such, it took them twice as long to return to the castello. The women shivered, their warm blankets turning into cold, heavy snow and freezing ice sheets.

When they finally reached the castello, a footman told them the house was in an uproar because they had not returned earlier. Renata rolled her eyes. She knew just who would be causing the commotion. She was proven right when Mama, the first person who greeted her, bellowed.

"You should never have gone to Arquà." Mama waved her arms frantically, turning in circles around Renata. "I will have that driver's head on a platter. We were worried you would get stuck and be late for your wedding. Between Placido gone, Vito injured and missing, and you, too, what a mess these few days have been. Hurry up to your room and change out of those wet clothes before you catch a cold. Eletta! Help! To think that—"

Renata could see her mother was not interested in a conversation, so Renata climbed the stairs, her mother's rant echoing as far as her bedchamber. Renata had started undressing when Eletta and several other maids arrived with jugs of hot water. They soon filled a small tub, and Renata sank into it, covering her head under the soothing, fragrant water. The ride home had chilled her to the bone, and the hot chamomile-scented water was a balm to her frayed nerves. Once all the other maids had left, Eletta washed Renata's hair.

"Signorina, did you enjoy yourself in Arquà?"

Renata detected a slight sarcastic note in the maid's question, but she did not probe. She did not have the energy. "Mostly, yes."

Eletta rinsed Renata's hair and dried it with a towel. She pinned it up until Renata was ready to leave her bath.

Renata traced figure eights in the water above her belly. "Sorry, I am distracted. We enjoyed ourselves, especially once Natalia found the baker that makes the bomboloni."

"Oh, I know the one you mean, signorina. He's near the entrance to the market. His doughnuts are delicious, and some say they are better than the fancy bakers in Padua."

"Mmm, yes. I ran into Fumo at the market. He was telling me about who was on the roof and what happened before Vito—"

Eletta dropped the shoes she was carrying.

"What is the matter?" Renata looked over the rim of the bathtub.

"I, uh, tripped. Sorry, signorina."

Renata thought back to Fumo surprising her at the market and not following through with her request to confess at Petrarca's tomb. It all made him that much more suspicious. He had disappeared, too, along with Dario, and no one had held them accountable for it. She would have to send word to their rooms that Ispettore Grasso wanted to see them as soon as possible. The groomsmen would ignore a request to see her but would make haste if they knew the inspector wished to speak to them.

The policeman was sharp. He would find out whatever Fumo was up to. She was sure of it. She had not entirely believed Fumo at the market when he had told her the inspector had already interrogated him. His answers had been too smooth. Perhaps the inspector demanding another meeting would rattle him. On seeing him, assuming Fumo did go for a second interrogation if she set him up, the inspector may initially act surprised, but she did not doubt he would catch on quickly.

"Oh, Eletta?"

"Sì, signorina."

"Could you find Signori Fumagalli and Rinaldo and tell them Ispettore Grasso wants them to report to the police immediately? I completely forgot he asked me to do that."

"He is not back, but I will look for Signor Rinaldo." Eletta brought around a big towel and held it up for Renata to step into as she got out of the bath.

Renata took the towel and wrapped herself in it. "I would have thought Signor Fumagalli left Arquà when we did." Eletta was not looking at her. Why was she behaving this way? "Eletta, do you know something you are not telling me?"

Eletta had moved to the bed and was laying out clothes. "No, what I mean is that I have not heard from the staff that he has returned."

Renata thought it odd that Eletta had her back to her and was about to say so, but she was cold and walked behind the screen to dry herself off.

"I heard he was going out into the storm to see if Signor Placido was on his way back. I did not realize he had gone to the market."

Renata poked her head out from behind the screen. "This snowstorm is a nightmare."

With Eletta's help, Renata dressed and sat by the fire to dry her hair, lamenting that what was supposed to be one of the happiest times of her life was one of the worst. Eletta emptied the tub while Renata opened a vanity drawer for some stationery. She quickly closed it when she saw another envelope with Placido's handwriting on it.

How were Po's messages getting through in this weather? Renata returned to her seat by the fire and pondered the answer while combing her hair. Then, another thought occurred to her.

"Eletta, where were you when the men rehearsed the tableau vivant?"

"Uh ..." Eletta had been emptying the tub and clunked the metal jug against the tub when Renata asked her about her whereabouts. "I was right here, preparing for your arrival." She stood and held up two jugs of dirty bath water. "Signorina, I will take these down and bring up a couple of maids to help empty the rest of the tub. Is there anything else?"

"No, thank you, Eletta," said Renata, but then she changed her mind. "Remember to look for the signori, will you? And let me know as soon as you find them."

Eletta knitted her brows and said, "Yes, signorina," then left.

Appalled at her attitude, Renata waited a minute before she yanked open the vanity table drawer and pulled out the note. She confirmed that it was Placido's writing. She brought the note to her nose and inhaled. It was scentless, and her shoulders drooped. She missed his earthy scent. It had been too long since she had smelled it. How could he justify being away from her?

Protecting his best man and his pregnant wife was more important to Po than being with her, the woman who would be his lifelong companion. Her heart hurt, and anger rose from her neck and spread to her cheeks.

An image of the inspector appeared in her mind's eye, and she swatted it away. Embarrassed, she sat with a jumble of feelings. Then, with no provocation, something shifted inside her.

She would assume the best intentions, not the worst. Po was not working against her. He had directed his energy where it was most needed, and his notes said so. It was not that Po had chosen Vito and Mariana over her. They were in a difficult situation, and he was helping them get through it. It would be over soon, and after, Po would be by her side forever. Perhaps he was using his distance and the blizzard as cover for his plan to protect a budding young family. Tears welled in Renata's eyes, and a warmth surged through her. Po was a good friend and a gentleman. He would keep his promise to her at the

Castle of Love. His temporary absence was never meant to suggest otherwise.

Sighing, she slid the letter opener under the wax seal, then read the note:

Hath, not a heart grown fonder
During a period of absence?
It is not a reunion among lovers
That much sweeter at the end,
Even after a tragedy?
Paycience can be a difficult virtue.

She made a note to get after him about his spelling, then continued.

And trust a welcome respite.
When the world thinks otherwise.
Behold, a mishap and a wedding, days apart
One is regrettable, while the other will be unforgettable.

Was Po spinning false hope? Was she a fool to believe it?

No, no, no, no. She stopped herself from letting her mind spiral into negativity. How quickly she moved from security to insecurity.

She was a tired bride for all the wrong reasons. If only Placido were——

A scream erupted from the hallway. Renata jumped out of her chair and ran to her bedchamber door. She yanked it open to see Eletta drop clay jugs on the tile floor, their shattered pieces strewn about. She ran to the maid and soothed her shaking, screaming body. Two more maids rushed up the stairs, and they, too, screamed. Martell was right behind them.

Martell held Eletta's forearm and then addressed the maids. "It's all right. Eletta is fine now."

"That's not it, sir." Renata looked at two young maids cowering and covering their mouths with cupped hands.

"Then what are you all upset about?" said Renata from the doorway. Eletta pointed a shaky finger behind Renata. Renata and Martell turned to look.

Prossima

The word was scrawled in red on her bedchamber door.

Now it was Renata's turn to scream. *You are next* was not something a bride should see two days before her wedding day. She had received two messages scrawled in red—one on the mirror and one on her door.

Ispettore Grasso passed Eletta on the stairs and arrived out of breath to stand next to Renata. He took in the scene, then put his classical Roman nose next to the door and inhaled. "That is blood. Unmistakable."

"How can you be sure?" Renata moved several feet away. She remembered the smell of blood on Fumo's handkerchief and forced herself not to gag. "It smells like rust."

"Paint does not smell like rust." He jotted something down, then turned to Renata. "Were you in your bedchamber?"

"Yes. I was drying myself after my bath. I was waiting for Eletta to return. She had gone to get jugs to empty the bath."

With his pencil poised, the inspector spoke. "How long was your maid gone before you heard her scream?"

She shrugged. "Not long, a quarter of an hour."

He frowned. "And you heard nothing in the interim while you were in your bedchamber?"

Renata shook her head. "No, Inspector, not a sound."

He flipped shut his notebook. "Martell, I will go down and speak to the kitchen staff to see if an animal was killed today."

Renata winced. "Martell, please let Cook know that I am skipping lunch."

Chapter 20

Renata left her mother to her correspondence and wandered over to the parlor's window to check on the status of the blizzard. The worst of it had stopped, but it was still snowing. All she could think about was that the evidence of Vito's accident was gone. Half a foot of snow had covered up all the signs. She was sure the inspector had recorded all he needed in his field book.

She pictured those soft-skinned yet strong hands writing away, then looked down at her hands and massaged them. The picture in her mind shifted to her hands interlocked with the inspector's, then his thumb grazing her knuckles left to right and back again.

Mama's words brought Renata's attention back to the room just as Martell entered. She touched the windowpane with each cheek to cool down the heat of her reddening face. She could not risk either Mama or Martell seeing her face like this or, worse, commenting on it. Renata thought she had sorted out her feelings earlier in her bedchamber.

What was happening to her? Was it this house? She thought of the strange things that she had witnessed. The sudden breeze in the Blue Room that had sent the tinsel flying. The three candles that had blown out when Eletta slammed the door. And the young girl who had appeared out of thin air in several places. Was she real or conjured? If real, who was she?

"You rang, Signora?"

Mama handed Martell some correspondence. "Could you see that these get to the post?"

"Of course. As soon as the storm clears." He nodded and left.

"Mama, I will be right back." Renata swept past the desk where Mama was clearing away her writing utensils. "I need to go down to the kitchens for a moment. I think I left my handkerchief there."

☙

"Oh, pardon me, signorina." Mrs. Trevisan exited the kitchen as Renata entered, holding the door for her.

"Thank you, Mrs. Trevisan." Renata walked through and into the room. The scent of warm spices and herbs filled the air. Fresh pies were cooling on long wooden racks. Jars of canned trout and pickled potatoes lined open cupboards. All these and more were signs that the spirit of Christmas in the Pelicani household was in full swing.

"Is there something you need, signorina?"

Renata turned to the housekeeper and shook her head. "No, I thought I dropped my handkerchief here the other day, and I came to see if it was on the mantle."

The woman entered the kitchen behind Renata. "Let me call someone to help—"

"No, please. 'Tis a trifle, and I should not like to interrupt your work. It is no trouble to search for it myself." The housekeeper pursed her lips, but Renata stood her ground. "Thank you again."

Mrs. Trevisan huffed and left, but not before lifting her chin and pressing her lips together even tighter.

Renata ignored the woman's sullen expression and surveyed the room. There was no sign of the errant girl child, and Renata wandered back to where she had seen her. There was no one there. She felt foolish spending what little time she had before the wedding on an urchin who probably was not real and did not matter to the investigation. She made a note to add her as her second case.

Looking out the windows and spotting the Inspector examining a skinned headless goat, he shivered and drew away from the gruesome site.

৩

Renata sat at her vanity and scrutinized her weary face in the mirror. Aargh. She reached into her drawer to pull out her rouge pot and slammed it shut after spotting another letter. "Dio Santo! My God, when will it end?"

She swore again and pulled open the drawer. She was surprised that the letter was not addressed to her but to Po instead.

It was fine marbled paper, in the Florentine style, and when she picked it up, it was rather heavy. When Renata handled it, she could feel a carved object inside. She carefully slid the letter opener under the wax and opened the envelope without breaking it—a technique she mastered as a young girl when she had wanted to find out what was in her mother's correspondence. A tiny key fell to the floor, and she bent to retrieve it, then read on the slip of paper inside.

Casella postale 99

It was a key to a post office box.

"Renata, the weather has cleared. It was not a blizzard so much as a heavy snowfall," said her mother, passing by her room. "I thought we might go into the village and visit Eletta's shop. You said she was there this afternoon and had invited you to stop in."

"Yes, she did. Let me get Natalia, and we will be right there." Renata stuffed the key and note into her purse and grabbed her coat, hat, and gloves.

৩

The village shops in Sica were very well preserved, and the shopkeepers took pride in maintaining the town's charming look. In the piazza stood a nondescript empty fountain in front of the Church of San Giacomo, with a row of quaint houses on each flank. It was small but picturesque, and with a thick layer of new snow blanketing the entire square, it bordered on magical.

Tiny stone-built shops with fanciful doors lined each side of the square. Candles were already lit in several windows. Strings of lattice paper snowflakes hung just below each top rail, drawing in visitors.

Unusually, the streetlamps were aflame in midday because the caigo that had rolled in from Venice had blanketed the village so thoroughly it seemed to swallow everything in its path. The pointy bell tower atop the municipal hall broke through the famous fog that engulfed the landscape and surrounded the town with a wall of mist.

Eletta had said that Moda Bianca was the second shop from the northeast corner, and Renata directed the driver to it. Just steps from the shop's door, a farmer was roasting chestnuts, and the nutty aroma permeated the dress shop as Renata, Natalia, and Mama entered.

"Greetings, ladies," said Eletta. "May we take your coats?" Eletta and her assistant helped each lady off with her coat and hung it on the nearby stand.

"Thank you, Eletta," said Mama.

"At least it stopped snowing, at least." The shopgirl's face was hopeful.

Ignoring the comment, Mama continued. "Perhaps there is a little something Renata could add to her trousseau. Could you show us something appropriate?"

"Of course, signora." Eletta nodded to her assistant, who disappeared into the back room.

"And not, too, um, costly." Mama was wringing her hands, and just when Renata wondered again what might be worrying her, Eletta returned.

"I carry some lovely handkerchiefs. Do you prefer Belgian, French, or Irish linen?"

Renata walked around the shop, fingering shawls, table runners, and doilies. "I have a few Irish ones, but if you have any with Burano lace on the corner, I could treat myself to a wedding present."

"Very well. Ah, here's some now." Eletta took the boxes from her assistant and beckoned Renata to the small table in front of a corner group of chairs. "Burano lace is one of the most renowned in the world. The pieces I have here passed through the hands of seven expert lace masters. Since the 1500s, the island's heyday, the same family has made these exquisite handkerchiefs by hand."

Natalia and Renata lifted each one and remarked on the fine craftwork. One with a sprig of lily of the valley caught Renata's eye. "Oh my."

"That happens to be one of my favorites," said the shopgirl. "The pomegranate and oleander are local favorites because everyone around here grows them."

Natalia held up one with a colossal, embroidered fig and showed it to Renata. "Perhaps Placido might like this one."

The friends roared with laughter.

"Hush, Renata! Your unladylike guffaws can be heard across the square. You sound like one of Alonzo's blasted pelicans." Mama fiddled with the cameo at her neck.

"Or perhaps this one is more his style?" said Natalia, holding up one with two figs on it and waving it around.

Renata's hand flew to her mouth to keep her laughter contained.

"Do not be vulgar, Natalia. Goodness. Sometimes, you two act like you are still in school. You had best remember your new place in society, Renata."

Renata lent Natalia a hand refolding the fig handkerchiefs. "We are just having a bit of fun, Mama. Is that not what the wedding week is all about? And Christmas, too? Po has practically abandoned me, Vito and Mariana are missing, and the inspector—"

A loud crash interrupted Renata. The sugar caddy on the corner of Eletta's tray had flown off and spilled on Renata's dress. At the same time, two cups fell to the floor, scattering porcelain bits hither and yon. All three women stood.

Renata shook out her dress. "I am afraid the sugar has landed on me."

Purple-faced, Eletta set the tray on a side table and approached Renata. "I am so sorry, signorina. My wiry body sometimes betrays me."

"What happened?" said Mama.

"I, uh, tripped," said Eletta. "Let me get a broom and dustpan."

Renata saw two thick beads of sweat roll down Eletta's face. How odd. That was the second person in one day that had tripped near her. The first was when Renata was bathing, and Eletta tripped in the room. Now this. A third one spelled some doom that Renata did not want to contemplate.

"I will help you." The shopgirl jumped up and followed Eletta to the back room.

"Tsk-tsk." Mama sashayed over to a plaid wool dress atop a dressmaker's form and examined the matching muff.

When Mama was out of earshot, Renata leaned toward Natalia and whispered. "What was I saying when Eletta tripped? Something I said triggered her."

Natalia whispered back. "The part about the inspector that you did not get to finish."

Renata pulled away. The friends looked at one another and then down at the broken crockery. Bad things happened in threes. The accident was the latest on the list of strange happenings. The fact that Eletta tripped here and at the house may mean she was nervous about the investigation. Something was going on, and in Eletta's case, Renata's mention of the inspector had caused her to stumble.

"What is it?" Natalia slid her arm through Renata's and pulled her to the glove cabinet. They bent over it, and Natalia whispered, "What have you conjured in that big, beautiful brain of yours? I can see the cogs a-whirling."

"Perhaps someone was trying to get us out of the house. Look." Renata handed Natalia the note and key, then disentangled herself from her friend to call Eletta. "Eletta, we must go."

Eletta came running in, her sweat worse than before. "So soon?"

"I am afraid so. I have things to attend to back at the castello."

Natalia looked up from the slip of paper with the postbox number, shrugged her shoulders, and handed them back. Renata tilted her head to the shop door. "Please put two lilies of the valley, two pomegranates, and two double fig handkerchiefs on my charge and send the receipt to the castello to my husband's attention. Better yet, address it to me."

"Sì, signorina." As Eletta lowered her head, Renata could have sworn she saw the maid raise an eyebrow.

The shopgirl helped Renata shrug on her coat, and Renata said, "Come, Mama."

Mama looked up from the muff she had been admiring and jerked. "But I have not picked anything."

"Add two oleander ones for my Mama," Renata said over her shoulder as she finished dressing for the sleigh ride home. Buttoning Renata's gloves in place, the shopgirl left to finish tying up the packages before coming back to help Natalia and Mama.

All the while, Eletta stood open-mouthed until she finally regained her composure. "There are plenty of other shops to see …" Her voice trailed off.

"They will be there for us another day. Thank you, Eletta. I will see you back at the castello." Turning to Mama, Renata said, "I need fresh air. I will meet you at the carriage."

Outside, Renata bought a small bag of chestnuts from the seller outside the dress shop and asked him to point her to the post office. It was beside the dress shop, so Renata hid her chestnuts away, flipped up her cape collar, picked up her skirts, and, as fast as she politely could, crossed the square.

Once inside, she dug into her purse and pulled out the key. She spotted a wall of postboxes and searched among them for *99*. How odd that she did not see her number there. She scanned the wall again to no avail. She walked over to the queue, waiting for the clerk. Two tall, though slightly stooped gentlemen stood in line before her. When it was her turn, she approached the rectangular window with the bars across it.

"Buongiorno, signor." She pushed the key under the bars. "I cannot find this postbox. It is number 99, but it does not exist."

The clerk picked up her key and turned it in his hand. "It looks like it should fit one of our older ones."

"Ahem, excuse me, signorina." One of the two gentlemen from the earlier line stood at her side. "I believe that key belongs to me."

"Oh, how so?" Renata put one hand on her hip.

"Anselmo Salucci. I own Salucci Books next door." He pointed to his chest and then behind him, presumably in the direction of the bookshop. "When the post office upgraded their boxes a few years ago, we rescued some of the old ones they had planned to discard. They are beautiful, and we could not let them be destroyed."

"And what does that have to do with this key?" Renata held her hand out, and the clerk returned the key. Then she turned back to Signor Salucci or Mr. Salt. What a strange name. She wondered if he knew the Pelicani's cook, Signor Succo or Mr. Sugar, and whether they had the opposite personalities of their surnames. She stifled a laugh and resolved to learn more about these two characters someday.

He raised an eyebrow but continued. "We were not sure what to do with them other than use them as decoration. Then last year, our store was not doing so well, and we were approaching Christmas, our busiest time except for Easter."

"Sir, please." She looked above him at the clock on the wall and said, "I am rather in a hurry."

He trudged on. "Well, we thought our customers could 'buy' a box for a friend or family member who loves books and quality treats from local merchants. We tailor every box for the recipient and occasion, not just Christmas—like birthdays, engagements, weddings, St. Valentine's Day, new babies, and more."

"What's your point, signor?"

"That key belongs to one of our boxes," said Signor Salucci, waving at a wall behind the bookshop, "so it will not fit one of the new post office boxes here."

Renata held up the key. "Perhaps you can show me these boxes and see if this key fits."

"Of course. Follow me."

She turned back to the clerk. "Grazie." He nodded and waved his hand at the door, indicating she should follow the bookseller.

They walked together from the post office to the door of the bookshop. The shop front looked like a postcard with snowy triangles on each windowpane. He held the door open for Renata. She shook the snow from her boots onto the coir mat and entered the store.

The inside was aglow with paraffin lamps, cedar boughs lining bookshelves, and red-orange embers peeking through the stove grate in one corner. The quaint decor put her at ease, and she wondered why she had never seen this shop. It was a very English-looking store, sure to fit into a Dickens novel.

"Let me put my coat away. I will be right back." The bookseller removed his coat, scarf, and gloves, and then, as he put a key into the cash register, her curiosity got the better of her.

"Tell me, Signor Salucci, how did you get your unusual name?"

"My name is Anselmo, a name that traveled here in the late eleventh century through Canterbury. You see, Saint Anselm was born in northern Italy and eventually became the Archbishop of Canterbury. I was named after the cleric."

"I meant Salucci, your surname."

"Ah, yes. My twin brother Osberto and I were abandoned by our mother in a foundling wheel just when the local bishop happened to be visiting Padua. He insisted on adopting us as his own and named us after the then-current Archbishops of York and Canterbury, respectively, both of whom he had befriended when he was in England. However, he gave us different surnames based on our personalities."

Renata shook her head and marveled at the story. "Well, now."

Signor Salucci laughed. "But you did not come to hear my story." He walked out from behind the register. "Let me show you the post boxes." She followed him to the back of the store, and as she did, she noticed a READ ME sign next to a book entitled *La Donna Delinquente* by Cesare Lombroso. She already had his *Criminal Man* book, and this one about female criminals would make a perfect companion, so she plucked it off the shelf.

"Here we are." His hand swept over the wall of boxes. "I shall leave you to it."

"Thank you, Signor." She handed him a one lira coin and the book. "And in the meantime, please be so kind as to wrap this up. You can address the invoice to me, care of Ca' Pelicani."

"Certo." Signor Salucci took the money and the book. He left so discreetly that she did not hear his footsteps fade away.

Renata eyed the wall. There were six rows of eight boxes per row, each box with a lock. She found the fourth row, then the fourth box from the left, number *98*, and a box next to it with no number, which she assumed was *99*. She withdrew the key and inserted it in the lock. It turned with some friction and then opened. Her heart gave a little jolt.

Renata pulled open the postbox door and peered inside. A velveteen box lay in the middle of the postbox in the dark, taunting her. When the doorbell jingled, Renata watched a stooped woman with an enormous hat stand in the doorway, slow to close the door.

Renata turned back to the task before her. Her shaking hand reached for the emerald box. For a split second, she debated opening it in the privacy of her room at the castello, but the thought dissipated as soon as it appeared. Afraid of dropping the box, she held it in both hands and lifted the clasp with her thumb.

Expecting jewelry, she was surprised to find a minuscule, folded note inside. Merda! She plopped the box back inside the post box to unfold the note with ten impatient fingers instead of five. At last, the message revealed itself.

This is your final warning.

Show yourself, and you will be spared.

Stay hidden, and your betrothed

pays the price for your deceit.

Renata's hand flew to her mouth to prevent her gasp from escaping. It was the same handwriting as Po's, but clearly, this note was addressed *to him* rather than written *by him.*

Were all the other notes from this messenger, too, instead of Po? And if Po had not been writing the notes all this time, who had?

Chapter 21

As soon as she alighted from the carriage with her book tucked under her arm, Renata excused herself. She made a hasty retreat into the castello, claiming she had to speak to the florist and check the flower arrangements in the ballroom. Mama and Natalia stood next to the carriage, chattering about Renata's erratic behavior, but she ignored them.

A maid called after her. "Signor Fumagalli wishes to see you in the ballroom, signorina."

Renata ignored her, too, and ran into the first open room she could find on the ground floor. It was the antechamber to the ballroom, and she leaned against the closed doors to catch her breath. A few minutes later, she walked to the other side to open the doors to the ballroom. Though the scaffold was still there, it was bare of any workers. The chemical scent of the paint and turpentine lingered in the air, but the gorgeous floral arrangements drowned out most of it.

She paced the length of the room away several times, thinking through everything that had happened. She could not make sense of all the accidents and incidents, the missing people, and the odd messages she had received. Now, a new message had come with a warning. Where was Po, and what was he up to? This message was almost as indecipherable as his last one.

"I had better not get any more notes," she said, shaking her fist at the ceiling.

As Renata was about to search for Natalia, two doors opened. She turned to the west entrance as Brizio entered.

"A scusi, signorina," said Brizio, backing out of the room. "I did not realize you had a guest."

"No, please come in." Renata walked to him.

He looked over her shoulder. "What about—"

"Do not mind me, Brizio. I am just talking to myself. Did you need something?"

"I came to get my apron. I left it here somewhere." He turned to the scaffold and craned his neck, looking for the apron.

"There it is." She pointed to the second story of the scaffold. Next to his apron was a folded piece of paper with her name on it. Renata grumbled as they reached across two planks to retrieve the apron and note. Brizio stabbed the note with a bloody knife, and immediately, she jumped out of the way just as the timber scaffold collapsed onto him.

Renata tucked the note into her bosom and screamed for help. "Aiuto! Aiuto!" Only then did she look around and watch in horror as a leg disappeared on the other side of the door to the east entrance.

Renata stood still for one second before she took off running. She flew through the open ballroom door. Skidding to a halt on the other side, she came within an inch of Po's face.

"What are you doing here?" Her voice rose an octave. "Did you see what happened to Brizio?"

"No," he said, holding Renata at arm's length before pulling her to him in a tight embrace. "Shhh." He buried his face in her neck, repeating *mi amore* until she pulled back.

"Where have you been?" She patted his chest and shoulders all over to confirm. "I have been so worried." She squeezed his hands. "I miss you."

"I cannot stay long. Too risky." He kissed her.

"Wait, what risk?" She gulped. "Vito?"

"Yes. I apologize that I had to be vague in my note," he said as he looked over his shoulder. "I am still trying to find who pushed Vito, but I wanted to let you know we were all right."

She searched his face. "Do you know how the accident happened?"

"He was pushed, and when he landed, Rodrigo helped him at first. Then Vito disappeared, and Rodrigo sent word to me in Orrico that

Vito had escaped. I returned by a different route to avoid running into my brothers. I am still trying to find out who did the deed without involving the police my uncle has brought in. I put Vito and Mariana someplace safe, and I am watching over them in case another murder attempt is afoot."

"What? How?" She waved her hands in the air. "Where are they? Oh my god, never mind all that. Come with me." She walked toward the ballroom. "We must help Brizio."

They heard running footsteps and raised voices.

"Oh good, help has arrived." Renata ran to another set of doors across the hallway and opened them for the arriving footmen.

"Where's the commotion?" said one footman. "We heard a loud crash," said another.

"In here," gestured Renata. "Hurry. A man is trapped under the fallen scaffold."

She followed them into the ballroom, but not before noting the empty hallway that moments ago had held a cowardly man. Fighting back tears, Renata turned to a footman.

"Go find Ispettore Grasso and bring him here."

She returned to the footmen who had started removing the beams and boards. Brizio's face was covered in dust, dirt, and blood. He was not moving. She remembered that Dr. Watson in the Sherlock stories often checked a person's pulse to determine if they were alive, and she did the same. She detected no pulse and gently put his hand over his heart. The bloody knife was next to him, but she did not see any blood on his hands.

"Please, Signorina Bombonatti," said a footman, pulling her arm, "step back and let us do our work. We do not want to see you injured."

She did as she was told. She plopped in an old chair near the window, waiting for the inspector. Scratching her head, she felt something scrape her chest and remembered the note. She pulled it out. Her name was on the outside of the paper, and a bloody thumbprint was on the inside, obscuring whatever short word or phrase had been written there. Otherwise, it was blank. Sweat trickled down her temples. Who was threatening her? And what did they want?

Just then, Ispettore Grasso burst into the room behind the footman she had sent to find him.

"Signorina! Are you all right?" He immediately came to her side.

"I, uh ..." She was stumped for words. He looked so gallant and romantic in his uniform, kneeling in front of her worriedly.

"Here, let me help you." He pulled out a handkerchief and tenderly touched her temples, wiping away the sweat.

She let him do it. When she saw a footman staring at them, she realized what it must look like to him and the others who were busy pulling a dead man out from a scrap heap. "Grazie, Ispettore," she said, taking the handkerchief from him, "but you have more important things to do than tend to me."

"I will come back to you. First, I must see to—" He pointed at the men around the debris.

Renata wiped the back of her neck. "Brizio is already dead. I checked." She stood and handed the inspector his handkerchief. "I will be in my room."

Climbing the stairs, she stopped when she heard voices on the landing above.

"You promised to help me convince Signor Marzano, and now you tell me you are going away. After all I did for—did *with*—you."

"Shhh. Do you want the entire castello to hear that you slept with me, woman?"

"But if you leave, I must fend for myself."

The next part of the conversation was garbled, and then Renata heard a man's boots clopping on the floor toward the stairs. She flew down the steps to hide behind the cabinet in the entrance hall while he rushed past her. She could not see who it was without revealing herself, nor could she place the voice.

Aargh. My suspect list is growing, not shrinking.

Chapter 22

A knock at the door awoke Renata from her slumber. She sat up. "Come in."

Natalia entered. "Are you done with your siesta? I came by earlier, but you were in a deep sleep."

Renata nodded, rubbed her eyes, and swung her legs over the bed. "How long have I been sleeping? What time is it?"

"Two hours, at least. You missed lunch, so now you will have to wait until dinner, but I managed to get you a bit of Cook's famous filone. I could not manage any cheese or fruit. Let me pour you some water, or do you want me to ring for coffee?"

"This will do. Grazie." Renata took the proffered bread and ate it with gusto.

Natalia came and sat next to Renata on the bed. "Why did you run off after we arrived back from Arquà?"

Renata finished chewing. "I had to think. Alone."

"And did you resolve anything?" Natalia played with the smoky quartz pendant dangling from her neck.

"No, and I am worse off than I started. Brizio is dead. The scaffolding fell on him. I think it was an accident. There was too much blood from a bulging gash on his head." Renata hung her head and cried. When she was done, Natalia stopped stroking Renata's arm and hugged her.

She would wait to tell Natalia about meeting Po and what she had learned about Vito and Mariana.

"I do not know what to say. A dead man under your roof with a wedding underway and Christmas around the corner. This is sad. And vexing."

"Yes." Renata agreed and then gathered the front of her dress to shake the breadcrumbs out of the window. She was about to stand when Natalia gasped and grabbed Renata's wrist. "Wait."

Renata looked down at her reddening wrist and then up at her friend. "What?"

"I think someone tampered with the scaffolding so that when you reached for the note, the falling wood slats and timber beams would maim, or worse, kill you."

Renata frowned, twisted her wrist away from Natalia's grasp, and stood. "No one knew I was supposed to be in the ballroom then. You cannot be serious ... oh, wait. A maid said Fumo was looking for me. And when I ran to get help after Brizio was trapped, I saw a leg disappearing out of the room. Whose it was, I cannot say. What I can say, and hopefully prove, is that to whomever that leg belonged, I will bet fifty lire the person had something to do with Brizio's death."

"From now on," Natalia stood toe to toe with Renata, "I am not letting you out of my sight. You must get married, not snuffed out!"

"But—"

"But nothing." She turned Renata in the direction of the window. "Look, Christmas is upon us! We know Vito and Mariana are safe. Let the inspector figure out who was responsible for Brizio's death."

"But I can help, and—"

"Enough, Renata. Now, shake out that skirt and pull on some thick wool socks. I am taking you skating. More of your guests have arrived and are all down at the pond. Oh, there's a little drummer boy and a girl flautist. They were my surprise, the one I mentioned when we went to Arquà."

"Oh?"

"I learned that they are a brother and sister team from Assisi and are quite talented. Their parents formed a group to carry on the tradition started by St. Francis of singing canticles. They go from village to village. This is their first visit to our area. They have already been to Sica and wanted to come here, too. You will like them. Besides, you need some divertimento. That is what one does at Christmas! You have not been enjoying the season as you should be, and I aim to do something about that today, at least."

"No, no, no, Natalia." Renata walked to the window and shook out the breadcrumbs from her skirt. She spotted a dozen or so of her and Placido's friends skating on the persimmon and pomegranate tree-rimmed pond below. She did not see the drummer but could hear his faint beat. She backed away from the window before anyone saw her and went to sit at her dressing table. "Thank you for the surprise, but there's a criminal on the loose. I am not going outside."

Natalia's shoulders slumped. "I may have been too dramatic about the scaffold, but at least come listen to the songs."

Renata paced, not answering.

"I suppose it could have been an accident. I should not have jumped to conclusions."

Renata bit her lip, remembering the bloodied note that was left for her. "And what if it was not?"

"There are plenty of people outside who are all our friends." Natalia sat at her dressing table and swept her hand in the direction of the window. "You will be safe, I promise. Besides, I will be with you and we can ask one of the footmen to accompany us for security's sake."

Renata clenched and unclenched her fingers. Natalia approached the dressing table and took hold of Renata's hands.

"There are still a few hours left of daylight." Natalia swung her and Renata's arms back and forth until Renata's face burst into a huge grin. "You are a bride who should be having fun, not cooped up here and bogged down in doom."

"You are impossible."

In a sing-song voice, Natalia said, "Come now, we will not sit in your rooms and be glum. Let us glide around the ice until we fall on our bums."

"Fine, but first, I must speak to the inspector. I will meet you in the foyer in twenty minutes."

&

Renata flattened herself against a wall. Two male servants walked past her in the connecting hallway across from the library. She hung back until they were around the next corner because she did not want anyone to see her enter the library. Witnessing Brizio's death and running into Po had sent her mind into a tailspin. She had to admit that the case was becoming more deadly by the hour. As much as she wanted to solve this case independently, she had an idea that might bring some answers, but she needed the inspector's help.

The coast clear, she dashed across the hallway and knocked on the library door.

"Vieni," replied its occupant.

She loved the expanse of the room, in width, length, and height— the latter giving the books room to breathe and readers space to think.

And thinking was precisely what the policeman looked like he was doing sitting at the desk. He had steepled his fingers and rested them on his stomach. His lips were pursed, and his eyes stared at the frescoed ceiling. He lowered his head as she approached.

"What can I do for you, Signorina Bombonatti?"

Renata handed the inspector the bloody note.

His eyes widened as he scanned the paper, his earlier detached demeanor now gone. "Where did you find this?"

She crossed her hands in front of her. "On the scaffold before it fell."

"Why did you not mention it before in the ballroom?"

She shrugged. "I forgot."

His pinched face did him no favors. His cheeks turned tomato red, and he bellowed, "Forgot? I am in the midst of a murder investigation, and you do not think this kind of evidence is important?"

She took a deep breath, counted to five, and then spat, "I was a witness to a near-death accident, albeit from afar, and one death up close. Am I not entitled to such symptoms as forgetfulness? Or do you expect me to conduct myself with fortitude even when enduring successive trauma?"

The policeman set down the paper and leaned against the desk, his fingers entwined and resting on the non-bloody portion of the note. "Signorina Bombonatti, you are a lady with sensibilities, I see that."

"Grazie," she said, wondering where he was leading the conversation.

"However," he continued, "you are also a woman possessed of astute observation. You would not have failed to bring this to me under normal circumstances, so I can only surmise that an aberration has occurred, and thus, I shall not hold you in contempt of obstructing justice."

Renata gave the man her thinnest, tightest smile. "We can go back and forth on withholding evidence, or you can hear me out about an idea I have regarding identifying that thumbprint."

He lifted his chin and nodded. "I want additional clarification on the matter."

She squared her shoulders, leaned on the desk's other side, and looked down at the man. "Ink the thumbprints of each of your suspects, and I guarantee we shall find the killer."

Ispettore Grasso raised an eyebrow. "You have studied Galton's classification system?"

"Somewhat. I have asked Mr. Salucci to order me a copy of Galton's fingerprints book. According to Galton's calculations, the odds of two individual fingerprints being the same are 1 in 64 billion." She turned the paper around on the desk so the bloody thumbprint faced her. "I suspect we will have no trouble confirming our suspicions."

"And if we fail?"

She shook her head. "I smell your doubt, Giorgio, I mean, ispettore, but I give it no credence."

He inched further across the desk and repeated his question, louder this time. "And if we fail, Renata, uh, Signorina Bombonatti?"

She had never sparred in a conversation with a man or anyone. Her blood coursed from her heart to her head as if it were a thoroughbred on a racetrack. She gripped the edge of the desk for fear that her lightheadedness might cause her to faint.

And he had said *we* twice as if she were his partner on the case. After reading The Strand in her mother's parlor, was it only days ago that she had imagined taking on a case? It was happening, and she wanted to play her part well without interference from her thumping heart.

She forced herself to slow her breathing, then said, "Ink the staff members first. Bring the note and the killer to the drawing room after dinner if you find a match to the print. Your revelation of the killer will bring much-needed relief to our guests. If none of the staff matches this print, you can infringe on Zio Alonzo's kindness and insist you be allowed to ink all of the guests who arrived two days ago."

Taking back the note, his eyes implored her. "Will you help me?" Renata and Giorgio locked eyes. *Too close too close too close.* The words reverberated in her mind, and she stepped back from the desk.

"I-I-I cannot, Giorgio ... uh, Ispettore Grasso." He dropped his gaze, but she continued. "I am to be married soon. My parents would be mortified if I intruded upon the wedding guests in such a fashion."

As much as I would like to do otherwise, she kept silent about that truth.

ꙮ

After dinner, the men left for the smoking lounge while Renata led the female guests into the ladies' parlor.

"This is lovely," said Mama, entering the well-lit room with floor-to-ceiling windows. All the other ladies agreed and twittered about the furnishings while Renata watched the scene unfold.

Candelabra-style wall sconces warmed the bisque walls of the largest sitting room Renata had ever seen, much less be the hostess of. Plush settees and armchairs ringed the room while a massive chandelier illuminated three card tables underneath. A portrait of a beautiful lady hung above the mantle. To its right, a polished walnut pianoforte Renata recognized as only the second Cristofori instrument she had ever seen outside of the University of Padua's concert hall.

She took a glass of amaro from Martell's serving tray and strolled to the painting to read the inscription:

Signora Paloma Pelicani, Contessa di Sica 1880

Your laughing smile draws me in, Paloma. I am envious of your cheerful disposition. I want to know why you are so happy. Or are you sporting a façade? I may never know.

Each guest had an amaro in hand and was sipping it after toasting Renata's future when Martell responded to a knock at the door.

"Now, who is that to interrupt us?" said Mama as she and Renata turned to the door.

Ispettore Grasso stood in the doorway and beckoned her to him.

"Where are you going?" Mama looked Renata up and down as she stood and smoothed her dress.

"I shall not be long." Renata walked toward Martell and drained her digestivo when she reached him. "Thank you, Martell." She handed him her empty glass and took another, stepped into the hallway to meet the inspector, and closed the door behind her.

"Thank you for meeting me, signorina. I apologize for disturbing your digestivo time."

She waved away his apology and handed him the amaro. "I thought you might appreciate some liqueur yourself."

"Grazie." He accepted the drink and took a long swig.

"So, were you able to match a thumbprint, ispettore?"

"No. The staff prints did not match. So, I shall send word to Signor Pelicani that I must meet with all the guests in the morning."

"Darn." Renata paced. "Not all, surely. Only the ones that were here when the incident occurred."

He removed his cap and patted down his hair. "Not necessarily. How do we know they did not have a hand in it before they arrived?"

She stopped pacing and whirled to face him. "Preposterous! Surely, these upper-class guests are above reproach. But that's—"

"That's how," he placed his hat back on his head and adjusted it, "an investigation is done. Even our nearest and dearest. No stone unturned in my business."

∛

Renata handed her evening gown to Eletta, who hung it in the wardrobe. She stepped out from behind the Oriental screen. "It has been a long day, and dinner tried my nerves. Good night, Eletta."

"Good night, signorina. I shall take this to the laundry and soak it overnight."

Eletta picked up Renata's dirt-streaked day dress, draped it across her arm, and left her mistress's room.

Renata opened the jar of face cream her mother ordered from the ancient pharmacy in Florence and faced the mirror. The skating had been good for mind and appetite, but her hair, eyes, and shoulders drooped from exhaustion. And hurt. How could Po be so insensitive? He had just left a broken man to die. For real, this time.

This behavior was not typical of the man she thought she was marrying—the man who had bombarded her with love tokens at the

Castle of Love, the man she had prayed for his safe return when he was in Africa, the man she had waited five years to marry. It was so unlike him to speak to her so harshly. It was a side she had never seen.

She finished her toilette and then stood, pacing the room. Good and bad thoughts flit through her head like a jaguar on a hunt. Could Natalia be right? Had she nearly escaped death? She shuddered.

Renata remembered the note from the ballroom and went to the bureau to retrieve it, along with the rest of the notes she had buried under her corsets and in the flap of her casebook. She laid the notes on her dressing table and carefully reread each one.

She needed to find out which were real and which were false. Her heart skipped a beat when rereading the postbox one with its threat scrawled across the paper in thick black ink. After staring at the other notes, she scooped them up and threw them into the fire.

Misdirection had caused mayhem. Falsehoods had provoked failure. She was done with this guessing game. These clues had led her on a wild goose chase, and none had proved their worth. The face of the inspector flashed in her mind's eye.

Noooo. I should have kept the notes for him. She stared at the fire. Within seconds, the flames had consumed the notes. It was too late. She gripped the edge of the table. His face popped out of her inner vision and into the middle of the roaring fire.

"Oh, what have I done, my lov—"

My what? She slumped to the floor. For a brief moment, guilt ripped through her shoulders and neck, causing them to spasm. She rubbed them until the tension subsided. She boxed her ears, trying to get the word *love* and the inspector out of her head. She pounded the floor in front of her.

Stop it, stop it, stop it. Have I no restraint? Must I fall in love moments after meeting a man? What is wrong with me?

Several minutes passed before she pulled herself together and stood, her arms crossed over her chest.

From now on, she would leave forbidden passion behind and follow facts. One fact that was indisputable was a man died today. Was she partly to blame? Had she and Brizio reached for their objects and put too much pressure on the scaffolding? What a ridiculous notion. The scaffolding was set up to hold two or three men at a time.

Another indisputable fact: a man who was supposed to be dead was not. So much for facts ruling the day.

Chapter 23

Eletta fastened the last button on Renata's right cuff and stepped back. "Blue suits you, signorina."

Renata turned away, not wishing to examine herself in the full-length mirror. This was her going-away outfit when she set out on her honeymoon, catching the ferry from Rome to Sicily. Instead, she was wearing it for a funeral her mother did not want her to attend because it was two days before she was supposed to be wed—if a wedding was even going to happen.

Her groom was on the run, his resurrected best man and his wife were missing, and there was a killer on the loose. Her winter wedding at a castello teeming with holiday decor turned out to be less of a dream and more of a nightmare. And as for Christmas ...

She dug into the pocket of her travel bag and pulled out a box. It was her Christmas present for Placido. Renata had gotten him a painting as a wedding gift but wondered if it was enough, so she splurged on some gold cufflinks as well.

She ran her finger over the engraving on the cufflinks: *mio cuore e mia anima.* But, turning them over and over in her palm, thinking about everything that happened, she was unsure if Placido was her heart and soul. If Natalia had questioned whether the scaffolding was meant to kill Renata, why had Po not done so as well?

"Signorina?"

Eletta interrupted Renata's brooding, stuffed the cufflinks in their box, and closed the travel bag. "Yes, thank you." She tucked a new black-edged handkerchief inside her cuff and put on the jet-black earrings she wore to every funeral. She adjusted a black bonnet she had found in Contessa Paloma's closet and said, "I should go down before Mama sends an altar boy to fetch me."

&

Renata entered the incense-filled chapel and sat next to Mama and Papà in the pew. Papà nodded and wished her a good morning. Mama leaned across Papà, and her harsh whisper was loud enough that people two rows ahead of them turned around.

"How rude, Renata, sneaking in here so late. The priest was just about to start. Will you ever be on time? Will you be late for your wedding, too? And where on God's green earth is your groom? Missing Brizio's funeral, for goodness' sake. Tsk-tsk."

Papà, an old hat at observing Mama's temper, picked up the hymnal and ignored the drama.

Renata wanted to do the same. However, she knew failing to respond to Mama's outrage would only escalate the situation. She wanted to share with Mama that her sleep was filled with nightmares after witnessing the crushing death of Brizio, not to mention the run-in with Po and the postbox note threatening to kill her if she kept up her sleuthing. Mama would be horrified and insist on a full explanation immediately. Something Renata was not prepared to give. Instead, she provided a platitude, knowing her mother could not be appeased for long.

"I am so sorry, Mama. You are right, and it will not happen again."

"Pfft," came the reply, and Mama leaned back. The woman refrained from anything further because the choir had begun to sing. "Kyrie eleison."

&

The funeral mass ended, and the parishioners sobbed while singing "The Lord Is My Shepherd" to accompany the men carrying the caskets out of the chapel. She looked around to see if Po had made it to the funeral, but there was no sign of him.

Mama had insisted the bridal party should not attend the burial at the grave site, but Renata was keen on observing who all were present at the chapel before they departed. Though there was no Po, Fumo and Dario stood up as pallbearers alongside some of the castello's footmen and Brizio's brother Rodrigo. While Renata had committed to sticking to the facts of the case—Sherlock would be so proud—she was curious to see people's faces. What expressions besides grief were written on them? In Fumo's case, his face was devoid of expression, his eyes dull.

Renata shifted her attention and caught Inspector Grasso glancing her way. Perhaps he, too, was keen to observe reactions. Or obvious masks. He had had more years than her to hone that skill. Renata made a mental note to ask him for tips to help sharpen her budding powers of observation.

She was surprised to see Eletta sitting in the pew behind the inspector. Renata was curious to know if her mind was playing tricks on her. She could have sworn a sly smile crossed her maid's face as Brizio's casket passed. Renata knew Eletta had an old score to settle with Vito's family, but she had nothing to do with Brizio's death.

Following the congregation outside, Renata shielded her eyes from the sun. It was much more blinding because of the reflection of the blanket of snow facing them after the dim interior of the greystone chapel. She felt a hand on her elbow and turned to face Fumo.

"Where are Placido and Vito?"

She did not like that he hissed at her, though it was a fair enough question. However, Renata knew those five words had meaning beyond what was being asked. At least she could answer it truthfully.

"I do not know." Unable to help herself, she gulped. An involuntary reaction to a feeling that came over her when Fumo's eyes narrowed into ominous black slits and pierced her with their fury. He looked around at the glum crowd, then took a step closer, lowering his voice.

"How is that possible? You are to wed my best friend tomorrow, and he is still missing. So are his brothers, who were sent to fetch him. And a manservant, and lest we forget, the best man, who fell from a tower. Very strange."

"I agree." Her response was sincere, and she hoped her face reflected it.

"So you honestly do not know Po's or Vito's manservant's whereabouts, do you?" His voice had softened, and she realized he was genuinely concerned.

She shook her head and motioned for him to follow her and move out of the way of the mourners.

He stared at her and then at the wintry scene around him as they walked. "I have looked in every possible corner of this estate. I thoroughly searched the wings, including the obscure ones, but neither Dario nor I had any luck. I remembered all the hiding places of our youth, and there was no evidence of him, Vito, or Mariana. This is so frustrating. Dario and I miss our friends." Fumo choked on the words.

She watched as his emotions registered on his face and nodded. They seemed real enough. Maybe he did not know where Vito was. Rodrigo had managed to hide Vito after his fall before anyone from the tower reached him. Po knew Vito was in good hands with Rodrigo, but he had left Fumo and Dario in the dark about the accident's aftermath. How curious. She thought they all trusted one another.

Why is the truth so elusive and secrets so abundant in this castello?

The sniffling behind her had lessened as everyone going to the burial site had already situated themselves in carriages or on the large donkey carts that Zio Alonzo had provided for the staff. All the others were walking under the portico from the chapel back to the castello to escape the bitter cold.

"We are going back with Alonzo." Mama and Papà indicated she should follow them back, and she acknowledged their request, though not before asking Fumo to escort her back. He offered his arm, but she turned him down, pointing to her heavy skirts, which she needed both hands to lift so the hem would not be dragged along a dirty, wet walkway.

"Tell me what happened when you all realized Vito had," she paused, searching for the right word, "um, fallen."

He winced hearing the word, then forged ahead. "Our world stopped, ever so briefly, until the wailing wind demanded we move. It carried us urgently down and down the steps of the tower. When we reached the tower door, we flung it open. That's when our breaths and cries and moans found us again. We skirted the battlements, our feet flying until we reached the laurel tree where we had seen him land."

"And ... was he already ... broken?" She bit her lip, her lies not sitting well on her tongue.

"He had to be, but no one is talking. From above, we all saw him on the ground, motionless. He did not fly away with all those broken bones."

"Why did none of you speak up when I started asking questions?"

"We—that is, Dario—took the accident to Zio Alonzo. The conte did not want anyone to know, including you. So many people were coming from all over for this grand wedding of the decade. Plus, it is Christmas. He did not want to upset you or your guests. You were already upset that Po was away."

"Hmm ..." The questions were coming at her faster than she could form them. Zio Alonzo did not mention that the groomsmen brought him the news. Rather it was Rodrigo. Was someone lying?

Fumo held the castello door open for her, and she walked through. "And the inspector? What did you tell him?"

"We were all paralyzed from the shock, but Dario wasted no time racing down to where Vito had landed. Brizio and others were on the scene moments after our arrival, and Rodrigo showed up a bit later, but they all said they did not see Vito and that Po had taken off running. I brought up the rear, but it was immediately evident that there was no—"

Renata mouthed her *body,* and Fumo nodded. They stopped walking and talking after approaching the back archway leading into the foyer. Servants rushed up and down stairs, helping more guests as they arrived. Renata tucked herself behind a pillar. She was in no mood for a conversation about her wedding, dress, honeymoon, Po's whereabouts, and the myriad other details she knew the new guests would thrust on her. Thank goodness none of them knew about Vito.

Eager to keep Fumo talking, she whispered, "Where do you think Vito went? Back home to Vicenza?"

Fumo threw his arms in the air. "This is what I have been trying to tell you. We do not know. We have been looking for him and his very pregnant wife for days. Perhaps they went to a midwife. Or a tenant farmer. Or to Sica or Arquà. We do not know. And we kept it all from you so you did not worry."

She put her hand on his forearm. "But I was worried all the same."

Fumo shrugged his shoulders.

Renata scratched her head. "Tell me again. How many men were there on the roof? I forgot. And about what time did Vito fall?"

His lip twitched in a repressed snarl. "What is this, an inquisition? Did Inspector Grasso put you up to this? I told him everything I just told you."

"I am just trying to—"

He cut her off and roared. "To what? Accuse me of foul play? He is my friend, Renata!"

She jumped. The unexpected force of his utterance threw her off balance, and he caught her around the waist. His grip tightened when he said, "It was an accident. No one is to blame, and now we must live with ... what happened. He's badly broken and hurting ... somewhere, and he has not let any of us know where he is or how we can help."

"You are hurting me." Fumo let go, and she rubbed the spot at her waist where his rough hands had indeed left a purple imprint.

He stiffened, then bowed. "I apologize," he said and strode away from her as fast as his long legs could carry him.

She stared after Fumo until Dario was at her side. "Did you hear all that?"

"Most of it."

She stepped in front of Dario and faced him. "Was it the truth?"

He gave her a slow nod and left, but not before she saw the haze over his eyes. This was one of the many signs her Nonna Bombonatti had taught her. Her grandmother had said haze is what happens to the eyes when someone is holding something back.

Chapter 24

Renata's head was buzzing. She knew she had to go somewhere to think, and remembering Zio's vast collection of books, she headed for the solitude of the library. When she opened the double doors of the hallowed space and spotted Inspector Grasso, her head pulsed with a growing ache. The silence was sure to elude her here, too.

"Ah, Signorina Bombonatti. I was hoping to speak to you today. Vieni, vieni."

He waved her over to the overstuffed armchair opposite him near the fire. She obliged, and while closing the doors behind her, she scanned her mind for questions. What could she ask that might be relevant to the investigation? She would not bring up what had happened between them on the tower. No, that incident was never to be mentioned. She could bring up what Po had told her. Instead, she nodded in the policeman's direction and slowly approached him.

"Ispettore Grasso." She removed her muffler, gloves, and short cape. After shaking the bit of snow that had settled on her cape, she placed it on the chair's right arm. Finally, she sat in the red damask chair, straightening the folds of her dress splayed on either side of her. "Any leads?"

He slammed shut his gray field notebook and peered over his spectacles. "You are not as subtle as many of your kind, are you?"

"My kind is human, no different than yours. Are you insinuating that women cannot get to the point as quickly as men?" The man infuriated her, yet she was angry with herself for being mildly aroused at how his eyes raked over her. "You certainly were not subtle when slamming that book."

He did not proffer a rebuttal. Instead, he said, "This is an active case. I cannot comment on the details or suspects or—"

"You have nothing then." She did her best not to smirk. She suspected he was upset that she had not immediately fawned all over him, either at the tower or in the library. Clearly, his powers of deduction did not extend to mating cues, and she blushed at the thought.

The inspector straightened his back and leaned forward. "Look here, signorina. I do not take kindly to—"

She changed tacks, remembering Officer Damiani's warning. "I am curious ... how much do you rely on what you feel instinctually?"

He raised his chin an inch, then removed his spectacles. "I trained to shoot at the academy in Rome, got put through my alpine training paces in Val Gardena, and earned my inspector stripe at the investigator specialist institute in Velletri. All that training helps, but my gut rarely steers me wrong. I have learned to trust it first. It bypasses the filters of the mental mind and emotional heart."

Renata's chest swelled. The policeman and she were simpatico. They could understand one another because they approached cases the same way. She told herself to stick to talking about the facts of the case, but the next question that came out of her was the exact opposite.

"Is that what drew you to the profession?" She choked on the words, her nerves getting the best of her when she realized their similarities made him more attractive than she had given him credit for. What was she doing? Sherlock would be most unhappy with her if he happened upon them, not to mention Po.

"There are two reasons why a man becomes a policeman," he explained. "In the main, what drives some is rivalsa. Over seventy percent of the force is from the south, and they cite revenge as payback. When you grow up in that mob-run, poverty-stricken environment, you must choose sides. For those officers, becoming a policeman is like making a statement to say, 'I choose legality.' They are tired of the gangsters."

She rolled her lips inward and back out again. "Yet your accent is from the north, so what is your justification?" Again, she wanted to slap herself on the head for going down what felt like a dangerous path.

"I fell in love with Auguste Dupin, the fictive creation of that American, Edgar Allen Poe. This was the world's first detective. Do you know this character? Have you read about him?"

"Yes, and yes."

"Well, well," he said, twirling his moustache. Renata knew he was surprised by her answers, and she forced herself not to blush.

He continued. "You see, he wrote the stories in the 1840s, and when my grandfather passed down these stories to me, I taught myself English so I could read them without help. The amateur detective's imagination was so great that he put himself in the criminal's mind. And as soon as I read all three of Dupin's investigations, I knew I wanted to be Italy's version of him." He chuckled. "The fantasy of a young, impressionable son of a pharmacist, but those stories had power over me."

She stroked the fur collar of her cape. "I suppose it was a calling then."

He tapped his notebook with his index finger. "So to speak, yes."

"I understand." They were quiet a moment before she spoke again. "It was Sherlock for me. I was in awe from the second he appeared on the page. '*Mr. Sherlock Holmes, who was usually very late in the mornings, save upon those not infrequent occasions when he was up all night, was seated at the breakfast table.*'"

He whipped open his notebook. "Which book?" He licked his pencil, ready to jot down the answer.

"His third, *The Hound of the Baskervilles*, and that was the first line. My mother—who regularly admonishes me for my dereliction of duty when it comes to time—does not look with favor on my imitation of Sherlock's habits. Far from ladylike, she often says." She held back a laugh but cracked a smile.

"'*As the strong man exults in his physical ability, delighting in such exercises as call his muscles into action, so glories the analyst in that moral activity which disentangles.*'" Grinning shyly, he continued, "From the first paragraph of Poe's *The Murders in the Rue Morgue.*'"

Nodding, she said, "Genius."

"Indeed." Clapping his hands and jumping out of his chair, he leaned against a corner of the fireplace and rubbed his chin. "Well, we have butted heads, discussed the motivations of an officer of the law, and compared notes on our favorite fictional detectives. Care to give me your take on the whereabouts of your fiancé's best man and the death of Brizio, the construction foreman?"

She arched a brow. "Who is being blunt now?"

They both roared with laughter.

Mrs. Trevisan threw open the library doors and entered. "Please be mindful. We are a house in mourning." She stood in the doorway with her hands on her hips, eyeing the occupants.

Renata squirmed in her chair. "You are right, Mrs. Trevisan."

The housekeeper squeaked out something unintelligible. She adjusted a few items on her chatelaine that had tangled themselves during her abrupt entrance, nodded, and then turned to leave.

"Mrs. Trevisan, before you go…" The inspector pointed his notebook at her, and she paused. "Could you tell me if …" he consulted his notes, "Ursino Fumagalli visited you just before lunch yesterday? He claims he did. Can you confirm his arrival in your office? Off the kitchen, I believe it is?"

Renata did her best to keep her surprise at the unanticipated question off her face. "Yes."

Renata saw the inspector's eyes bulge. "And?"

The housekeeper crossed her arms at her waist. "You asked for a confirmation, not a novella."

Attempting to cover her laugh, Renata twisted her head and coughed into her hand. "Mi scusi."

"Very well. You may go." He scribbled something in his notebook, then waved a hand at the doors, dismissing the housekeeper.

With an exaggerated "Signor, Signorina," aimed at both of them, the older woman turned and left.

Renata's heart thumped erratically, and sitting still was impossible. Fumo had told her he had gone to his rooms after Vito's fall but had said nothing about a visit to the housekeeper. Why lie?

Renata turned to the inspector for an answer. "Ispettore, why this question? What did Fumo visiting the kitchens yesterday have anything to do with what happened to Vito?"

"In my bag of tricks, Renata, er, Signorina Bombonatti," he blushed and pulled himself together, "whenever I am a bit stuck, I often pull out a question to which I already have an answer just to see how someone reacts and responds."

She peered over at him, wondering if he had done this to her, and she had been oblivious to it. "Hmm ... and what did you learn?"

"She is telling the truth, and so is Mr. Fumagalli." He flipped to a page of his notebook, and she could see by how his hand moved that he had drawn an X. "Thus, I have just eliminated two suspects."

The rush of that truth made her heart skip a beat before it returned to its usual self. Talking to the policeman like this—one professional to one amateur—brought a feeling that descended on her like the sweetness and thickness of honey. She was not sure what this was or whether she liked it. She knew that she had never felt it before, including with Po. How could a man make her feel like this when she was engaged to marry another?

"Signorina Bombonatti?"

"Sì, scusi," she said, returning to the present with a jolt, her cheeks flushed. "Uh, yes, yes. It is as I thought, too."

She had sensed the same during Fumo's emotionally charged speech. If she had only paid attention to his words and their ferocity, she would not have missed her stomach's signal. The entire incident had affected

Fumo, and as a grieving friend, it was clear he was a jumble of emotions, many of which, as sinister as they had first appeared to her, did not equate to motivation to commit murder.

So where did this revelation leave them?

Chapter 25

Mama handed Renata several notes, all sealed with wax. "These came for you."

She had entered Renata's bedchamber uninvited, breezing right past a dumbstruck Renata, who had just reclined on the chaise lounge to recuperate from the funeral and her flirtatious talk with the inspector. With Mama's arrival, she could expect no rest.

Renata sat up and flipped through the stack—bypassing all those that looked wedding-related—until she got to one that was not. When she opened it and pulled it out, she gazed upon a light blue card in a proper envelope, not just thick paper stock convolutedly folded into an envelope. The card was embossed with what looked like a salt block atop a book, and underneath was one word: *SALUCCI.*

She tore it open, eager to learn why the bookshop owner had contacted her.

Cara Signorina Bombonatti,

It seems you may have opened the wrong box. Please return to my store to claim what is rightfully yours.

Saluti,

Sig. Salucci

If she had received the wrong note, then Placido was not in the danger she thought he was. Nor Vito and Mariana, for that matter. Renata did not know what was waiting for her in the correct postal box, but a calm settled over her. She took that as a sign that whatever was in the box had to be good news. She tucked the note inside her sleeve and almost somersaulted to Mama.

"Mama, I must take the carriage in to—" Renata whirled around the room, picking up gloves, scarf, and hat.

"You will do no such thing, young lady. Tomorrow is Christmas Eve and the day you will wed."

"Yes, I know."

Mama patted the space next to her on the bed. "I want you to tell me what is going on. Since we arrived, I have hardly seen you. You and Natalia have been running around all hours of the day with no fiancé in sight. Where IS he? And what does he have to say about you carrying on like this? It is not befitting a lady of your stature nor the future wife of a conte."

"A contessa? So soon." Renata tried not to panic, knowing her mother could smell it miles away.

"Yes, Alonzo reminded us that you will be la contessa to his nephew Placido, the lady of this castello and his grand estate upon your marriage." The following words tumbled out of her mother so fast that Renata was not sure she had heard them correctly. "That's all fine, of course, though it would be better if you were the contessa now and not a contessina ... well, once Alonzo is gone, you will have the full title."

Renata wanted out of the suddenly stifling room. How odd that Mama wanted Renata to be to the contessa now. If this were any other time, Renata would demand an answer, but she did not want to dally. "I ... uh ..."

"What's the matter with you? We talked about this before. Why have you forgotten already?"

"My memory has just ..." Renata shrugged her shoulders while she racked her brain, trying to find a way out of the room.

"You must be vigilant at all times, my dear." Mama straightened her dress and checked that her hair combs were secure. "You see, in these provincial towns, people remember how you behave long after you have forgotten. And they talk."

"Mama, being a countess will take me years to perfect, and that is all right. I am in no hurry. Let the country folk talk. They know I am young and will need to forgive my early mistakes. By the time I am the contessa ..."

"You do not understand. There are not enough distractions or near enough polite society in the country. Talking about others is their main source of entertainment, and you will be in the center of it long before you ever earn your real title of contessa. Everything you do between now and then will be watched and dissected down to the—"

"Placido never mentioned this to me." A stunned Renata stopped pacing and then lowered herself next to her mother.

"If you had not been running hither and yon yesterday, you would have sat with Papà and me to hear Alonzo tell us of the history of his family and this town, how they got their title, and his plans for the place when he gets too old to be master of it." Renata wanted to wipe her mother's smug expression right off.

Contessa di Sica. Titles had a nice ring but were no match for solving crime. Renata shook her head free of all that.

Time was ticking by, and she was still no closer to helping the inspector find the person or people responsible for two accidents, one leading to death. And while she *had* been busy with her sleuthing, she had not let herself ruminate and seethe about the predicament Po had led her into—both natural and not. Oh, she missed him so. Her heart had not been the same these last few days, and this was not the time for indecision, hurt, and doubts.

"Why were you holed up in the library with Ispettore Grasso for over an hour?"

"What?" Jarred, Renata returned to the present. "I was not there long, Mama."

"Oh yes, you were. Do you dare question Mrs. Trevisan's pocket watch? That woman's timepiece is calibrated by the camerlengo at the Vatican himself, and every year, she attends the Pontiff's Easter Mass. She knows and sees everything in this house. Martell may think he does, but she holds the true power. Remember that."

Renata squeezed her eyes and then opened them again. "The woman could not be so important that the Pope's right-hand man makes himself available to her." Nor could she know everything because she had not witnessed who pushed Vito or who set a trap in the scaffolding.

"The camerlengo is her brother, so he helps her with it because it is important to her work. Now, stop stalling and tell me what you discussed with the policeman. Was it something about Placido or ...?"

Renata heard a tremor in Mama's voice when she said Placido's name. How odd. Renata took a deep breath. Po was her friend, then her confidante, and now her man. Also, her liar. Her body softened and then hardened in the blink of an eye.

"So, was it about Placido? Is there a problem you are not telling your mother about? Out with it!" Like most in Italy, her family could have entire conversations without saying a word because their face, hands, and other body parts did all the talking. At this moment, Mama was like a windmill in a hurricane—arms and words flying everywhere.

How could Po have run away from a crime scene like that? With a man trapped and quickly bleeding to death under heavy scaffolding. Scaffolding had been set up to make decorating the ballroom for their upcoming nuptials easy. Nuptials that might not even happen, though she could not let Mama think that.

"Answer me, child." Mama's arms had stopped flailing, but the hot energy she had created with her arms seconds earlier had transferred to her neck. Red and white blotches spattered across her skin like the onset of leprosy.

"No, no, no, nothing like that, Mama." She looked away from her mother's neck. "The ispettore was regaling me with his time at the police academy."

"Those are *not* stories a lady about to be wed should pay attention to. What violence and nonsense has he been filling your head with? And at Christmastime, too. Ack!" Her mother raised her hand, letting it fall with a thunk on her knee. "These past few days have been pure chaos, and I told Papà I am not having it. I must get this family and household into some semblance of order. I cannot imagine what our guests are thinking."

Renata wanted to shout at the top of her lungs that she did not care what her parent's society guests thought. Damn, bella figura! It was a cursed custom. If she had her way of righting all the wrongs of Italian societal norms, she would kill that one first. But actual murder and attempted murder were not topics to be swept under the rug like dust mites. Guests would sooner or later find out what was happening under this roof.

"Renata. Renata. Are you in there?" Mama had been snapping her fingers in front of Renata's face with no response.

"Yes, I am here." Renata rubbed her knuckles up and down her cheeks to help the blood flow back.

"Stop that. You cannot go out there with streaks on your cheeks. What would peop—"

Here we go again, thought Renata, biting her tongue. Bella figura. What would people think? Sometimes, she wondered if that was all her mother cared about.

Mama growled and continued. "Have you inspected the flowers in the ballroom?"

"Yes, and I am satisfied with all the decorations and my bouquet, so no need for you to—"

"Fine, but you and Placido should know that in your absence, Dario and Fumo have been entertaining your guests in the glaciarium, where they plan to reenact the Battle of the Aegates tonight."

"Yes, Mama. I saw them practicing yesterday when Natalia and I went skating." The more her mother talked, the more Renata's impatience and anxiety grew. She had to get to the bookshop!

"Also, the gardeners and stablehands have been busy melting snow and filling up the inner ring of the glaciarium with water for the big event. A naval battle reenactment in the glaciarium has not been performed here since Alonzo's grandfather brought the famous soprano Giuditta Pasta to perform at his wedding and ran away with her. She was just 17!"

Renata nodded. She knew about the Battle of the Aegates Islands between the fleets of Rome and Carthage over 2000 years ago. It had been fought off the western coast of Sicily, reducing the massive Carthaginian convoy to just a few vessels. It almost felt like Po was reducing her *mass*, her presence, and her *significance* by staging such an event.

Zio Alonzo would not bring an opera singer to our festivities and then fix it, so Po ran away with her instead of marrying me, would he? Could that be part of the family curse, and why "everlasting" did not apply to the weddings and marriages in the Pelicani family?

Irked at the thought, Renata said instead, "The tableau vivant from Shakespeare that Po and his friends are going to perform tomorrow is enough entertainment for one wedding. Must we have a battle, too?"

"Oh, my dear. You are so droll." Mama clapped. "Your wedding is the talk of the entire region. Of course, you must have a grand affair, and everyone must see it. You know how important a union is between two noble families, especially this one." The last phrase was said almost sotto voce. Something itching to be scratched ever since Renata announced her engagement six months ago just got scratched.

Renata turned to her mother. "You want me to tell you what has been going on? You start. You, and less so Papà, have been acting strange for days."

"How dare you speak to me in that accusing tone? Wha-a-at do you mean I have been acting strange?" Mama shifted on the bed. "I have been here the whole time except for a few hours at Eletta's shop. But that was a necessary diversion to obtain—"

"That is not what I mean." Renata put her things down on the bed and paced the room. "Why is this wedding so important, Mama? Is it more for Papà and getting him more connections? Or you? To grow your social circle? Because right now, it is not about me, and maybe never was."

Mama's hand flew to her heart. "How can you say that? All we ever wanted—"

"No, Mama." Renata held up her hand. "Stop right there. You are being theatrical. I would not change my mind about Placido, nor was he about me, so why the rush?"

"Because your family is running out of money, that's why." Natalia had entered the room without either Colombina or Renata noticing. She had spoken the unsaid so matter-of-factly. Colombina's mouth opened, and though her fist was in the air, her protest was devoid of words, lies, and more lies.

Renata knew Natalia spoke the truth when a pang clanged in her chest like a bell. Renata curled her fingers into both palms to steady herself and asked her mother. "How long? How long has this truth gone unspoken between us?"

"After the Fatti di Maggio and then again after the downfall of Generali Pelloux." Every word from her mother's mouth was like a little dagger to Renata's stomach. For once, her mother did not try to counter.

"Ah," Renata said softly. Natalia nodded in agreement, her face grave with the news she revealed.

During the Events of May or *Fatti di Maggio,* as the time last year was referred to, riots in Milan killed at least eighty citizens, demonstrating against the rising cost of wheat. The military had overreacted to the widespread protests, and two successive governments had failed as a result, throwing the entire country into turmoil.

Renata knew Papà was heavily invested in wheat, and his harvest, like all landowners and farmers across the peninsula, was poor. His attempts to divest and diversify his investments had failed. She had never heard that from him, of course. She had caught snippets in whispered conversations around the house, and many a conversation was curtailed when she entered a room. Though she suspected, she did not want to confront Papà and embarrass him. Servants had left and not been replaced.

Why had she not paid more attention? She had been too focused on her many pursuits. Her embroidery classes, her plein air painting classes, and, of course, the adventures of her man, Sherlock. Beyond that were the literary salons for women proliferating around the University of Padua campus, where she and her learned friends dissected titillating prose from Petrarca and Dante.

And there had been her pining for entry into the non-academic salons such as the Baronessa di Calandro's, which had been so stressful. Oh yes, and in the last six months, her wedding had distracted her from the concerns of the real world. And now look where they all were.

Any joy and energy that might have been in the room, even a corner of it, had been sucked out, and Renata went limp. Natalia threw her arms around Renata. "Many are in your family's situation. You cannot hold it against your parents that they seek to see you safe with Placido and his wealthy family and not concern you about their finances."

Renata did not want to be mollified. Heat crept down from the edges of her hairline and spread over her cheeks and neck. She squeezed her eyes tightly, wanting to fend off this news and cast blame on anyone in spitting distance. When she opened her eyes, Mama's tear-stained face stopped her.

Natalia kissed Renata and then moved to the window to give mother and daughter privacy. Then Renata got up and knelt at Mama's feet, putting her head on Mama's lap. "I am so deeply sorry. I wish you had told me. I have a stubborn head, but I could have seen sense sooner."

"Papà and I are the ones who are sorry." Mama stroked Renata's head. "Parents should not have to rely on their children, particularly a daughter, to get them through a rough patch with money."

"Shhh, Mama."

Mama moved her hand from Renata's head to her cheek. "You must know we love Placido. We did not think getting married earlier would bother you, so we remained silent about our difficult circumstances. We did not want to intrude on your happiness or ruin your nuptials or Christmas." Mama wept, and Renata hugged her waist. "And we never imagined so many things going wrong."

They stayed like that for a while, comforting one another and whispering soothing things, until Renata forgot all about Signor Salucci and his summons.

Chapter 26

Renata watched as a thin-framed, raven-haired beauty alighted from her carriage, helped down by the steady hand of Alonzo Pelicani.

"Welcome to Castello Pelicani, Signorina Pinto! Our nation's newest operatic star. We are thrilled you are here." Alonzo kissed her hand, then waved his arm in a wide arc. Amelia Pinto marveled at the gray splendor of the fortress, majestic despite the uncooperative cloudy sky. He offered the woman his arm, and he steered her to Renata. "And this is the bride-to-be and my future niece, Renata Bombonatti."

"Grazie, Signor Pelicani." When the petite songstress smiled, her teeth were so white that the reflection could pierce the dark clouds in the morning sky. "Piacere, Signorina Bombonatti."

"Piacere, Signorina Pinto." The two young women acknowledged one another, their expressions full of admiration. "Please call me Renata."

"I shall," said Amelia, laying a buttery-soft gloved hand on Renata's bare one, "if you do me the courtesy of addressing me as Ama, which all my friends call me."

"Sì, certo." Friend? How forward of her, considering they had just met, but Renata was not about to stir a new pot.

Mrs. Trevisan, Martell, and all the footmen greeted the performer as Alonzo offered his other arm to Renata, leading them both into the castello's foyer.

∞

After Mama left Renata's bedchamber an hour earlier, Natalia had shared all the gossip with Renata.

The Neapolitan soprano was about to make her début on the 29th of December at the Teatro Grande in Brescia, where she planned to sing in Amilcare Ponchielli's *La Gioconda.* Alonzo had been entranced when he had met her in Rome in the autumn at a student recital at her school.

He had begged her to rehearse her role on Christmas Eve at the wedding of his nephew and heir at Castello Pelicani, and the soprano had agreed. Zio Alonzo had announced his surprise guest last night, and the entire castello was abuzz. Renata had skipped dinner, so she did not hear the news until moments before her dramatic arrival.

"My maid learned that the reenactment in the glaciarium plus the tableau vivant are only two of the three surprise entertainments Placido, his brothers, and their uncle have planned for everyone during the wedding week."

Renata stretched her neck to the left and the right. "Dare I ask about the third?"

Natalia had clapped her hands. "The third revel is a visit and aria by the soprano, Amelia Pinto."

Renata had groaned at the news. "All of this fuss. With no Po or Vito—and an actual murderer wandering in our midst—will we marry?"

Natalia tightened her jaw. "Shall I go on, or do you wish to complain further?"

"Please continue, O great orator." Renata winked, and Natalia sat up, eyes blazing.

"There is hope that the soprano's arrival will break the curse of eight attempted weddings at the castello that all failed to materialize in the last century." This last fact was one Renata knew but had failed to inform her parents lest it cause an unwarranted hullabaloo. Neither she nor Po had paid much mind to the old curse.

"I ought to feel grateful that no expense is being spared for me and Po. None of this would have been possible if the wedding had proceeded in Padua like my parents had planned. No wonder they did not want to be responsible for such an extravagant affair with their dwindling resources. The Pelicani family is taking care of everything."

℘

As Zio Alonzo escorted the soprano and Renata into the foyer, Amelia Pinto looked around and uttered the one question everyone had asked for days. "And the groom, your nephew? Where is he?"

Zio Alonzo's arm stiffened. He turned to Amelia so Renata could not see his face, but she imagined he had flashed her his broadest smile. "He is in charge of the wedding entertainments and is busy putting the finishing touches on things. Is he not, Renata?"

Another lie. Soon, she would need a horse to carry them around for her. "You will meet him soon enough." Renata knew her smile was not as dazzling as Alonzo's, but just enough not to betray Amelia that anything was amiss. While they had been waiting behind the castello's gates for the soprano's carriage to come up on the final stretch, Zio Alonzo had told Renata, "Do not mention Placido. If she asks, I will answer."

Renata observed Alonzo run a finger under the collar of his shirt and pull it away from his sweating neck. Renata suspected Natalia was right again with her hunches. She had thought Alonzo was worried that the latest Pelicani wedding might be number nine in the curse, and he did not want to let on how worried he was in front of the bride.

"Well, Signorina Pinto," said Alonzo, bringing her to the first step of the stairs. "You must be exhausted after your long journey from the Eternal City. A footman will show you to your bedchamber. You missed lunch, but we shall have a tray sent to your room."

"Thank you, Signor Alonzo." She picked up her skirts. "And the schedule?"

"Yes, of course." Zio Alonzo tipped his hat at her. "The program is in each guest's room, but I am happy to give you what I remember. The reenactment is at five tonight, and we dine afterward at seven-thirty. Dinner is at nine tomorrow, after the wedding at eight. My nephew has a tableau vivant planned for midnight, so we would love to hear your aria before his performance."

"Very good." Amelia turned to Renata. "And you, my dear, must have plenty to do to prepare for your nuptials."

Renata threaded her arm through her future uncle's arm. "Thanks to Zio Alonzo, most of it is done. I am so fortunate to be marrying into this wonderful and thoughtful family."

"Indeed, you are, but I imagine," Amelia paused and gazed up at the frescoed ceiling, the paintings, and the sculptures dotted around the foyer, "you most deserve such familial harmony and unparalleled luxury. They ought to be the ones to count themselves fortunate."

"We do," answered Zio Alonzo, patting Renata's hand.

"Excellent. I look forward to getting to know you all better these next few days. Ci vediamo See you later." She turned and followed the footman up the stairs while everyone watched her sashay her tiny behind from below.

"She is lovely, Zio Alonzo," said Renata. "I can see why you are infatuated with her."

He did not respond, his eyes glued to Amelia's retreating form. Coming to, he dismissed Renata's comment, yelling out, "I am not," before stalking off, his cheeks a tad pinker than they were before the songbird arrived.

And yet, Renata saw the fire in his eyes and perhaps a longing. He had been without a wife for eleven years after she had perished with their daughter in a sailing accident near the glassblower's island of Murano. The soprano had come from Rome with neither a male or female companion nor a maid. Perhaps she would become the Contessa di Sica before Renata. No, she must not let her mind go there. She had enough troubles of her own without borrowing more.

⮞⮜

"Ah, there you are."

In the foyer, Renata and Natalia were bundling up for a carriage ride back to town when Ispettore Grasso came upon them as he entered. The strange note she had received from Signor Salucci had piqued Renata's interest, and she had been itching to get into the village since Mama's confession. Amelia's arrival had also waylaid her. Mama did not want Renata to do anything but lie around all day, waiting for Placido to turn up. Renata knew he would, but she was anxious to see what postbox she *should* have opened, according to Signor Salucci.

"Yes?" After her long talk with the policeman in the library yesterday afternoon, Renata's skin turned to gooseflesh whenever she thought of him. She did not like this and had vowed to stay out of his way lest her feelings get the better of her, yet here he was. Unable to ignore him but needing to get out of the castello before Mama saw them, she asked again, "What is it, Ispettore? We must keep an appointment before the day gets away from us."

"I was hoping we could talk, and uh …" He cleared his throat. "Discuss the case. I have—"

Renata walked past him. "Unfortunately, we must go, so we will not be able to—"

"That is no problem. I shall accompany you and keep you, er, safe." He fell in step behind her.

Renata stopped, and he slammed into her. She turned to face him. "Ispettore—"

"Mi scusi." He stepped back, but not before he stroked the front of her coat as if he had deposited dust or dirt by running into her. "Please, call me Giorgio, and may I call you—"

Natalia brought up the rear and turned to the policeman, pointing between him and Renata. "What is the meaning of this?"

"It is the night before your wedding, and your fiancé is missing. Perhaps something has happened to him that could affect your safety, and you need protection until he returns to, er, wed you."

Uncharacteristically, the inspector was wringing his hands. If Renata had not known better, she would have thought her presence made him nervous. And his nervousness was making her anxious.

"It is not far to the village, and the coachman will wait for me outside the post office." Renata did not want to let on that she was going to the bookshop. "I feel perfectly safe with just Natalia and the coachman."

"I must insist." They were outside now, and he jumped before her as she was about to enter the carriage.

Renata barely registered Natalia's gasp at his rude maneuver.

The proximity of Renata's body to his was not something Renata thought would ever happen with anyone other than Placido. The scent of his olive oil soap wafted up to her nose, lingering. She recalled her reaction two days ago when the wind above the tower carried the same scent, making her dizzy—how her skin, heart, and stomach reacted so strongly.

"You cannot insist." Natalia stepped up and slipped her arm through Renata's. "Step aside, Ispettore Grasso." Natalia elongated his name, irritating the man to the point where his left eye twitched. "Soon-to-be la Contessina di Sica has an appointment to keep."

The inspector did as he was told, and the coachman helped the women inside.

After the doors were closed, Natalia peered out from behind the curtain of the coach.

"What is he doing?" Renata glanced furtively at the parted curtain.

"The inspector is standing immobile as if he has been asked not to move an inch. His eyes are trying to bore a hole into mine, but I am not having it. I believe his face was turning an unnatural shade of purple." Natalia let the curtain fall back in place.

If I recall Officer Damiani's warning correctly, the inspector's temper takes a while to calm down. I wonder ... how long that while is and what the consequences might be for the person to whom that wrath is directed.

The coach lurched, and they were off. The women rode in companionable silence until Natalia said, "Do you want to tell me what that was all about? And do not 'what' me. You know very well what I am asking."

Renata squeezed her eyes shut, unwilling to discuss what was stirring inside her. The stirring did not have a name. *Not yet*, a little voice said, and that is when her eyes flew open.

"Oh my." That was all Renata was capable of. Two words. Not positive, not negative. Just neutral. It was an observation, not an absolute. "How can I admit something to you, my dearest friend, when I cannot put a name on it myself?"

Natalia patted the empty spot next to her, and Renata moved to sit beside her friend. "I gather 'it' is not only a reference to the moment I witnessed back in the courtyard, correct?"

"Correct," Renata whispered.

"Did you say 'correct'? Because I was not sure I heard it."

"Yes," said Renata, louder.

"Has anything ... happened ... between you and—" Natalia pursed her lips. "I do not think I have to state the obvious for you to understand what I mean."

"Nothing physical. We have done nothing in that regard." Renata shook her head slowly. "I-I-I do not know why I feel this way. I waver back and forth. One minute, he is just an annoyance, a country policeman. He should mean nothing to me. Another minute, my heart reacted violently, full of a feeling I could not name. This ... thing that is happening between us scares me a little."

Natalia nodded, "Happening? Hmm ..."

Renata bit her lip and did not answer. The two women turned away from one another to stare out their respective carriage windows. A silence fell between them until Natalia finally said, "What can I do?"

"Can you tell me it will pass?" pleaded Renata. "I am about to marry the love of my—"

"No, I cannot." A sad little smile appeared and disappeared on Natalia's lips so fast that Renata wondered if she would see it.

"Do you think I ought to tell Placido?" Renata was not sure she should have asked the question.

"I cannot answer that. Only you can." Once again, her smart, stalwart friend did not give Renata the answers she sought. Instead, she helped her find the answers with just a little prodding.

Renata nodded at Natalia, then marveled at the snow-laden trees and fields they passed into town. She brought an index finger to her. What was happening to her? Was she so weak a woman, a weak fiancée, that another could tempt her in only a few days away from her man? She did not know if she should be disgusted with herself or happy that another man had found her attractive.

It had been almost a year since she and Placido met again, became friends, and fell in love. Her friends all told her that they were perfect for one another. Renata thought they were, too, and then Ispettore Grasso walked into her life.

Chapter 27

"Do you remember when we were at Mont Choisy, and the landscaper's son only had eyes for me?"

Renata shook her head as she returned to the present and faced Natalia.

"What brought up that memory? It has been three years since we left that finishing school."

Natalia squared her shoulders. "And do you recall what you said when I told you I wanted to run away and marry a Frenchman?"

Renata could feel a lump growing in her throat. "No."

"You said," Natalia leaned against Renata and patted her knee, "that he was 'fine for right now but not right for later.'"

Renata knew what Natalia was saying, and she knew she was right. There was no future for her with a policeman. And she now had the added weight of her family's misfortune to consider. But as much as Renata's feelings for the ispettore were inappropriate, she could not shake them, and Natalia could see it, too. What she could not admit to herself, much less to Natalia, was that her tumultuous feelings for the ispettore were unlike those sweet ones she had for Po.

She could feel Natalia staring at her, waiting. "I am about to wed Po tomorrow. Giorgio is just a distraction—"

"Giorgio? I see." Natalia removed her hand from Renata's knee and sat back.

"It is not like that. I just learned his name at the same time as you did. It does not mean anything."

Natalia narrowed her gaze and said, "Are you going to tell Po how you feel?"

Renata rubbed her eyes. Her fatigue was catching up to her. "I just said—"

"You are trying to deny—"

"Natalia, there's nothing to deny because there is nothing—"

"There *is* something. It is not nothing, Renata." Natalia wagged her finger at Renata. "You are fooling yourself if that is what you think and say to yourself."

"All right," Renata said through gritted teeth. Mama always scolded her when she did that, telling her that a proper lady would not behave that way. "All right," she said more softly. "I do not understand it. I told you before, it scares me. I cannot tell Po. This is a temporary aberration. If Po were here instead of God knows where, this would not—"

Natalia shook her head. "No. Do not blame him. This has nothing to do with him."

"The ispettore is only trying to help us find out what happened to Vito and now Brizio, and he asked my help. And I wanted to help." Renata looked down, crossing and uncrossing her ankles. "That is the only reason we spent time sleuthing together."

Natalia narrowed her gaze. "The lure of a crime to be solved."

Renata sat forward and tapped her gloved hands in the air. "And an important one at that."

"Well, it is no secret that you do have a fascination, shall we call it, with that British writer and his macabre stories."

"You say fascination, and I say I have an appreciation, as do many others, for Conan Doyle's Sherlock Holmes."

"Appreciation, then," said Natalia.

Renata nodded. She was glad she got her point across before Natalia continued. "At that level, there would be no holding you back from trying to be involved in an investigation. Plus, Vito is Po's best man, *and* Po has not been seen other than by you since you arrived, so working with the police would not be an improper activity for a curious fiancée."

"As for all that ..." Renata scratched her ear.

Natalia knitted her brows. "What 'all that'?"

"Po has been in hiding with Vito and Mariana. He has been trying to find out what has been going on."

"He … they … what?" Natalia clasped her hands together in prayer fashion. "Dear Lord, what am I about to hear? You did not think to tell me before now?"

Renata lowered her voice. "After the scaffolding fell on Brizio, I ran out into the antechamber to the ballroom looking for help and ran into Po. I was too upset to tell you yesterday. Besides, he stayed with me for only a moment. He told me Vito was not missing and that Mariana was with him, but he did not say where."

Natalia's eyes widened. "Did he say how he fell or whether someone pushed him?"

Surprised by Natalia's curt tone, Renata answered. "He did not specify. However, I have deduced that Vito's costume, which he was wearing during the rehearsal of the tableau vivant, was caught on the horizontal flagpole near the base of the tower when he fell the first time. When it tore, he fell further into the laurel tree below, and it broke his second fall. He lay on the ground without moving, knowing that everyone was looking down from atop the tower."

"So, he pretended he was dead, but really, he was alive?" Natalia's voice rose, and a blush appeared on her cheeks.

"Correct." Renata leaned forward. "Once he thought everyone had left the roof, he scuttled off to the tobacco barn and hid there awhile."

Natalia frowned. "A barn?"

"Yes. Eventually, he made his way inside the castle, grabbed Mariana, and hid in the old tutor's room. Mariana had her maid send a note to Po, so he knew they were safe, and asked him to hurry back from Orrico."

"But I thought there was a thorough search."

"There was. It seems everyone forgot about the old tutor's quarters."

"Is Po with them now?"

"Rodrigo sent word to Po that Vito had escaped, so Po took a long route home, bypassing the roads his brothers were using to fetch him from Orrico. He told no one he had returned in case Vito was still in danger. He immediately knew where Vito and Mariana were hiding and went straight to them."

Natalia pulled at her earlobe. "So when will we see Po?"

Renata brightened. "Po told me he would show himself tonight when he thought everything had calmed down after the funeral."

"Does Po know that the falling scaffolding could have been another attempt on a life, namely yours?"

Natalia brought a hand to her drumming heart. "That is why I have been spending time with the ispettore and trying to get to the bottom of it all before the wedding, before more guests arrive, and before Po and Vito return."

The carriage slowed, and Renata could tell they were in the center of town by the sound of the horses' hooves on the cobblestone streets.

"You should not have kept any of this from me. What does your Shorluck say about—"

Renata ground out, "Sherrrrrrrlooooooooooock, Natalia. Sherlock."

"Yes, same thing." Natalia waved a dismissive hand.

"No, it is not." Renata pounded a fist on the seat next to her. "Aaargh, oh, never mind."

"Well, you still did not answer me: why did you not confide *all* the details? But we can have that discussion another time." She took her fan out of her purse, bringing cool air to her reddening cheeks. "In the meantime, I want to know why Vito did not tell us where he was. Honestly. Worry lines do not become me."

Renata leaned over to Natalia and lowered her voice. "It involves Vito's wife Mariana and keeping her safe from a, uh, potential murderer."

"Murderer?" Natalia screeched, then clutched her throat. "I know, I said it myself, but I did not think it could be real. I thought Vito's fall was … an accident."

"Keep your voice down." Renata slapped her glove against Natalia's knee. "That is what everyone is trying to figure out." Renata pulled her gloves up and adjusted her hat. "If he was deliberately pushed, why? And if the culprit finds out Vito is still alive, he may come after Mariana and the baby, too."

The carriage stopped, and Renata looked out the frosted window. They were in front of the bookshop, though at a bit of a distance, as three other carriages were ahead of them. Renata rose and reached up to pull the knocker that would tell the driver it was okay to stop and let them out here.

"Natalia, while we are in the village, let us leave all this talk be. We can discuss it further later." Thankfully, Natalia did not argue.

∞

"After you." A man held open the bookshop door, and Renata and Natalia thanked the man and stepped through.

Once again, the fire was blazing, and there was pleasant chatter among the bookshop patrons. The shop owner had red and green bunting on several shelves, and he had put little signs pointing out which books would make good Christmas gifts. He was busy wrapping books for a customer, so Renata and Natalia waited by the post boxes.

He approached them when he was free. "Buongiorno, Signorina Bombonatti, and…?"

"Signor Salucci, this is my friend, Natalia Nunzio."

"Piacere," they said in unison, greeting one another.

"I realized after you left that you did not open 99. You opened what looked like a blank box. It was an older box whose number had fallen off and was never replaced. I do not know what you found in it, but post box 99 was not intended for you."

"Oh." Renata scanned the boxes again, and sure enough, there was number 99. "You found the right one, then?"

"Yes, my assistant had sent it out to the locksmith to clean the locking mechanism, and it only came back yesterday. He had set aside the contents of the box with a note in case the person to whom it was intended stopped by, and we could hand it to them. When the locksmith returned the box, he returned the contents to it, and that is when I realized you did not get what was meant for you, so I gave you the same key and the correct box this time."

Signor Salucci handed Renata the key, bowed, and walked away.

Renata repeatedly turned the key in her hand and tried to recall what the note from the wrong box had said. Some warning about showing herself and being spared, but Po would pay the price if she stayed hidden. But it did not mention Po by name. It just said, "betrothed." Who else in the town of Sica was engaged and potentially in trouble? It did not seem possible to be anyone other than her, but she was a stranger here, so how could she know everyone's marital status?

No, wait. She was misremembering. It was Po who had been warned to show himself.

"Renata," Natalia waved her hand in her friend's face, "what is it?"

The key had mesmerized Renata. She was not sure she wanted to see the new note. There were many, too many. None of them good. How could she be sure this one was from Po? Would it bring her anything but worry or hurt? What price would she pay if she just left it? Perhaps it was a distraction to get her out of the castello?

"Hello? Are you there?" Natalia shook Renata until she came out of her reverie.

"We have to go." Renata turned, but Natalia gripped her forearm.

"We came all the way here. I think you should at least look in the box."

"No, I do not need to see what is there." Renata released Natalia's grip.

"Really? It might be important. Then give me the key. I will open the box."

"No." Renata tucked the key into her coat pocket and paced in front of the post boxes. "I think something might be happening back at the castello, and I need to get back there. This excursion was a fool's errand." She had been had, just like the last time a note brought her to the bookshop. She had to be more discerning and follow the facts. This had been a distraction, and she had had enough of them.

"What are you not telling me? Again!" shouted Natalia to Renata's fleeing back.

Renata stopped in her tracks. What kind of investigator refuses to follow every clue? Sherlock would surely admonish such behavior. She whipped around and strode past Natalia, pulling her back to the bookstore. Waving to an astonished Signor Salucci, they hurried past him and headed for the postboxes. They stopped in front of box 99, and Renata paused, key in midair.

Natalia raised her hand to take Renata's key. "Do you want me to—"

"No, I will do it. I am preparing myself for finding something awful inside, that's all."

Natalia began to whistle the Italian farewell serenade, *Dormi, piccina dormi.*

"All right, all right. You can quit your lament now." Renata fit the key in the lock and turned to open the box, laughing at the song traditionally sung in the Veneto when a girl was about to wed.

Renata reached into the box and pulled out a photograph of a little girl. She flipped the card over and read, "Palomina." It was the same wisp of a girl Renata had seen here and there around the house, which she had chalked up to her fatigue. Who had put her photograph in the postbox and for what reason? She must ask Po about her.

"Who is that?" asked Natalia.

Three young women interrupted Renata's reply when they entered the postbox area, their faces animated and their conversation giggly. Each of them had a key and, without hesitation, opened their postboxes. They began pulling out and unwrapping small books, floral bookmarks, dainty handkerchiefs, and perfume bottles.

Renata looked again at the faded photograph before stuffing it into her purse. The girl resembled the Countess Paloma from the painting in the ladies' parlor, except that the dress was not from the same period as when the countess was a girl. How curious.

Chapter 28

"Renata, where you have been?"

Mama and Eletta greeted her in the foyer when she and Natalia returned to the castello.

"The servants have been running all over the house, barn, and fields looking for you." Mama's hands were flying as she blustered about. "And so has Placido."

Placido.

"He's ba-a-ack?" croaked Renata.

"Yes. He has been so worried. And Papà and I have been, too. Between you and Placido going here and there, and then the inspector interrogating everyone twice, why, it is enough to make one—"

The fingerprints! "Where is he?" Renata peeled off her gloves and scarf, setting them beside her muffler on the foyer table. Eletta scooped them up and offered to help Renata with her coat.

Natalia walked past Renata and greeted Signora Bombonatti.

"He is in with Ispettore Grasso in the library," said Mama nonchalantly.

Renata stopped unbuttoning her coat and Natalia froze after leaning in to kiss the signora on her cheeks. On the ride home, Natalia and Renata's conversation had gone back and forth between anger, frustration, silence, and back to anger. One minute, they talked about Po; the next minute, it was Giorgio. No doubt Natalia was glaring at Renata knowing she was going to meet the inspector, so Renata did not dare look at her friend.

"How long has he been in with the, um, inspector?" Renata composed herself, passed her coat to Eletta, then unpinned her hat in front of the mirror and smoothed the stray hairs back over her ears.

The signora threw her hands up. "Oh, what does it matter now?"

"How long?" Renata's voice was sharp.

Natalia and Mama stared at Renata without answering her. Finally, Renata said, "I think I will go to the library and find out for myself."

"I will tell the servants they can stop looking for you." Natalia strode out of the foyer without another word.

∞

Bepi, Po's manservant, waited outside the library. After opening the doors, he stepped aside to let Renata pass through. "Signorina Bombonatti, inspector."

"Renata!" Placido jumped out of the armchair facing the inspector in front of the fire and ran to Renata.

She embraced him, and he whispered, "I have missed you."

"And I, you," she whispered back. "I have so many questions."

"First, Signorina Bombonatti, I have some questions." The inspector was waving his field book at her.

"They will have to keep, ispettore," said Placido. Through her corset and dress, Renata could feel the warmth of Placido's hand on her lower back seeping through the fabric. The warmth traveled between her legs, a new and very welcome sensation. He turned and guided her to the exit door, his eyes not leaving hers.

"No, questions about the investigation will not keep." The inspector ran to the doorway and stood in front of it, arms akimbo.

"Very well, Ispettore, but ten minutes is all my soon-to-be wife will give you." Po steered Renata back to the two chairs facing the fire. He poured two nips of grappa, then came to stand behind Renata's chair, handing her a glass.

After taking her first welcoming sip, Renata said, "What questions can you have for me that have not already been answered by my fiancé?"

"I, well ..." He paused, looked down at his notebook, and flipped through it. "Well, uh, ..."

"Ispettore Grasso," said Po between gritted teeth. "Have you narrowed the suspect list further?"

The inspector's head snapped as he looked at Renata. He waved his familiar book in the air. "Yes."

Renata stared at the policeman, a lone trail of sweat rolling down his forehead. "Really? Who are they?"

"This is an active investigation and, as such, is not open for discussion." Every second word of his answer was clipped. She sensed he was stalling or purposefully withholding information because Po was in the room with them. His famous temper was on full display.

"You said that before, and yet I recall that you enjoy discussing a case."

"What do you mean?" Placido came around from behind the chair and faced Renata.

"Just that the inspector and I—"

"You and the inspector? You and the inspector, what?" Placido placed one hand on his hip while stretching the other hand in front of himself, the grappa sloshing over the rim.

"When I first arrived, you were not here, Po. Nobody knew what was happening, so your uncle needed someone to escort the inspector around the castello. He needed a guide, but we were gathering evidence, searching for clues, and meeting with the staff to question them and find out what they knew."

"You are not a detective. Why would you pretend to be one? Why did you not just let the inspector do his job? Besides, my uncle would have gladly provided a servant to handle a man's job."

"Do not raise your voice when speaking to me." Renata stood with her chin jutting out. "I have had enough of it from your disrespectful servants, thank you very much. And what exactly makes investigating the attempted murder of my fiancé's best man and the accidental death of the castle's construction supervisor a man's job?"

"You are right, my love. I am sorry." Placido shook his head. "I did not realize you have a penchant for this, er, work."

Renata did not want to bring her secret obsession up in the middle of an argument, so she continued. "Are you saying I could not handle showing the policeman the castello? Or are you upset that I was spending time with him? Or both?"

"You were a great help to me," said the inspector, his voice softening. Placido shot Ispettore Grasso a look. "I so appreciated the many hours of your assistance, Signorina Bombonatti, but there is still the matter of—"

Renata blushed and looked away from the inspector's gaze.

"What was that look?" Placido pointed between Renata and Ispettore Grasso, his lips pinched straight. "Was that assistance with or without a chaperone?"

"Placido, please." She wrung her hands forward and backward and moved closer to him.

"When the cat's away, the mice shall play," said the policeman under his breath.

"Placido, no!" Renata's hand shot out and landed on Po's shoulder, keeping him from slugging the inspector. She felt a pang of betrayal at his sudden outburst.

"Arrgh!" Placido roared, shrugging off her hand and storming out.

❧

After chastising the inspector and leaving him to stew in the library, Renata searched every nook and cranny of the castello but came up empty-handed. When she reached the kitchen, Signor Succo barked orders at his staff. Seeing her, he paused, then continued.

"May I help you?" Mrs. Trevisan appeared with her hands behind her back.

"Yes. By chance, did you see my fiancé?"

"No, Signorina Bombonatti," said the housekeeper, raising an eyebrow. "Should we have? We do not typically keep track of all the family's comings and goings. If this is a new directive you wish the household to observe, please speak to Martell."

Renata swallowed hard. The housekeeper still had not softened toward her. "No. I just thought ..."

Mrs. Trevisan relaxed her arms and winked. "I believe he may be out in the arena seeing how things are progressing for the reenactment of the *naumachia* in precisely..." She checked the timepiece dangling from her chatelaine. "Three hours."

"Yes, of course, that is where he would be." Pacified, Renata said, "Thank you very much, Mrs. Trevisan." Finally, a servant who respected her and felt comfortable enough to display a sense of humor. Because God knows even amid tragedy, Renata could appreciate it.

❧

"Over there! Next to the second trireme on the right." Placido shouted commands to the workers to get everything in place for the massive naval battle he was staging for this evening's entertainment.

The workers had flooded the old jousting arena weeks before, and the basin was now solid ice, ringed by dozens of giant torches. Eight men were busy arranging wooden sea creatures in various positions on the ice, and another dozen men were securing small-scale replicas of the ancient Roman boats—biremes, triremes, and a few of the imposing ones, quinqueremes.

Racks of weapons were stacked diagonally to one another on opposite ends of the ice. Spectator seating had been constructed four levels high on the long sides of the arena. Po had been overly excited about orchestrating the combat on ice, and she had been hearing about it for months. It had only been cold enough to practice on the ice two weeks ago, but Po seemed confident that he and his friends would be declared the victors after fighting against his brothers and their friends.

Renata walked up behind Po, and only when her shoe scuffed the walkway did he hear her and turn. She saw him stiffen, and her heart sank.

His lips stretched into a thin, hard line. "Why are you here?"

"I did not get a chance to explain. You left in such a hurry." She ran her gloved finger along the railing.

"Why did you spend so much time with the inspector?" He spat the words.

She clasped her hands and shook them near her chest. "We thought Vito was dead."

"Well, he is very much alive."

She winced at his tone. "Look, the inspector needed help. This is a massive castello, and it is easy to get lost. Between Vito and Brizio, everyone was a suspect. Plus, your uncle wanted ..." Renata was listing things off her fingers. "Do I need to go on?"

"There was a look he gave you that made you blush." Po pointed at her face. "He looked at you and talked about you as if there was something more between—"

"There is not, and there was not." She pronounced each word slowly so he would not misunderstand. "Yes, perhaps there is an attraction, but—"

"I knew it." Placido balled up his fists. "Just marry him then and save us all this bother." He shook his fist in the air at the castello.

Renata's frustration boiled over. "How dare you make such accusations! You know my heart belongs to you and you alone. This is not the time for your jealousy, Placido."

Renata raised her voice without shouting. "But, let me finish. I am marrying *you*. I-I-I do not want him, and I certainly do not want to marry him."

"Are you sure?" Despite the twilight, she could see his eyes were full of fire. "Your voice cracked."

She shivered. "Why are you reacting like this?"

"I thought you had changed your mind, and my absence had contributed to that."

Her heart surged. "No, my mind was made up ages ago at the Castle of Love, and then it was confirmed when we walked around Il Prato afterward and made that first vow. I have never wavered from it. I also waited for you while you were soldiering away in Africa, unsure if you would return with a spear tip in your head."

"Oh. Right." Placido looked down at his feet.

Renata squeezed her eyes and shut out all the noise around her. It was an effective technique she had adopted as a child in the raucous nursery school her governess had taken her to break through her shyness. She stilled her mind, heart, and nerves that had built up from racing around the castello looking for Po.

Moments later, she opened her eyes and broke the silence. "Po, we need to talk. I have not seen you for more than five minutes since I arrived three days ago. I do not understand everything that has happened, but I have spent much time trying to—"

"As have I." Every word he spoke to her was an effort.

She put her hands on her head. "And I have wracked my brain trying to decipher all your cryptic notes."

"I only sent you love notes." He stepped closer to her. "Did that inspector send you love notes, too?"

"No!" Renata stomped her foot. "For the last time, stop asking me about him."

"What is that famous line from Shakespeare about protesting? Your vociferous protests feel too forced."

"Then maybe my feet rather than my vocal cords need to do the protesting instead." This time, she stormed away from him, though as she did so, a lump formed in her throat when he failed to stop her.

Chapter 29

Renata slammed the door to her room and flopped on her bed, crying. Po was infuriating. God forbid he reveal what he had been up to, though he expected her to provide him with every detail of her sleuthing with the inspector—sleuthing she had been doing to help Po and his friends.

The inspector! I forgot to ask him about the fingerprints, and now that I think of it, I wonder if he suspects Eletta at all.

Renata pulled herself together and walked behind an Oriental screen. She picked up a pitcher painted with the Pelicani crest and poured water into a wide-mouthed ceramic bowl with a matching design. She scooped up handfuls of cold water and splashed it on her face. Now, not only was she fully awake, but she had washed away all evidence of her crying.

She was about to open her door to go downstairs and find the inspector when she stopped herself. He would not reveal who was on his suspect list. However, he might have relented if Renata had offered to share her own, including the photo of Palomina. They would be on a more equal footing if she had. She closed the door and returned to her dressing table. She picked up her glass dip pen, uncorked her ink bottle, and opened her casebook.

Renata found her suspects list and frowned. A list of names and some evidence was only part of the puzzle. The rest she would have to assemble with observations and facts and the very nature of the human soul. What would cause someone to commit a crime? What was it about their mental life, its phenomena, and conditions that would lead someone to murder or attempt to murder a fellow human?

Sighing, she crossed out Brizio's name and replaced it with Rodrigo, but then she thought better of it and put Brizio back. There had been blood on his knife, though perhaps that was not unusual for a man who worked in construction. Also, the note was written on the same stationery used by whoever sent her the notes. Could Brizio have harbored ill will against Po from childhood and wanted to take it out on Renata? Maybe *he* had tampered with and loosened some screws on the scaffolding, and the note had fallen out of his apron pocket then.

Brizio had entered the ballroom moments after Renata. Perhaps he had intended for the scaffolding to fall on her, but her guardian angel had acted fast and saved her from doom. But how could Brizio have been sure she would go into the ballroom *and* over to the scaffolding? She could not think of any logical reason to do so. However, she had only entered the room because the maid told her someone had wanted to talk to her there. The maid's name escaped her, and she put a star next to Brizio to remind her to return to it later.

Rodrigo was the groundskeeper who had helped Vito escape, but could he have been the small fellow the footman could not identify at the rooftop rehearsal? Could he have run down from the tower before everyone else? But what motive did he have for pushing Vito?

When she had lied to him in the stables, he had been gruff towards her, and he had lied back at her. He had a very responsible job, but it was outdoors and not as interesting as that of his brother Brizio, who spent all his time inside the castello, among warmth and finery. Could there be a rivalry there? Could he have also left the bloody note with Renata's name on it? But why would he have cause to threaten Renata? Or Vito? Or Po, for that matter, with that last note?

She scanned the list of the rest of the servants. The only one that could have had the time and motive was Eletta. Vito's family had wronged Eletta's family, and they were about to be thrown out on the street when their lease ran out in a few days. But what would Eletta have been doing on the roof? Though she was not part of the tableau vivant, she might have worn a disguise. Plus, she had the time because

Renata had yet to arrive and had no one else to tend to. However, Eletta would not have had the strength to mess with the scaffolding.

That latter point eliminated all the women on the list.

Renata had not spent as much time at the crime scene as the inspector had, and she had just taken him at his word that the scaffolding had been tampered with. A few loose screws were not an absolute determinant. A judge certainly would expect more proof. She marked the entry with a question mark, signaling an open question.

Po's half-brothers may be jealous that Po was inheriting the title, the castello, and most of the land when their uncle passed away, so they had a motive to harm Po but not Vito. Could one of the brothers have intended to do away with Po but, in frustration over Po's absence, pushed Vito off the tower instead? A chill ran through her body, and she pulled on a shawl. She had not interviewed her future brothers-in-law, but she knew the inspector would have.

What had he learned about these men? She knew nothing of their whereabouts before she had arrived and had barely seen them afterward except for dinner. They had also contributed little to the nightly conversations around the table. Their personalities were still entirely foreign to her.

What about Dario? So, too, Renata had had little interaction with the other groomsman. What did he know? What had he seen on that roof? How had he spent his days since Vito's fall? She was sure by now that Ispettore Grasso had questioned him thoroughly. So, was he a worthy suspect? And how determined had he been about searching for Po?

Like Fumo and Po's brothers, Dario had been close to Vito since they were boys. However, this did not absolve him from suspicion or further interrogation, and Renata added a star beside his name.

Though he had been on the roof, Fumo did not seem likely a suspect. She had seen him moved by the injuries Vito would have suffered and was upset by his absence. However, Renata remembered how he had acted toward her in the hallway, at the market, and at the end of their conversation after Brizio's funeral.

And what of the blood spots she had found on the handkerchief that he used to wrap the Algerian knot he had given her? As well as those on his cigarette case. He had also been unhappy about the amount of attention put on Vito, and then he was disappointed at being passed over for the role of best man. A jealous, temperamental man? Yes. A loyal friend? Perhaps, to a point. An attempted murderer? She added two question marks to his name.

Martell. The footmen. Mrs. Trevisan. The maids. The brothers Succo and Salucci. The kitchen staff. The carriage driver. The stable hands. Oh, and Alonzo. She crossed off each one until she came to Zio Alonzo. There, her glass dip pen hung suspended, and drops of red-black ink dripped onto the page, creating a patterned oval around his name. She put neither a star, a question mark, nor an *X* next to his name. It deserved something, but her instinct told her to leave him without facts.

She tallied up her list. Eight solid suspects and none to whom she could point a definitive finger. Her hands started to shake. Could it have been one or more of the guests? She shuddered at the thought. Perhaps the inspector had a shorter list and possibly a working theory of whether it was family, a staff member, or a guest or two that had done away with Brizio and Vito (almost). It was time to seek out the inspector and compare notes—amateur to professional.

და

Martell told Renata that he had not seen the inspector in the library, kitchens, ballroom, or breakfast room. Mrs. Trevisan confirmed that he had fingerprinted the entire staff, and she had let him know that she was none too happy about his intrusive methods, accusatory tone, and arrogant attitude. Renata sat slumped on a bench in the hallway leading to the library when she heard loud voices trailing up from the foyer. She walked to the top of the stairs and poked her head out over the railing.

The Baronessa di Calandro and her entourage had arrived.

The party could start now that she had deigned to lend her presence for a country wedding after all. Renata wondered what she would make of the kerfuffle that had beset Ca' Pelicani. Might she leave if she learned what had happened? Might it put her stellar society matron reputation in jeopardy?

Renata reminded herself that she had shifted her perspective about Po and assumed the best about him. Yes, she had faltered, but not for long. She should also apply the same kindness and take the best about la baronessa. Time might be a better judge, though it was now ticking away. Renata decided she would let Mama deal with the guests and backed away from the railing so neither la baronessa nor her coterie would see her. Meanwhile, Renata would dress and skate to the pensione where the inspector was staying. That would be a far more productive use of her time than waiting on la baronessa.

Chapter 30

The Canale Vingenzone was busier than she had expected at this hour. Many couples had sprigs of holly pinned to the lapels of their coats and capes. Some older children pulled more minor children and their pet dogs on sleds up and down the icy canal. The gay laughter and talk of Babbo Natale bringing gifts was music to Renata's ears. She needed to see and hear and participate in the Christmas activities of the castello and the village, but she had not had time to enjoy such revels.

Renata had to slow down so she would not run into a child. She knew she only had a few hours of daylight left before sunset. Her desire for answers from the inspector grew as she neared the Pensione Cavallini, where he was staying temporarily.

She bent to remove her skate blades and kept her balance by leaning against a tall boulder. Walking up the path to the inn, she looked up to see the inspector bent over a desk, holding up papers to the oil lamp in his room. Too intent on his work, she did not want to shout and frighten him.

Even in absentia, Renata could hear Mama's voice scolding her about acting like the countess of the county that she was soon to be. Failing that, she would be reminding her she was still a lady and shouting was bad form. Though Sica was four hours from Padua, Renata wondered if Mama's voice would ever stop being a permanent and pesky occupant in her head.

Renata opened the front door of the inn. The bell on the inside rang and awakened the proprietress, who had dozed off over her desk, and she eyed Renata from afar. Smiling, but not too much, Renata approached the desk.

The silver-haired woman in a plain gray dress with a pearl paste bar pin at her neck shook herself awake and stretched her back. "Buon pomeriggio. How can I help?"

"Good afternoon to you, signora." Renata put her skate blades down in front of the reception desk. "I am Signorina Bombonatti, and I have come from Castello Pelicani to speak with Ispettore Grasso. Could you let him know I am here, please?"

The owner peered over her spectacles at Renata. "Ca' Pelicani, you say? Why, I have never heard your name before today."

Renata could feel the heat rising and spreading across her cheeks. "Yes, well, Signora Cavallini, is it?" The woman nodded. "I am new to Sica, but tomorrow, I shall be the Contessina Pelicani."

"So, you are the one." The signora grinned from ear to ear. "At last, the castello will have a hostess. It has been too long without one. I am afraid the Pelicani men have forgotten how to behave in polite society without a woman in their midst."

Renata raised an eyebrow and nodded. "There's little time left to outrun the setting sun before getting home. If you could let the inspector know I am here ..."

"Yes, of course, my dear. Please sit in the parlor, and I am sure he will be right down."

"Grazie," said Renata, picking up her skates and walking across the small lobby to a sitting area.

It was a cozy room with rose-patterned voile draped over the windows against sage green walls. She spotted a group of four vermillion-toned bergère armchairs and chose to sit there because they were near the fire and the furthest from the reception desk. Signora Cavallini seemed kind enough, but Renata was here on police and castello business. She did not want to be overheard.

She removed her cape and hung it over a rack near the fire to dry out guests' outdoor clothing. It was like the ones she and Natalia had had at their boarding school in the wintertime. This way, the girls would not drip water from rain-soaked coats or snow-packed capes along the halls, making the hall or dormitory floors slippery and dangerous. They were not always successful.

Renata had just sat down and was pulling out her casebook when the inspector arrived, field notes in hand.

"Hello, Signorina Bombonatti. To what do I owe this disturbance?" He stood outside the circle of chairs with his hands behind his back. He was not in uniform but in a tailored woolen suit in brown check and a maroon necktie.

"I thought we could start again or at least agree to a detente." He did not react, and she continued. "You see, I have assembled a suspect list, and I thought we could—"

"We could what?"

His reply was coated with a frostiness she had not heard before. Their last encounter in the library, when she had failed to respond kindly to his flirtations in the presence of Placido, may have bothered him more than he had let on. Perhaps he wanted to take her down a notch or two when he had treated her like a colleague, and she had rebuffed him. Renata recalled Officer Damiani telling her to watch out for his sudden tempers. She realized she would have to try a different tactic to get him to open up to her again.

"Please sit," she said, pointing to the chair across from hers. "I will ask Signora Cavallini if she might bring us some coffee."

Mollified, he took the chair next to hers and unbuttoned his jacket. She could see his physique form from how stretched his vest fit against his chest. Ripping her gaze away from his body, she hurried away to speak to the owner and returned a moment later.

"She is bringing coffee and some lovely Pazientina she baked this morning." Renata sat and picked up her casebook. "So, I thought I would share my suspect list, and we could compare it to yours. With your keen eyes, you might see something in my notes that will help your investigation." In an attempt to get back into his good graces, she complimented him and emphasized *your*.

He crossed his legs without saying anything.

I will not be defeated, she thought.

She found the page with her list of suspects and the notes she had written beside them, took a deep breath, and held out her casebook for him to peruse. After an interminable time looking over the two pages of her notes, he opened his notebook and began comparing what she had surmised to what he had written.

The proprietress arrived with a tray and bent to set it on the low table between them. "Shall I pour?"

Renata jumped up and took the tray. "I will do it, thank you." The woman harrumphed and strode off, her shoes squeaking too loudly on the floor. Too bad, but Renata did not want the woman hovering. She and the inspector had business to attend to, and by the long shadows stretching across the room, there was not much time to do it before she had to head back and hope no one had noticed her missing.

She poured them each a cup and then held up the sugar bowl. "One lump or two?"

"Three," he said without looking up.

If she had three sugars every time she had a coffee, she would have to visit the dressmaker far too often to have her seams let out, to say nothing of the beaded wedding dress she had ordered from Milan that had taken four women months to sew. She put a slice of St. Anthony's cake on his plate, smiled, and handed him his coffee. The cake was calling her name, though she managed through sheer will to abstain.

She sipped her coffee for several minutes, then lost her patience with his silence. "Well, do our lists match?"

He nodded, and she was pleased, taking it as a good sign.

She pressed on without smiling. "And what of the bloody thumbprint on the note left on the scaffolding?"

He closed her casebook and handed it to her. The inspector picked up the decadent layered cake and took a few bites. Then, he took a sip or two of his coffee and another bite of the pastry creation and repeated it a few more times while he savored the moment.

He's torturing me and enjoying it, too. The cake may have been called Pazientina because of the patience it took to make it, but the inspector's slow eating only caused Renata to grow irritable and impatient. *I am not sure I can last much longer at this pace. I may have to—*

He set his cup and plate down, then brushed a crumb from his vest before turning to her. "It was smudged near the bottom, so we could not make an identification." He stood and looked down at her with a piercing gaze. "But I have one more trail to trod, which I shall keep to myself for now."

Her heart thudded in her chest. She was sure inking everyone's fingerprints would have brought closure to the ordeal of Brizio's death, at least. She felt like she was back at the beginning. As the gears turned in her head, she sprinted to a cliff, ready to throw all her gains over it.

℘

Renata's skate home was uneventful except for her churning thoughts about Palomina. Was the castello playing tricks on her mind? Did the girl's haunting presence play a role in Vito's fall or Brizio's death? Or was she just some dead benign relative that bore no role in the drama unfolding at the castello? And who had put her in the postbox? All good questions Renata would scribble into her casebook, though she doubted she would ever receive an answer to them.

Renata made it back just as the sun sank into the horizon. The sky was pigmented orange and magenta, but she was in no mood to marvel at it. It was one of her favorite things, yet she had wasted precious time with the inspector the last hour or so. He had refused to share his

219

findings after she generously shared hers, nor had he offered up a theory about the identity of either Vito or Brizio's culprit.

Vito was the one person who could provide the most definitive answer yet about Vito. Po knew where he was, but he was not telling. If Vito did not plan to surface until the wedding, she would have to go to him. It was the only thing she could think of doing, and because she knew more truth about the Brizio matter than Ispettore Grasso, she was in an enviable position to get a leg up on him. She could not join him, and therefore, she would beat him.

Though her powers of persuasion had not helped her with the inspector, she prayed as she entered the castello that she had better luck with her future husband and his best man. She had a theory and wanted to test it out on her own. If unsuccessful, she would wait for Po to reveal what he knew.

Renata snuck up the servants' stairs and exited on the third floor. She stood still, listened, then followed a hunch. Hearing no voices in the hallway or anyone coming up the regular stairs, she dashed down the women's wing of the old servants' floor and put her ear to door after door.

Martell had told her that when Signora Paloma had set herself to remodeling downstairs, she spent some money redecorating the servants' and tutor's quarters, too. But it looked like these old ones had been left to the ghosts and were ripe for hiding. This being the women's wing, it now made sense why no one had discovered the Marzanos. Neither the Pelicani brothers nor the groomsmen would have ventured down this way.

At last, Renata spotted a concealed door at the wing's end. She recognized the voices and checked the hallway before knocking.

The voices ceased, and all movement stopped.

She knocked again but dared not say their names aloud. "It is me, Renata."

The door opened, and an arm reached out and yanked her in.

"What are you doing here?" hissed Vito.

Renata took in her surroundings. A corner suite with a heavy oak bed and a tiny crib is near a roaring fire. A mattress with a pillow and some blankets on the far side of the room. A suitcase by the bed. Po's temporary bed with his sweater on it. He had been sleeping here to protect the Marzanos. She wanted to run over, wrap herself in his blankets, and wait for him to join her under them—cold, naked, and raw.

A creaking noise broke her concentration. An uncomfortable-looking woman had shifted in a rocking chair, rubbing her swollen belly and staring wide-eyed at the visitor. With messy hair and dark circles under his eyes, Vito stood protectively next to Mariana.

"Hello, Mariana." The woman offered up a weak smile. "I am sorry to barge in here," Vito scoffed, but Renata continued. "I have just come from seeing the inspector assigned to your case. He has a list of suspects, which he has refused to share with me, so I decided to come straight here. To the one person who can tell me what happened on that roof. If we can narrow the list—"

"Po said you were sniffing around. He has been trying to find out who did this to me, so you do not need to be involved as well. Surely, it would be safer if you avoided this mess."

Renata was surprised by Vito's opposition. She pressed on: "I was, *am*, trying to help. No one had any answers to what happened to you after your, er, fall. No body was found at the scene. It was quite vexing. Dario and Fumo mounted a search, but it came up empty. There was no blood on the ground, and the torch mount was bent, so we all suspected you had lived, but where were you?"

"I hid in the tobacco barn. Rodrigo helped me into the barn. When he went to fetch bandages, I escaped and found Mariana. We have been holed up, healing, and staying alive since then. With a potential killer out there, hiding is paramount to me and my family's survival."

"Ahhhh." Mariana gritted her teeth and held her belly.

Vito squeezed his wife's shoulder. "She is close to her time. Po is discreetly arranging for a midwife. I cannot compromise the safety of my wife and child by leaving here."

Renata shifted her gaze from Vito to Mariana and back again. "I understand. What else can you tell me?"

"I knew I could trust Rodrigo to get word to Po in Orrico. He returned to protect us and stayed here until he could find out who was responsible. He could not be seen, but he needed an ally on the inside."

"Brizio was his man?"

Vito nodded. "Not much good he is going to be for us now."

"You think he was found out?"

"Yes. He was killed, was he not? He may not have betrayed us, sacrificing himself to protect us, but we do not know. So, our position here is even more precarious because of what happened to him and maybe because of you, too." Vito was jumpy and eyeing the exits.

"I was not followed. I can assure you."

Vito snorted.

"Aaargh." Renata paced in front of the couple. "I was threatened. I received notes, one with blood. I did my best to help the police, but I could not see any progress, and time was marching on with my wedding day and Christmas Day drawing near. Zio Alonzo told the inspector that the case had to be solved by my wedding day. And then I ran into Po, but he refused to explain everything. He left me with more questions than answers. I could have died under that scaffolding, too. So, forgive me if my wild guess about your whereabouts has led me here."

"You should not have come." Vito pointed at her and punched the air thrice with his index finger. "You are putting us all in mortal dang—"

Renata cut him off. "Who do you suspect pushed you? Does Po know?"

He shook his head. "We have been over this so many times."

Renata's shoulders drooped, and she switched her focus to Mariana. "Mariana, I am sorry. You have been through a lot, too, and you should not have had to endure any of this in your condition."

Mariana stretched her hand to Renata, and Renata gratefully took it. "I could say the same for you. You are a bride. This is a magical time. Once in a lifetime, and it has been marred by disaster." The two women held hands and looked at one another for a long while until Renata broke the silence.

"Have you and the baby been getting enough to eat? Has Po been bringing you—"

"Do not fuss, Renata. I … we … are *fine*. Po has thought of everything." On a console table, Mariana gestured to some pantry items, such as fruit and cheese. A few logs were stacked next to the fireplace. Cloth diapers were rolled vertically in a basket. "No one has bothered us—"

"Until now," Vito grumbled and paced behind his wife, raking his hands through his unruly hair. "It was no accident. Someone pushed me. I do not know who it was."

Renata had found a chair and sat. She opened her casebook to a blank page and scribbled in it. "And did you get a look at their face or eyes?"

"No. We were all wearing masks, yet I did not recognize their eyes. As a jeweler, I have witnessed many expressions in people's eyes when they purchase a piece from me. I can tell what they are thinking and feeling through their eyes. Those eyes that pushed me were foreign to me, and though I thought of my impending death as I fell, I could never forget them. The eyes were full of malice, but to whom they belong, I know not."

Renata tapped her pencil to her temple. "Think hard, Vito. Who might wish you harm?"

Vito put his hands in his pockets and shrugged. "I told Po that if the man had not died of influenza a month ago, I would have said a rival jeweler one street over from my shop in Vicenza. If the old coot had been alive, it still makes no sense that he would have followed me here unless he knew someone who could get him in."

Renata drummed her fingers on her casebook. "Did he have a spouse or children who may have wanted to continue the rivalry?"

Vito shook his head. "None that I know of. I knew very little about the man."

"The motive is as clear as mud to us." A tear rolled down Mariana's cheek. "We must find whoever did this."

Renata bit her lip. "Vito, look, I know about the lease issue on Eletta's shop. Could Eletta have something to do with this?"

"That is a business matter that has nothing to do with what happened." Vito stretched his neck. "Besides, she was not on the roof. How could it have been her?"

"Po has been unable to find the man who pushed Vito," Mariana sniffled.

"Po is trying his best, and I suppose Renata has been, too. I am sorry I was stern and doubted you, Renata."

She smiled. "I forgive you. This has been a trying time for all of us."

Mariana continued—her voice shrill. "He must be found. We cannot let him ruin our Christmas. Or the birth of our firstborn."

Vito tried to kneel in front of Mariana but groaned from the pain and gave up.

He returned to stand behind Mariana and stroked her head. "Oh, my love, it is okay. I am here. We are safe—me, you, and the baby."

If Vito had a good memory for eyes, then it could not have been anyone he knew, which ruled out Po's half-brothers and the groomsmen Fumo and Dario. "Then the other conclusion must be true." Realizing she had spoken out when she had not intended to, Renata dropped her head and focused on writing in her casebook.

"What must be true?" Vito's knuckles were turning white as he spoke.

"You are right. The villain had to have someone on the inside. They knew, or perhaps suggested, that the rehearsal would or should take place on the roof. They were involved in the planning from the beginning. Masks. Costumes. Weapons. Fighting. With all that, it would be easy to stage an accident."

Chapter 31

On either side of the glaciarium, the spectators had already filled the topmost benches. All benches were lined with thick blankets, and the spectators brought heavier blankets to cover their legs. There was much tittering among the guests as they took their place and snuggled under their blankets, awaiting the spectacle to begin.

The night sky was slightly overcast and cold, but not unbearably so. Tall torches were ablaze wherever one looked. A panoply of painted ocean creatures, from seahorses and octopi to jellyfish and whales, were scattered among the ancient-style boats. The teams reenacting the sea battle were outfitted with pads over their arms and legs and sturdy blades strapped onto their boots so they could quickly skate on the ice-filled battlefield.

A military band had struck up *Bersagliere Ha Cento Penne* The Marksman Has 100 Feathers. Many former soldiers in the stands swung their old military-issued wine skin bags up to their lips, taking a swig as they sang along. Renata thought it a fitting tribute to both teams as they prepared for the "battle." She hoped Po and his team would win. He was already sour over her supposed affection for the inspector. He needed a win. They, as a couple, needed a win. Tomorrow, they would be husband and wife, and she did not want to go into this marriage with him, thinking she would like to be with anyone but him.

The band ended their song, and the sole drummer began a slow drum beat. The crowd turned as Zio Alonzo and Amelia Pinto entered the rink through the arch placed on one end of the ice for the teams to use. No one rose. Perhaps they did not want to disrupt the blankets they had settled under, but everyone clapped enthusiastically for their host. Alonzo and Amelia waved to the crowds. Even from where she sat, Renata could see that Alonzo was smitten with Amelia, so she relaxed her fear that Amelia was brought in to replace her in Po's affections.

Then Martell handed Zio Alonzo a megaphone.

"Signori e signore, welcome to tonight's festivities." The crowd's applause grew louder. "Tomorrow, my nephew and heir is marrying his inamorata, Renata Bombonatti." The crowd roared. When Alonzo finally quieted them, he inquired, "Where are you, my dear?"

Renata looked to her parents, who beamed and encouraged her to respond.

"Stand up." Zio Alonzo gestured for her to rise. She stood and waved. Two rows down and three benches over, la baronessa stopped clapping when she focused on Renata. Remembering to assume the best, Renata waved. The Baronessa di Calandro nodded, then turned to her companions.

"Before you tonight," Alonzo continued, "you will see a reenactment of The Battle of Aegates, the last in the two-decades-long First Punic War. As these reenactments were called, Naumachiae took place in ancient Rome, and Romans thronged the banks of the River Tiber to view the novelty. In tonight's crowd, I sense there is as much excitement as there would have been back then, though, in our version, the bridegroom and his brothers are on opposite sides, so be careful about whom you applaud."

The spectators cheered, and the teams rushed out behind Alonzo and Amelia and lined up on either side of them. Renata's hands shook. Was the killer on the field? In the stands? There were weapons everywhere. Indeed, one could go missing and not be noticed for some time. The shaking moved to her legs, and she tucked the blanket tighter around herself, watching everyone.

Alonzo paused, waiting for them to settle. "This week has been difficult and unexpected when it should have been easy and joyful like a wedding week and Christmas week ought to be."

The audience stilled, straining to hear what the lord of the castle had to say.

"After the wedding, we have a special treat for the guests and staff here at Ca' Peli." He bowed low in front of Amelia. "May I present Amelia Pinto, the rising opera star from Naples whom I met in Rome. She will sing a rendition for us from Amilcare Ponchielli's *La Gioconda,* which she will debut in Brescia at the Teatro Grande, but she's giving us a sneak peek. And she promises some festive tunes, so you are in for a treat."

The crowd stomped their feet and waved at Amelia. She curtseyed, laughed, and waved at everyone.

"Until then, let us watch my nephews in mock combat. May the best team win!" Alonzo offered Amelia his arm, and they left the rink to get to their seats.

The teams assumed their positions in their makeshift boats with wooden weapons in hand. When they were ready, Martell walked onto the middle of the ice, raised the family standard in his hand, and seconds later lowered it to signal the start of the battle. For the next hour, the men threw pig's bladders filled with red dye through alternative cannons outfitted with slingshots. They maneuvered their crude boats around the "bloodied" ice and crashed into one another. Swords with dull blades either slashed the air or clashed against their opponents' weapons.

The fight continued for another half hour, the men shouting war cries while the band played on. The spectators for each team hooted and hollered, trying to outdo one another and encouraging their respective teams to win. Tommaso signaled Fabrizio, who fired off another shot of a pig's bladder and took down the mast of the quinquereme, the largest ship, thus almost ending the battle.

At one point, Renata jumped up when she lost track of Po in the battle. Where had he gone? And where was Fumo? He was supposed to be covering Po's right flank. The spectators behind Renata shouted for her to either sit down or leave because she was blocking their view. She sat and bit the inside of her mouth until it bled.

Finally, Placido was back in the front where she could see him. She scanned the crowds, looking for a murderer—not that she would recognize one if she saw one. Po had been missing for too long, and she would have to ask him his whereabouts later.

He and his sailors whipped themselves into a frenzy of victory for the next ten minutes before clambering out of the four boats they had been commandeering. The defeated team and crew climbed out of their respective ships much more slowly and without fanfare. They shook hands with and congratulated the winners, then bowed while the audience whooped it up, including Renata and her parents.

Renata clapped profusely, then looked down to see Placido turn away and follow his friends off the ice. A jolt went through her heart. She thought he would be happy to see how enthusiastically she supported him, his work to pull off the reenactment, and his win, but she had thought wrong.

Renata and Placido were supposed to sit at the head of the table tonight. How could they when he would not look at her, much less talk to her? She had to reach him, and fast.

"Come along, Renata." Papà was waiting for her to precede him off the spectator stands.

"Sì, Papà."

She followed him along with everyone else as they gathered to return to the castello. The wind had picked up, and she pulled her cape tighter to keep out the cold.

"Renata, or should I call you 'contessa' now?"

She recognized the voice as the one and only Baronessa di Calandro and paused. Clenching her teeth, Renata turned to see the noblewoman with her friends

flanking her on either side. Renata forced herself to smile and ignore the taunting.

"Contessa, hello." Renata pointed at the ground filled with ice. "How did you enjoy the spectacle?"

"I enjoyed it very much indeed." She pulled her coat collar up around her neck. "And at least one thing ended well … for I understand that so much that has happened at the Castello since you arrived … has not."

Renata looked away so the daggers she was sure had replaced her eyeballs would not fly out and stab the woman.

"Pity that the best man is missing, and how very unfortunate that there has been a death after him. Tsk-tsk. How is it that such tragic circumstances have befallen the betrothed? Such bad luck. Here's some advice: I do hope that no one and nothing else interferes with the preparations for your wedding or the wedding itself …"

Renata whipped her head around to glare at the woman. She would see that the contessa was placed far away from her and Placido at the wedding banquet.

The countess continued. "I cannot imagine what the society in these parts would say if they did. These ancient families have long memories and are not inclined to forgive easily. Oh, and I also agree that they prefer a seasoned hostess in their noble midst. So be careful of your next move. Potential usurpers abound. As for my last advice, they can say what they want, these handsome snake charmers, but the Pelicani men are not renowned for their faithfulness."

Then, she touched her hair and exaggerated her lips' pout. With that and a flourish of the hand from her noticeably younger male companion, la baronessa strode past Renata without so much as a glance.

Renata stomped on the ground and raised a fist behind la baronessa's back.

"Oh my, why so angry?"

Renata whirled to face Amelia. "Pardon me, Amel—, I mean, Ama. It is just that the woman infuriates me. It seems I slighted her more than I thought at her recent salon, and she has decided the slight cannot be forgiven. She means to take my place."

Ama raised her eyebrow. "At your wedding?"

"Perhaps, and more." Renata hung her head.

"So very uncouth of her. I must say she travels with quite a coterie of—"

"Hmm, yes," replied Renata, cutting her off and watching la baronessa's retreating back. Renata expected Amelia to reassure her about Po's fidelity, but she said nothing on that score. Renata clenched her teeth. Amelia's remark felt like she was trying to throw Renata off the scent of the illicit goings-on of the Pelicani men.

Renata also realized that la baronessa had quadrupled the number of guests she had invited to accompany her at the wedding versus the doubling of guests Renata had brought to la baronessa's salon. Not only had she brought uninvited guests, but she had also expected Zio Alonzo to put them all up in the castello. The woman was militant about her boundaries but felt no compunction about adhering to anyone else's.

"Well," said Ama, slipping her arm through Renata's and guiding her forward, "turn the other cheek and be the bigger woman, for it shall serve you well in your future role. As 'La Contessa della regione,' there will be many wagging tongues, biting even, and you must learn to act more like the pelican from which your new family takes its name."

Renata raised an eyebrow at the soprano. "How so?"

"When Placido took me to see the aviary, he explained that the pelican's large bill is used to gather food and store water. However, for the family, the bill represents a token of a unique aptitude for gathering important ideas and information."

"I see." Renata nodded nonchalantly and tried not to show her surprise that Placido had spent time with the songbird. Alone. All while the whole house had been looking for him. "Is there more?"

"When pelicans fly, they do so in the form of the letter *V*, each bird knowing its place in the greater whole of the colony. These aerialists are adept at soaring and gliding throughout their journey, whether long or short. There are legendary stories about these winged wanderers and their great sacrifices for their children and families, ensuring they are always properly cared for and protected. In some areas of the world, pelicans are renowned for their ability to control storms."

Renata waved to her mother, who had turned to look for her, and then returned to the conversation. "Goodness, Ama, you learned all this from one visit to the aviary?"

"Why, yes! I had never seen these prehistoric-looking birds before and was curious about them. Are you not fascinated with them, too?"

Renata shrugged. "Fascinated? No. Intrigued? A little."

"Well, I suggest you reconsider because the man to whom you are affianced is transfixed by them. When Po—"

Renata coughed and apologized.

Amelia burst out laughing. "You have a deep, throaty grunt, just as a pelican

does when it wants to communicate or attract a mate."

Renata curled her fingers into her palm and squeezed. Here was another woman mocking her and telling her how to be. "You were saying…"

"Ah yes, when Po shared how the birds have been featured in many mythologies throughout history and how they have equally inspired writers and artists, I became as full of love for him, for *them*, the birds, I mean, as he does."

What had she said? How could Po do this? No. Renata had already let the baroness get under her skin. She would not allow another woman to add fuel to her outrage. But Ama had spent time with Po, and he never mentioned their time together. And Ama had said *love*. It was indeed just a slip of the tongue. Surely. The attraction she had seen between Ama and Alonzo at the battle had not been a figment of her imagination.

Having reached the castello, Renata was glad to untangle herself from Amelia and beg off once she spotted Eletta coming her way. Renata strode through the entrance and tapped her boots on the boot jacks near the door. Eletta came over just as Renata started at the bottom of the stairs. "Miss, I picked your jade green taffeta dress for dinner tonight."

Renata nodded. "That's fine, thank you." Renata picked up her skirts. "Eletta, have you seen Natalia? She was not at the naumachia."

"Yes, but ..."

Renata stopped and faced Eletta. "Yes, but what?"

"Well, I do not know if I should—" Eletta twisted her lips aside while looking at Mama and Papà retreating backs.

Renata leaned in, "I demand that you tell me whatever you know about Natalia. You will not get into trouble, I promise."

"I saw her coming out of Fumo's room before I left to come outside."

Renata's eyes widened. "Did she see you?"

"No, her back is all I saw, signorina, and I quickly hid in the alcove in the hallway before she turned around."

"Good. Very good." Renata removed her gloves and scarf and handed them to Eletta along with her cloak. "Anything else?"

"She was with another man. I think it was her husband, but perhaps it was another."

Renata sensed Eletta was too eager to engage in gossip rather than truth and stepped up her pace. She climbed the stairs two-by-two with Eletta hurrying after her. At the landing at the top of the stairs, Renata turned right and said, "Please go and fix my bath. I will be there in a moment."

"Yes, signorina." Eletta turned left, and as she turned, Renata thought she saw a smile spread ever-so-slowly across her maid's face.

ℰℭ

Renata strode down the hall to the men's wing. At Po's room, she pulled herself together, then knocked on the carved oaken door.

"Come in," he shouted.

She opened the door and then closed it behind her. As she entered his suite, he was in the tub behind an Oriental screen, and she looked away.

"I looked for my gray cravat, Bepi, but could not find the thing." He was splashing about and referring to her as his manservant. "Did you already move it to our new marital suite?"

She mumbled something. Unsatisfied, he repeated. "What did you do with it, Bepi? I want to wear it tonight."

Looking around the room, she was unsure what to do. She knew she should announce herself yet felt incapable of doing so.

"Never mind. I shall look for it myself."

Renata could hear him grunting, and she panicked. She ground out a low-toned "yes, sir," then grabbed a nearby towel. She unfurled it and held it up near the screen, frightened that Po would stand up and jump out of the tub to get it. She was not yet ready for that sight. There would be plenty of time for anatomical revelations tomorrow evening.

Right then, someone knocked on the door.

"Who is it?" asked Po, still slathering himself with soap. No response. "Bepi, go see who it is."

Renata froze, staring at the door. If she moved, Po would see her. If she did not, he would stand and grab the towel from her and not see her until then.

"Bepi? Good God, man! Do I have to do everything?"

Next thing Renata knew, Po had jumped up and grabbed the towel from her just as Ispettore Grasso and Zio Alonzo entered the room.

Chapter 32

"Renata!" shouted all three men at the same time.

Po hastily wrapped his lower half with the towel. He strode over to the bed and pulled on his robe over his half-naked body, letting the towel drop after he had covered himself.

"What is going on in here?" Zio Alonzo approached Renata, who had turned away from Po and stood near the window.

"I came in here to have a word with Placido before dinner, and he was, er—"

"In flagrante." The inspector's brows were knitted together, and his mustache twitched.

"Your parents and I, Amelia, the Baronessa di Calandro, and all your guests expect you in the salon before dinner." Alonzo waved his arm in the direction of the downstairs salon. "With all the, uh, troubles we have had, I asked the inspector to help me find you, boy. You were gone for days, came home, and disappeared again. The policeman wanted to ask you some questions. As for you, Renata…" He walked over to the window where Renata was standing. "Grasso insisted I accompany him to your room. Eletta said she has been waiting for you for some time. My dear, how long have you been in Placido's rooms?"

"Not long, Zio Alonzo, and I swear, nothing improper happened." She looked at Po, and he nodded at her. "I do not mean to cause anxiety or to keep everyone waiting, but I must speak to Placido alone. It will be but a moment."

"This is most irregular," said Ispettore Grasso, his eyes narrowing.

"Seeing my fiancée alone is none of your concern," Po growled at the inspector. He stretched his neck to give the illusion that he was taller than he was and then pointed at his uncle and the inspector. "Please leave, both of you, and give us some time to talk."

The two men left, but not before Zio Alonzo looked at Renata and Po and said *behave*. Alonzo left the room first, but when the inspector reached the door, he paused and turned to address Renata. "Please see me when you are, er, done here. Before you go into dinner."

The door closed, and neither the bride nor the bridegroom moved. An eternity passed before Renata chanced a sidelong glance at Po. The glow of the gaslights cast his jaw, chest, and legs in tender shades of ochre marble, like those of a smooth sculpture that begged to be stroked. And in that moment, that is what she wanted most. To touch him. To feel his skin ripple beneath her fingers. To sense his muscles harden. Her anger, her jealousy, her disappointment—all dissolved.

She did not hear him repeat her name until he walked across the room and stood inches away. She broke her stare and directed her gaze to the wall behind him. Of all the paintings he could have hung, it had to be a nude one of Bacchus looking adoringly at Ariadne. Its provocativeness caused Renata to be even more flustered. It was almost as sensual as the painting she had bought Po as a wedding present.

Renata dared to turn her attention back to her beloved. "Yes?" Her voice rose at the end of the word.

"I did not ask a question," he said softly. "I was merely calling your name. I wonder what or who was distracting you?"

She blushed and looked down at her shoes.

"Dostoyevsky once said, 'Beauty will save the world.'" He traced his finger down her cheek and rested it on her lips. He moved his finger to her bottom lip, and it quivered.

"Wh-why would you say that?" The tremor in her lips triggered a full-body shiver. He was a hair's breadth away from her. The shiver turned into a song in her head that she hoped he could hear.

"Because mi amore," he took her face in his hands. "amidst the chaos and suffering in the world, beauty holds the power to inspire, transform, and save."

Renata sucked in a breath, unsure what to say. She had wanted to hear him flatter her and shower her with poetry *after* their ordeal was done. There was so much to talk about. She not only wanted to know where he had been for part of the naumachia when she had lost track of him, but she wanted to warn him a killer was still on the loose. She was loathe to bring up the dark when all she was feeling, finally feeling, was light. Hers. His. Theirs.

"My darling, your inner beauty has held me in its thrall—when I was studying at university, during my military training, when I served in Africa, and especially so these past few days while I have been kept from you. You gave me hope, and I could not have lived without it."

She found her voice and began. "I apologize that I doubted you and your love for me. I can see it in your eyes. It is unmistakable. I know you were missing a few days, yet I needed that mirror of truth. Now and always."

"Amore, amore, amore." He buried his face in her hair and then pulled back. "I am sorry I put you through so much leading up to our special day. I should not have treated it like a game nor expected you to go through it alone or, er, leaning on others without proper answers from me."

"No, you should not have." She said this part quietly but without wavering her gaze or the strength of her voice.

He held her hands. "In these situations, where working clandestinely is paramount to maintaining safety and sanity, code is what I know best. Protecting Vito and Mariana put me back in the African jungle where every day was a struggle to stay alive. I was doing it for all of us. As a civilian, I must improve my communication skills in difficult situations and not revert to my military training."

She knew he referred to Ispettore Grasso when he referred to "leaning on others," but she did not want to mention the inspector's name—not while she and Po were patching things up. His presence stirred something unbidden in her. All that she had wanted to discuss, all the case details, his absence, Vito and Mariana, just … disappeared. The most important thing was what was happening in this room between them, and she wanted to be present for all of it.

"Renata, you were *and are* a brave, strong, and resilient woman. I believe you always will be. I hope we will be all that and more to each other, forever, come what may."

She took his hands from her face and squeezed them. "Me, too, my love."

He searched her face as if memorizing every beauty mark, curve, and pore. And then he kissed her. Deeply. Hungrily. At last, they came up for air.

He touched his forehead to hers. "Never again shall we be parted."

"And never again shall we let doubts come between us." She wanted to add "and others" but left that out.

Chapter 33

Renata stood poised at the top of the stairs and smoothed her dress. Eletta had chosen a taffeta in jade green, the traditional color for an Italian bride to wear at the rehearsal dinner. It was a sign of good luck and good fortune for a long life ahead. She caught herself in the ornate gilt mirror at the end of the corridor and tried but failed to keep from blushing. She had finally been alone with Po, and his warm kiss had sealed him to her forever.

Things made sense to her now, and though she disagreed with his methods, she had to concede that they had kept Vito, Mariana, and the baby safe. She could have used stronger assurances of his plan and love these past few days, though she knew now that she would never doubt him or his feelings again.

Po told her that he and Fumo had gotten into a one-on-one altercation behind one of the ships, just as she had suspected. He believed Fumo's temper had gotten the better of him these last few days with the "death" and mourning of Vito.

Also, the fact that Po himself had been missing for days had left Fumo fumbling for answers to everyone's questions, fueling his already short fuse. He claimed he was an aggrieved friend who wanted to offer Mariana his condolences. He accused Po of keeping her from the family, though Po explained that he had fibbed and told him that he had sequestered Mariana in a convent as she had asked and had been tending to her while she grieved.

Renata lost track of how many lies and half-truths Po had been spinning. Sighing, she fixed an earring escaping her ear and headed down the grand staircase. As she came around the bend, Ispettore Grasso stood there with another policeman tapping a baton on his open palm.

Renata gasped. "What is the meaning—"

The policeman rushed forward and clapped his hand over her mouth, dragging her to an open door.

The inspector followed behind and, in what sounded like a sing-song voice, said, "You are under arrest for the murder of Brizio. Come with us to the dungeon."

℣

Carved from ancient stone, the dungeon's corridors wound unpredictably, creating a labyrinthine maze that disoriented and confused Renata. The passageway was so narrow that Renata and the men needed help to pass side by side. Torches flickered sporadically, casting eerie shadows that danced along the walls. Darkness and despair hung in the air, and the weight of centuries-old secrets and suffering echoed off the walls.

Shivers crawled down Renata's spine. She could almost hear the screams and moans and guttural cries of previous prisoners. Soon, her desperate utterances would join the ghostly voices of those trapped before her.

"Come on, keep up." The policeman had not cuffed her, but his grip on her arm was unrelenting and unnecessarily painful.

Four iron-barred cells lined the walls, each bearing the marks of countless lodgers who had no doubt languished within their confines. Rust clung to the bars, evidence of the dungeon's neglect. Some cells were empty, their occupants long forgotten, while others still held remnants of their former inhabitants: straw strewn across the floor, torn clothes along a worn bench, chains hanging from the walls, and etchings carved into the stone—silent testaments to the despair and longing for freedom.

"This one will do, Damiani,"

They had reached the end of the row, and the policeman thrust Renata into a corner chamber. She stumbled but grabbed hold of the hanging chain to steady herself. The policeman closed the cell door, and the inspector locked it. He nodded to the policeman, walked away, and left the inspector alone with Renata.

Renata rushed to the door. With one hand, she grabbed a cold cell bar and, with the other, the inspector's coat. She wailed, "Why am I here?"

He swatted her hand away. "You were the last person to see Brizio alive. No one else witnessed you killing him. And as a rich noblewoman, you thought you could get away with killing a commoner. What did he have on you, hmmm?"

Renata shook her head vigorously. "How can you prove I did anything? Do you honestly believe I could or, more importantly, *would* loosen screws on a scaffolding that men were using to touch up a ceiling in a room where my wedding reception was to take place? Why would I sabotage my wedding? Or hurt people that will eventually work for me?"

"I think a jury," said Ispettore Grasso, pacing in front her an arm's length away, "as Mancini called it, that 'palladium of public liberties,' might see it otherwise."

"How so?" Renata slapped her right calf after sensing a bug crawling up her leg.

He laughed. "I will let you stew on that while I finish my report."

"No, Giorgio. Noooooooooo. Please. I beg you. You are making a big mistake. I am innocent. You are doing this to punish me."

He ignored her and turned to leave. "The torch should last another hour before you are plunged into black and the starving rats begin their feeding frenzy."

"You unfeeling, lowly brute. People are expecting me at dinner, including my fiancé. He and others will come looking for me." Her shrill voice was already raw, but she tried one more time. "What will you tell them?

"Nothing. I am going out the back. No one will know I was here." He swung the key, and it hit its ring repeatedly as he walked out of the dungeon.

Her mouth hung open, bereft of words. Then a few came—not on her tongue, but in her mind's eye. The frame was blank until the phrases rhythmically rolled across the space like a teacher's cursive writing on a blackboard.

Tomorrow, I am going to be wed. Or will I?

Ꝏ

Her voice had abandoned her hours ago, but her mind was still working on the case. She was holding onto her sanity by a thread, and she was not going to let what that barbarian of an inspector had done to her shred it any further than it already was. Her pacing had displaced much of the straw and revealed the cracks in the floor through which, she imagined with disgust, the rats would crawl through at any moment and gnaw at her. Awake or asleep, they would find her and chew her down to her marrow.

She shivered in the dimming glow of the torch. The dampness and decay in the air mingled with the faint odor of mold and mildew. She tamped down the nausea that was rising in her. Water dripped steadily from unseen sources, forming puddles on the uneven stone floor. Her hands and arms were tired from holding up her skirts to prevent them from dragging through the wetness. She slumped onto the bench and rubbed her arms to warm herself.

With a weary resignation, Renata looked around her cell.

Chains hung not only from the wall but from the ceiling, too, their ends disappearing into the darkness above, while instruments of torture lay scattered across the floor from her cell, their twisted metal grotesquely gleaming in the dim light. These devices were relics of a bygone era when cruelty and suffering were commonplace. Things, awful things, had happened in these rooms—carried out by Pelicani ancestors. Is this what the woman in la baronessa's salon was trying to warn her about?

In the deepest recesses of the dungeon, in the castello's underbelly, hidden away from prying eyes, true horror awaited Renata. She was alone in a strange place with no one by her side—the ultimate torture. The anguish of her loneliness and fear was catching up with her. Deep in her bones and heart veins, she knew this place would linger in her dreams and haunt her forever, even if she managed to escape.

She imagined the most awful, blood-curdling scream she could muster rising from her throat. Consumed by the hurt and anguish of these past few days, she would let it all out, and she did. Long, gut-wrenching, and complete.

And when no one acknowledged her suffering, she summoned that same strength from earlier. The one that had helped her shift her perspective. She waited. She closed her eyes and waited for it to fill her up. Filled to bursting, her eyelids flashed open, and a sense of calm washed over her. She saw the words in her mind's eye, and then they formed on her lips.

"You will not be bested. You will not."

She continued with the refrain until even her whisper was no longer a whisper. She leaned against the wall. All the while, the damp, near-frozen walls seeped into and numbed her skin. She lay on the bench and tried to stay awake, thinking through her suspects list.

Who had she left off?

Who had she dismissed too soon?

And then it hit her.

Chapter 34

"Will you ever forgive me?"

Renata kept her eyes closed. She knew she was not dreaming but did not want to awaken either. Her imagination played tricks on her because she could have sworn she recognized that voice. It sounded disembodied initially, though that could have been because of that state between sleep and awake. Then, the voice came into its own. Or maybe she had. The next time she heard it, there was no mistaking who was talking to her. Indeed, Inspector Grasso was her alarm clock.

"Will you ever forgive me, Renata dear?" he repeated. "I saw red when no other suspects made sense, and you were an easy mark. I do apologize for my temper and incorrect judgment. I am wholly out of character to act in this brusque manner."

The voice was louder and closer, next to her ear, and someone gently shook her.

"Will you ever forgive me, pleeeeeease, Signorina Bombonatti?"

Today, the man had manners.

Her right eyelid fluttered open. His left eyeball and a flaming torch were inches from her face. She sat up in a flash. "Get away from me, you brute, and move that torch away. What time is it?"

"Sì, scusi." He apologized and affixed the torch to a wall mount before standing before her. "Around midnight."

She rubbed her eyes and looked at him. His eyes darted back and forth and sweat beaded his brow. She was suddenly conscious of him leaning over her. At some point in the night, she had unpinned her long hair and pulled it from the back of her head to cover the revealing décolleté of her evening gown. Renata had tried picking the cell lock with one of her hairpins to no avail.

A glance at the open cell door and her heart leaped. No second policeman. She could bolt. If the inspector caught her, she could bite him, poke his eye with her hairpin, and then escape. Calming herself, she decided to take advantage of the current state of things another way.

"You are back, Grasso, and begging for forgiveness. Well, I am not granting it. Not now, not ever."

The inspector winced, then said, "Begging is a strong word, Signorina Bombonatti. I came to, uh, check to see that you were—"

"Still here? Well, I am, no thanks to you and your ignorance, nay, vengeance." She pushed him away, and he stumbled back. "I suspect you have someone in custody; otherwise, I think you would have left me here to rot indefinitely, yes?"

"Not custody, no, because, er, well, signorina ..."

Renata was re-pinning her hair. She did not have a mirror to style it, so she piled it high at the crown with soft waves on the sides and back. Finished, she said, "Because he's dead?"

"The one set of fingerprints I did not have was Brizio's. I managed to get them, and they match the bloody thumbprint on the note you found on the scaffolding."

She shook her head, "Brizio's knife was bloody, but I do not recall seeing blood on his hand. Besides, he did not push Vito off the tower."

The inspector pulled his shoulders back. "Oh?"

"The person who did is connected to the one who loosened the screws of the scaffolding."

"How can you be sure?" The inspector placed his forefinger on his chin. "I did not see such connections in your casebook."

"I only made them while being stuck in here." Renata waved her arm in a wide arc.

Ispettore Grasso stomped his foot and raised a fist in the air. "Who is it? I will arrest them now!"

"Oh no, you must wait and do it tomorrow morning for all to see." Renata stood and brushed the errant straw off her soiled gown.

With his pencil poised in midair, he said, "Give me a name and how you deduced they are the culprit."

"Tommaso. He and Eletta have been having an affair. I overheard them arguing about how much he had already done for her, though he did nothing to fix her lease issues with the Marzanos. At first, I thought she was with Fumo because she had mentioned him a few times, though perhaps that was to throw me off the scent."

The inspector wrung his hands. "But where is the proof she was on the roof and pushed Signor Marzano off it?"

"Vito and the footman described an unrecognizable figure on the roof as "wiry." Eletta described herself this way when she had an accident with a tray at her shop. I believe she went undetected on the roof because she was in costume, like the others, and it must have been Tommaso who had got it for her. I made the connection here while I had time to think but not move."

"Ahhh." His cheeks flushed, and he busied himself, pulling out his notebook to hide his embarrassment. "Well, you are not the only one with revelations. I had already determined that it was Tommaso who rigged the scaffolding. I believe he was not expecting Brizio to be with you when you reached for the note."

"You may be right, ispettore. I know Brizio was surprised to see me."

"Tommaso arrived in the ballroom shortly after you left. His first question was whether you were involved or hurt in any way. He appeared to be grateful you were spared, yet I think he was putting on an act. He was visibly angry at Brizio's death, which seems out of character. His entire demeanor was suspect."

"So he *had* intended for me to die." Renata swallowed a lump in her throat.

"Yes. Fortunately, your guardian angel protected you, and you are still with us. However, it means that I must speak to Signor Pelicani at once and inform him his nephew is going to jail, as is his maid Eletta."

"I suggest you wait until morning, Inspector. Post a man outside the men's wing and another outside the women's wing. Arrest the Tommaso and Eletta in the morning before they try to slip away."

"Very well, signorina. It looks like it is going to be a fitful night."

"Indeed, though I must try to get some sleep. A bride should be well-rested before her wedding day. It is all your fault that I missed dinner, the entertainment, and the opening of Christmas gifts. There will be a furor when I am discovered in the morning. Rather than blame you and ruin your reputation, I will claim to have gotten trapped behind an old door that locked me in, and you found me."

The policeman took a deep breath and sighed. He straightened his shoulders and nodded. "Thank you, Signorina Bombonatti. Again, I apologize for the trouble I put you through. What can I do to make it up to you?"

She looked down her nose at him. "I have also given this much thought. There will be a time when I will come to collect payment and you will brook no argument. Now, will you kindly escort me to my room?"

"Of course. Lead the way."

"If you wish, because it is late and the snow will make it difficult to get back to your pensione, you can probably find an empty room in the servant's wing where you can stay overnight. In the morning, speak to Martell, and he will send someone to the pensione to fetch whatever you need."

"Yes, signorina. Now let us get you to your room."

"Ah ha! Nothing is happening between you two, eh? Going to your *room*, you say."

Placido had jumped in front of them, and the inspector reared back, almost knocking Renata to the ground.

247

"Hey! Stop! Listen!" Inspector Grasso was blocking the blows Placido was raining on him.

Renata screamed to cut through the commotion. The men halted their scuffle immediately, and she separated them to put some space between them.

"Listen, Po, the Inspector made a huge mistake putting me here, and yet, I forgave him. That's all you need to know about that. Then I asked him to *accompany* me to my room, not *enter* it."

"Hmmpf." He wiped the saliva off his face with the back of his hand.

"It is late, and I need my beauty sleep. You will be pleased that I have solved the case of who pushed Vito, and the inspector knows who attempted to kill Brizio. The three of us can reveal it all at the wedding breakfast tomorrow. You can share in our glory."

He took a step forward. "But how—"

"Stop." She put her hand against his chest. "Amore, your questions can wait. The inspector will explain more in the morning, but I will fill you in on the basics on the way to my room. Let's go before I change my mind."

Chapter 35

On Christmas Eve, Renata woke to a ray of sun streaming through the leaded glass window and warming her left cheek. She opened her eyes and squinted at her wedding dress hanging on the front of the wardrobe. She pulled back the duvet, rubbed her eyes, and walked to her dress, bathed in sunlight.

Pearl beads were sewn into a large heart shape on the lace-covered bodice, while a string of smaller hearts lined up like sentinels from the top to the bottom of the sleeve. A layer of Burano lace covered the silky underdress, and both fabrics hit just below the ankle, creating a small puddle at the back.

Much to Mama's chagrin, she had decided against a train, but she got back into Mama's good graces when she chose to wear her grandmother's veil. Nonna's veil was twice the length of the dress and would trail behind her as she walked down the aisle of the Pelicani chapel on Papà's arm.

Eletta had laid out the new peach-colored corset, matching bloomers, and silk stockings on the overstuffed armchair near the now-cold fireplace. Renata ran her fingers over them, a heat rising in her cheeks that she could not blame on the sun. Tonight, for the first time, her husband Po would see her in her lingerie and undress her. Renata sat at her dressing table and let a warmth envelope her body as she imagined Po's hands and lips all over her.

Their talk last night and the long kiss that followed cleared the air and brought them back to the closeness they had had before she arrived four days ago. She felt compelled to give him the personalized cuff links to wear on their wedding day, and he ran to his rooms to find the bracelet he had commissioned and gave it to her. He had the back of the diamond-bar bracelet engraved: *mio cuore e mia anima.* The same heart and soul sentiment she had put on his cufflinks. Their love was destiny.

The chaos of the last few days had driven them too far apart, and they both vowed that nothing would drive a wedge between them ever again. That had sat right with Renata, especially after she and Po had reconciled despite the debacle in the dungeon. He had escorted her to her room, and she had fallen asleep with an ease of mind and body that she had not felt in some time. Her only regret was that she had not asked him about Palomina. The timing was off. Her questions about the waif would keep for another day.

A knock at the door jarred her thoughts. "Come in."

"Good morning, signorina."

Eletta entered with three other maids carrying buckets of hot water, which they poured into the tub.

"Good morning, Eletta," she replied. Renata thanked the other girls as they left to fetch more water. Eletta uncorked a miniature bottle of the renowned local scented oil, emptying the aromatic liquid into the water.

When she was done, Eletta came to Renata, her fingers contorting. "I am glad to see you here. We were not sure what happened to you last night. Your parents, not to mention your fiancé, were very worried, but the inspector said that you were working on a surprise for your wedding day and that we were all supposed to stay away."

Ah, he had not told her that. It was a good enough excuse, and it sounded like everyone bought it. She would not have to use her lame one. "Yes, quite right. A big surprise. And no one came looking for me?" Renata held her breath.

"No one that I know."

Renata exhaled and moved away from her wedding gown, not wanting to look at Eletta and give away what she knew was coming to the girl. Renata stood near the window with her back to Eletta and looked over the snow-laden glaciarium where Po's team had roundly beaten his brothers' team last night. Beyond it, she spied the bent torch mount that had caught Vito's tunic when he fell and landed on the laurel tree that broke his fall. Behind the tower were the barns, stables, and the pelican pen.

She moved closer to the window to gaze further afield to where Arquà Petrarca lay where she had encountered Fumo. Her roving eyes surveyed the estate, and she gulped, realizing that the people tied to the land would be hers and Po's to manage and govern over one day.

"Signorina, is everything all right?" Eletta stood next to the tub, jug in hand, an inquiring look on her face.

"Oh yes, yes. Excuse me." Renata turned behind the painted screen to relieve herself before bathing and dressing for breakfast.

꩜

Ding, ding, ding.

Zio Alonzo rose from the breakfast table, a glass of Prosecco in his hand and a spoon in the other where he had tapped the glass. The guests quieted, and he began.

"Welcome everyone to Ca' Peli. Thank you for joining me, Sandro, and Colombina Bombonatti as we celebrate the joining of our two families. To Placido and Renata, may you live long, happy, prosperous, and child-blessed lives. Salute!"

The guests joined in the toast with three rounds of *salute* until Ispettore Grasso appeared next to Zio Alonzo.

"Before you start your breakfast, the inspector would like to say a few words. Ispettore Grasso, please proceed."

"Buongiorno, everyone. I would also like to congratulate the happy couple and hope they live joyfully, trouble-free lives."

Everyone clapped.

"I say trouble-free because this week of their wedding has been anything but." The inspector paused and scratched behind his ear.

"You see, unbeknownst to many of you, there has been miscommunication, misunderstanding, distance, and a host of other problems, including a serious accident and a premeditated murder."

The table erupted, and people turned to one another to find out what they knew.

"Please, could I have your complete attention for a few moments? All will be revealed." The chatter died down. "As these two betrothed head to the altar today and then leave the chapel to begin their new life as husband and wife, let us help them start fresh. Signor Placido and Signorina Bombonatti, please come to the head of the table and share the news."

Renata and Placido flanked the inspector, and he began again.

"Some of you may know that a few days ago, atop the roof of the castello's tower, the groomsmen, some footmen, and all the Pelicani brothers practiced the tableau vivant you will see tonight. During this rehearsal, Signor Marzano claims he was deliberately pushed off the tower and headed for certain death. To his good fortune, his tunic caught on a torch mount, and he was saved except for some severe bruising and a broken arm when he fell further, and a laurel tree broke his fall."

Vito held up his right arm in a sling. Appropriate murmurs reverberated around the room.

"Signor Marzano was convinced his fall was no accident but attempted murder instead."

Gasps filled the room. The inspector held up a hand, and the room quieted again.

"As such, he was so afraid that the villain would track him down and try again that he enlisted the help of the castello's groundskeeper and Signor Placido Pelicani himself. He asked for protection for himself and his wife and that they be hidden until the perpetrator had been found and arrested or until the wedding day, whichever came first.

Placido, his manservant Bepi, and Signor Marzano's manservant took turns in shifts to protect this growing family."

A few guests politely smiled at Mariana, who put a protective hand over her swollen belly. The rest of the guests' eyes were glued to the front of the table.

The policeman continued to pontificate. "A few days ago, Signor Alonzo Pelicani summoned me here to investigate and root out this perpetrator. Before I could do so, another accident occurred with the scaffolding in the ballroom. It collapsed on the construction foreman and killed him instantly."

The guests were all a-twitter again, and the inspector asked for silence. "Please let me finish."

"When I inspected it, it looked like the scaffolding incident was planned. After further investigation, we learned that the man who is responsible for tightening all the screws at the end of each workday had not done so."

A string of "oh my" and "oh dear" raced around the table.

"Silence. Please. The faster I finish this, the faster the delicious food that is warming over on that console table will be served to you."

"The revelation of a true accident had us back to the first incident. By taking Signor Marzano at his word, we interviewed everyone, some multiple times, and fingerprinted them. For most of the interviews, we used the traditional interview method of our esteemed Padua police force, yet it yielded nothing."

"Nothing?" said Mama, but when the Inspector narrowed his eyes at her, she apologized. "Scusi, please continue, Ispettore Grasso."

He pulled his shoulders back. "You might be wondering what evidence we found that offered a solution to the crime of attempted murder. Well, a strange combination of *un*traditional interview methods, regular conversation, lots of observation and physical legwork, notetaking, arguments, perseverance, some luck, and the nose of a bloodhound."

The room erupted in laughter, then died down as they all anticipated the big reveal.

"Officer Damiani and Officer Verga," thundered Ispettore Grasso, "please bring in the villainous duo responsible for the attempted murder of Vito Marzano and the murder of Brizio."

The officers entered the breakfast room, gripping the arms of a handcuffed and struggling Tommaso and Eletta.

Signor Alonzo hung his head at seeing his nephew in handcuffs.

"These two, Tommaso Pelicani and Eletta Bianca, were in cahoots together. One was jealous of Signor Placido—his inheritance, his fiancée, and Vito for being chosen as the best man. The other villain was a non-paying, rude tenant who was woefully behind on her rent and claimed she had an ironclad lifetime lease. The plot came together when these two learned of one another's grievances, thickened when they fell into one another's beds, but ultimately fell apart when they were found out."

Several "boos" were hurled.

"Signorina Bianca wanted a lifetime lease from Signor Marzano for her dress shop. When she did not get what she wanted, revenge was the only payment she would accept. Tommaso wanted to be the best man. The only way to achieve his goal was to secure the premature death of Signor Marzano.

"With their mutual goal set, Signor Tommaso got to work. Signor Tommaso convinced the tableau players to flex their machismo atop the castello's tower as the venue for the rehearsal. Anyone who disagreed was ridiculed. He secured a costume and mask for Signorina Bianca so she would not be recognized when attending the tableau vivant rehearsal.

"Signor Tommaso paired her up with Signor Marzano on the roof. She managed to maneuver their fight ever closer to the crenel until there was nowhere else to go but down. And when Signor Marzano did go down, thanks to a nudge from her sword, Signorina Bianca was the first off the tower, never to be seen again. She and her lover used all manner of trickery to deflect suspicion, but they failed."

Renata looked at Placido and grabbed his hand to stop him from clenching it.

The policeman intoned. "These criminals will be spending a lifetime behind bars atoning for—"

Eletta and Tommaso fought to escape, and several male wedding guests jumped up to help the officers subdue them.

"Show us some compassion, signorina," begged Eletta.

"Yes, show us true Christmas spirit, Po," wailed Tommaso.

Renata suppressed a laugh. "Those who do not embody the Christmas spirit do not deserve to experience it."

"Well said, mi amore." Placido leaned behind the inspector and motioned for Renata to meet him there for a kiss.

"All right, you two. I see you cannot wait until you are before a priest." Ispettore Grasso shook his head and chuckled. "Officers, please take the prisoners away, put them in the police wagon, and wait for me there."

The room exploded with spontaneous applause. The inspector allowed it and then hushed everyone.

"I shall conclude with this." He adjusted his cap and raised himself on his tiptoes. "You all heard me say 'we' throughout my speech. 'We' is a word that means 'two or more people.' The criminals failed, plain and simple, because of the power of the Bombonatti intellect and the Pelicanis' resourcefulness." He turned to the betrothed couple. "The police are very grateful to you, Signorina Bombonatti, and you, Signor Placido, for your enormous assistance in the case."

Renata looked over at Po. She saw him say, "I am so proud of you, my crime-solving contessa."

He said contessa, not contessina, and a warming sensation radiated through her.

Chapter 36

A maid was wielding a buttonhook like an expert as she finished buttoning up Renata's boots when a knock at the door halted her progress.

"Who is it?" Renata called out, and her parents entered.

The maid finished with the boots and moved to put away the hook. Renata's father held out his hands to Renata as he approached. She stood, and then he kissed her on each cheek and embraced her.

"My dear, you are a vision, more beautiful than I have ever seen you look."

"Thank you, Papà. Glad you approve." She twirled and curtseyed, and both her parents clapped their hands.

"Your twirl reminded me of another time. Do you recall when you were dressed in armor and announced you were ready for the Castle of Love?"

Renata laughed. "Yes."

"Back then, you were headed for Padua's grandest event of the year, though your garments were not so fine. I dare say your wedding today is not only the city's and countryside's grandest event but maybe for the whole of the Veneto, too."

"And for at least the next decade," scoffed Mama, "no other wedding shall match the importance of this union."

"That's quite a proclamation, Papà and Mama." Renata teased them. "Do you have a crystal ball so accurate it can foretell such grandiose promises so far into the future?"

"Certo." Papà winked, and she shook her head.

"All right, you two. That is enough nonsense on such a grand day. Now, maid, please fasten every button on the signorina's dress. You missed a couple of loops." Renata's mother motioned for the maid to attend to Renata, and the girl did as she was bid, beckoning Renata to sit at her dressing table. "We cannot have the soon-to-be contessina half-dressed before the priest!"

"Perhaps he might enjoy it," said Renata, winking.

"Renata! You are incorrigible." Mama shook her fan at Renata. "Stop that kind of talk at once."

After the maid was finished, Mama came over. "Now, before you put your veil on, I want to give you this." Mama handed Renata a bronze velour box. "I have worn this several times, sometimes in parts. Two of the pieces can be reworked into earrings."

Renata opened the box. A ring of diamond brooches of different sizes and patterns were arrayed inside. "Oh, Mama."

"This jewel was given to me by Princess Milena of Montenegro when I wed your father. The piece is called a traîne de corsage, a mix of several brooches often clipped together and draped over the neckline of a dress or into the hair. I think between the maid and me, we can do wonders with putting some sparkle into your hair."

The maid oohed and aahed at the glittering set. "Which one would you like to add first, signorina?"

"See here," said Mama, picking up one enormous brooch and showing the girl, "depending on how they are grouped, the brooches can look like a garland of flowers because the design includes wild roses, leaves, and buds created in an array of differently cut diamonds."

"I see what you mean, signora." The maid took the proffered brooch and clipped it to Renata's hair. She had elaborately curled Renata's thick hair and piled it up high atop Renata's crown in tight coils and curls with a fringe over the forehead. The maid tucked a few more brooches below so they trailed down to the nape of Renata's neck. "There, signorina. Let me get the hand mirror."

Renata turned her head this way in front of the big mirror, then adjusted the hand mirror. She loved seeing all the diamonds tucked into her coiled hair. "A mane of magic. It makes me feel like a princess,

Mama. Thank you. This may be the best my hair has looked this week."

The maid blushed and put away the jewelry box.

Mama leaned down and kissed Renata's forehead. "Likely, you will receive a tiara from your husband's family when you become Contessa di Sica, though Alonzo may have something for you now as la contessina. I have no such extravagance, but I think you will find this set quite versatile."

Renata searched Mama's eyes. "I am sure I will. Are you certain you do not want it back after the wedding?"

"Once we have recovered our, er, recent losses, I shall use its absence as a reason for why your father needs to buy me some new sparkly thing." Mama patted her hair under her enormous, feathered hat. "Or I might lean toward a modern trend with something enamel from Giuliano. His jewelry is all my friends talk about, though not always in a complimentary manner."

"Mama, you are too much. I shall have to powder my face three times if you keep me in laughing tears." Renata dabbed a pink puff into a round box, then powdered her nose and cheeks. After finishing her toilette, Renata put her hand on her hip and tilted her head at Mama. "Am I acceptable?"

"Indeed, you are." Mama beamed. "Well, if you are finished and sure you are *ready ...*" Mama cleared her throat several times and winked at Renata. "Let's not keep your handsome groom waiting."

The winking and "ready" was Mama's way of asking if she was prepared for her marital duties. Renata blushed and nodded.

"I am sure your father has something he wants to say before you head down, so I will see you downstairs. Do not dawdle. It is bad form for the future contessa to keep her subjects waiting ..." Her voice trailed off as she left the room.

Subjects? thought Renata. Where does Mama get these notions?

"Will that be all, signorina?" The maid adjusted Renata's nightgown on her arm. "I shall take this to the laundry, then meet you at the chapel entrance. Your carriage is already at the front door."

"Thank you. We shall be down in a minute."

"Very good." The maid turned and hurried out of the room.

Renata watched her go, and a lump formed in her throat. She shook it off and then inspected herself in front of the mirror. Papà walked over to stand behind Renata. He placed his hands on her shoulders and squeezed them. "You are marrying a good man from a good family, one of the best in these parts. Your mother and I could not be more pleased. We are blessed that you chose so well."

Renata raised her eyebrows. "I know mother wanted me to marry royalty, but—"

He gave her shoulders another squeeze. "Hush, child. I meant what I said."

"Papà, do not keep your troubles from me again." Renata frowned at her father's reflection, reached up, and patted his hands. "I am a woman who is about to marry. I can face these adult situations without shirking from them. Whatever happens, Placido and I will help you. You know that, right?"

He kissed her head. "You are a true blessing. We have nothing to worry about now. Andiamo!" He circled his index finger above his head, his sign for *let's go*.

Chapter 37

"Whoa there." The driver reined in the horses to slow them and then pulled up to the chapel's front door.

Renata looked down at her bouquet—a mix of white roses and camellias with pinecones and cypress twigs tucked in. She tweaked the seeded eucalyptus but stopped in her tracks. Peeking out beneath the budding holly, the only hint of red in the arrangement was a note. Not today of all days. She could not take another troubling message.

She looked at her father, who was busy fiddling with his cufflink. Her fingers shook as she hurriedly pulled the card from the envelope and read:

Se so cos'è l'amore, è grazie a te

If I know what love is, it is because of you

Smelling a trace of his cologne on it, Renata kissed the card and then tucked it inside her dress. How sweet of Placido. He had signed the card in a most elegant hand. Even if he had not done so, she would not have doubted *this* message came from him.

"Ready, daughter?" said Papà.

Renata looked out the coach's window. Mama stood to the left of the fir and holly-laden archway, and Renata waved at her. Then, she turned to Papà. "I could not be more ready."

Renata grabbed the strap above her. The coach jostled as the coachman jumped off the back and approached the side door. He opened it and then pulled down the folding stairs. Papà stepped out first and held his hand out to help Renata.

Mama held the veil aloft, and the three entered the chapel. They stood in the vestibule and waited for the music to accompany Renata down the aisle. As a maid arranged the veil behind her mistress, Renata looked over at the far end of the room, where a log and sawblade lay in wait.

Po had yet to tell Renata that he wanted them to do this. She was surprised yet glad he was observing the ancient ways—another reason she loved him. Her heart danced, and she put a hand over it. She closed her eyes and pictured Po standing at the altar, his heart beating in rhythm with hers. Once she was satisfied their hearts were simpatico—in her mind anyway—she opened her eyes.

The first bars of the new romantic melody, O Sole Mio, wafted through the vestibule doors.

Che bella cosa, 'na giornata 'e sole

n 'aria serena doppo na tempesta!

What a beautiful thing a sunny day is!
The air is serene after a storm.

…

"Ma un altro sole, più bello c'è

O ragazza, il sole mio, sta in fronte a te"

But there is another sun, more beautiful
O girl, my sun is in front of you

…

Renata recited the words in her head. It was a perfect song for a perfect day. She took a deep breath and linked one arm with Papà's arm and the other with Mama's.

"Open the doors," she nodded to the usher. "My beloved awaits."

The congregation turned to the door where Renata stood with her parents. She could see the shock on everyone's faces as the three of them strode slowly down the aisle. Mama had protested outside, but

Renata insisted on her accompanying her. The further they progressed, the more the shock on people's faces became smiles.

The entire village was here—bedecked in top hats and feather concoctions, woolen coats and gloves, and fur-lined muffs and capes gracing the bodies of the chilly guests. Free-standing candelabra lined the outer reaches of the nave, engulfing the church in soft golden light. The ends of the pews were lavishly decorated. They alternated with either holly berries on evergreens or grape vines atop white netting.

As Renata and her parents walked, their feet released the sweet, grassy aroma of the grape leaves strewn on the floor. The village maintained a few old pagan traditions, and owing to their heart-health benefits, it was thought that the bride and groom would enjoy a long marriage if they walked on grape leaves to and from the altar. Months ago, Cook had been instructed to store bags of the leaves from harvest time and freeze them, anticipating this day.

Placido was facing forward and not watching her walk to him. Renata swallowed a lump in her throat. Why did he not look at her? A quiver began in her heart and wiggled up her throat, drying her mouth. She gulped.

Renata forced herself to calm down, glancing at the heavy, red-bowed baskets of holly and fir boughs lining the sanctuary's edge on either side of the altar. She squeezed her mother's arm tighter, knowing she had a hand in all the beauty before them. Her mother nodded but kept her head forward.

Nearing the base of the altar and the two blue plush stools situated before it stood Po and Vito. They both wore black cutaway coats with gray trousers. Po was not moving, so she could not see if he was sporting the cuff links she had given him last night, but she secretly hoped he was.

Tears formed. She lowered her head and then blinked to stop the water from pooling in her eyes. Renata raised her head, and Po turned. When he caught her gaze, he, too, had tears in his eyes.

Her parents took turns whispering congratulations to her through her veil. She heard Po thank them both, and then they went and sat in the front pew. He returned from accompanying them and then paused to take her in. She could not look at him, so she cast her eyes at the priest, then up at Jesus on the cross, and finally back at Po.

His smile reached his glassy eyes, pushing up his cheeks and making the corners of his eyes crinkle with crow's feet. He held out his hands, and she took them. Then he released her to grasp the lacy edges of her nonna's veil and gently lift it, leaning into whisper:

"Mi amore, per sempre."

My love, forever.

Chapter 38

Like a Boldini painting, the banquet hall was a gaggle of swan necks and radiantly powdered faces, a cornucopia of satin gloves and opulent fans, of graceful aloofness and elegant poise. Mustachioed men in tailored evening suits and gleaming spats exuded an air of refinement as they glided across the Christmas-themed dance floor.

The lively banter and clinking of Prosecco glasses halted when the doors swung open, and the blissful, newly wedded couple entered the room.

"Presenting … Signor Placido and Signorina Renata Pelicani, Conte and Contessina di Sica."

Martell announced the bride and groom and then stepped aside to let them enter the hall. Applause greeted them and reverberated off the lavishly decorated walls.

As they crossed the threshold, Placido lifted their clasped hands overhead while bowing his head toward his family, who raised their bubbly-filled flutes to them. Renata laughed and blushed at the three hundred guests filling the great room, and she soon chatted with everyone who passed through the receiving line. That is until Ispettore Grasso stood before her, the buttons on his uniform shining ever so much brighter than they had at breakfast.

"Surprised to see me?"

"Yes, a little," Renata admitted. "I gather Il conte Sica invited you?"

The inspector's chest puffed out. "He did, to thank me for all my efforts in solving the case."

Renata wanted to admonish the man. He knew very well that it had been a joint effort, and she tried to remind him that he had said as much at his speech earlier that morning. He was back to his old ways.

Sigh. She knew this was neither the time nor place to point out her contributions *again* or how sorry he should be for arresting her and throwing her into the dungeon *again*, so she took the high road.

"I want to thank you, too, Ispettore." He beamed, and she lowered her voice. "Should you ever need assistance in another case, I would love to, er, appreciate an opportunity to express my gratitude, that is, my family's gratitude, once again for all you have done."

The policeman could not conceal his astonishment. After a moment's pause, he winked and moved down the receiving line.

℘

As the clock struck eleven, those remaining revelers left the castello for the chapel to attend midnight Mass. Others continued their celebrations and good cheer until the early morning hours. They staggered home on a crisp early morning after spending an enjoyable night wishing the newlyweds a lifetime of happiness and ringing in Christmas Day at dawn.

The band took a break, and when they returned, they struck up an Italian version of "My Wild Irish Rose."

"Oh, my wild Italian Rose
The sweetest flower that grows
You may search everywhere
But none can compare with my wild Italian Rose ... "

As the song neared its end, Placido wrapped his arm around Renata's waist. "Close your eyes and come with me, my love, my wild Italian Rose," he whispered, whisking her off the dance floor.

At the north end of the ballroom, he led her behind an enormous tapestry, through a hidden door, and up three flights of stairs.

"Where are we going?" Still squeezing her eyes tight, she shivered. "The cold is seeping into my bones."

"I know, but keep your eyes closed. We are almost there," said Po, guiding her up the last few steps. "It will be worth it, I promise."

"Why are you being so mysterious? Is this going to take long? What about our guests?"

"Patience now. All will be revealed soon." They continued until they reached the door leading to the outside. A sharp gust swept past them as Po opened the door.

"Ow." Renata's face cringed at the chill, slapping her face and leaving her shivering once again.

"There's a riser here. Lift one foot then the other." He held her hands and steadied her as she crossed over, then steered her to an opening in a crenelated wall. "You can open your eyes now."

Renata's eyes flew open. "Oooh."

They were on a minor parapet overlooking the glaciarium, and she placed her hand on the wall to keep herself from swaying. She could see couples and small groups wending their way along the snowy, torch-lit path to the chapel. The moon was in its last quarter phase and had risen on the eastern horizon, its left flank illuminated. The stars were like twinkling buttons in the celestial quilt of the night sky.

"It's beautiful out here with the Yule moon shining on us."

"Not quite a full moon, but I agree, it is beautiful, as are you." Po gently pulled Renata to him so she could lean her back against his chest and he could warm her with his embrace. "This last moon of the year is sometimes called *Luna Lunge Notte*, the Long Night Moon."

"Hmm, I know." She loved being in his arms and knew they would spend many nights this way. Just the two of them facing the universe together. Forever. "Should I wish upon it?"

"In Tunisia, many do. When I served there, protecting our railway interests against the French invaders, I learned it symbolizes peace and reconciliation. The Arabs would gaze at it while reflecting on their past year before setting intentions for the new one ahead."

"I see." She was glad he could not see her bemused expression. "Anything else?"

He ran a finger down her cheek, and she leaned into it. "On one of my free days, I met a wise man in the capital city of Tunis. He was a renowned seer, so I thought I would seek his counsel about something."

"Which was?" Renata held her breath.

He held her tight against him and kissed the hair on the back of her head. "I told him about you. I asked if he thought you would still be waiting for me when I returned home."

Renata stiffened. "And what wisdom did he impart?"

Po rubbed Renata's arms to warm them. "An ancient proverb which has stayed with me. 'If the full moon loves you, why worry about the stars?'

Her brain was slow. Renata was unsure if it was the drink, the fatigue from a long day, or both, but if the answer took a lot of explaining, she had better face Po to hear it. Leaving his embrace, she turned to look into his eyes. "I do not understand."

"All the other soldiers were chasing one girl after another, but I never did. Years ago, when we were young, and some might say stupid, we made that pact at the Castle of Love. Since then, I never doubted we would be joined on a future Christmas Day."

Renata held back her tears and allowed her heart to swell.

"I always counted my blessings that we met on that fateful day. I knew we would always support and appreciate one another, no matter where we were or what happened. You may have cursed and doubted me these past few days, for which I would not blame you, but our love, though separated by physical distance these last years, stayed true."

She kissed him then, and in that kiss, time melted away. Delicately, she rediscovered the contours and textures of his lips that had become distant memories. She tasted joy and the bittersweet flavor of time lost. The kiss was a languid dance of longing and familiarity, five years and three days apart, unity and love everlasting.

Finally, she pulled away and held his face in her hands, a thumb tracing his lips.

"Me to you and you to me, we stayed true. Christmas spirit true."

THE END

Author's Note

Dear Reader, It is important to note some cultural references, preferences, and creative license. Your understanding and appreciation of these elements will enrich your reading experience and deepen your connection with the Italian culture portrayed in the book.

When Italy's republican constitution took effect on January 1, 1948, it significantly changed the country's system of nobility. The new constitution no longer legally recognized noble titles, though it stopped short of outright abolition or prohibition. The Consulta Araldica, the state body previously responsible for regulating these titles and ensuring their proper use, was also dissolved.

However, the constitution made provisions for certain aspects of noble heritage to be preserved in surnames. Specifically, it allowed for the retention of *predicati*—territorial or manorial designations often linked to noble titles through particles like *di*, *da*, *della*, or *dei*. Individuals who possessed these designations before October 28, 1922 (the date Fascism came to power in Italy) could apply for judicial approval to incorporate them into their legal surnames.

For example, in 1897, when the story starts, the protagonist's uncle-in-law, Alonzo Pelicani, an aristocrat, holds the title of Conte di Sica or Count of Sica, representing his title and fiefdom. Note that Sica is a town I invented, as is the nobility to which the protagonist gains membership.

Post-1922, well after my story begins, Alonzo would have become "Alonzo Pelicani di Sica" in official contexts. The noble title was dropped, but the territorial designation remained part of the surname.

Despite these legal changes, noble titles hold informal significance in certain social circles. Today, they are used unofficially in some villages, private clubs, and among particular social groups, reflecting the enduring cultural impact of Italy's aristocratic history.

A few titles are also standard in diminutive form as terms of affection for young people (like Contessina for "the Little Countess"). Though the protagonist is not a child, she is offered this honorific title or that of Nobildonna, which is a noblewoman—written as N.D. before her given name on stationery—as a courtesy until her uncle-in-law and head of the House of Pelicani dies, and she becomes Contessa.

Throughout most of Italy, mother is referred to as Mamma, except in the north, where Mama is the norm. As the story is set in the Veneto and because my family has had roots in the north (Friuli-Venezia Giulia region since 1640), I chose this spelling, too.

Italy has long adopted siesta, a Spanish word for a midday pause when most of the country takes a break from work. Riposo is used interchangeably with siesta in the north, while controra is preferred in the south, but I kept siesta as it is more commonly known to most readers. These terms are not to be confused with words for a nap, such as pixolotto in the Venetian tongue or pisolino in Sicilian.

The publication dates of some books and songs, as well as the name of one popular song, Wild Irish Rose, were slightly altered to fit the narrative.

Finally, Castello Pelicani exists! Not under that name, of course. I will share its actual name in a later book. In the meantime, be sure to subscribe to my newsletter—www.tessafloreano/newsletter—for more information about the book, the inspiration for it, photographs of the actual castello in the Veneto, and to learn more about future books!

Printed in the USA
CPSIA information can be obtained
at www.ICGtesting.com
CBHW020854061124
16873CB00001B/2